Carl Weber's Kingpins:

Memphis

Carl Weber's Kingpins:

Memphis

Raynesha Pittman

www.urbanbooks.net

Urban Books, LLC
300 Farmingdale Road, N.Y.-Route 109
Farmingdale, NY 11735

Carl Weber's Kingpins: Memphis
Copyright © 2020 Raynesha Pittman

ISBN 13: 978-1-62286-274-0
ISBN 10: 1-62286-274-0

First Trade Paperback Printing January 2020
Printed in the United States of America

10 9 8 7 6 5 4 3 2 1

*This is a work of fiction. Any references or similarities
to actual events, real people, living or dead, or to real
locales are intended to give the novel a sense of reality.
Any similarity in other names, characters, places, and
incidents is entirely coincidental.*

Distributed by Kensington Publishing Corp.
Submit Orders to:
Customer Service
400 Hahn Road
Westminster, MD 21157-4627
Phone: 1-800-733-3000
Fax: 1-800-659-2436

To Memphis, a city full of lessons that forced me to grow, and the only place I've lived that harmonized my blues. I'll always be a Memphian at heart. Thanks for the tough love!

Prologue

The moans of disapproval intensified as the recreation room neared capacity. It was Darryl Johnson's turn to command the gadget that made channel surfing push-of-the-button easy. Although everyone dreaded the days his name was written on the schedule, he accepted the power the remote control gave him like a brave knight holding his faithful sword. In preparation for his moment of power, he turned the volume down on both of his hearing aids. It was his subliminal way of telling the other veterans of life to kiss his ass beforehand. With fifteen Silver Sneakers or disabled bodies in the room on any given day, complaining was a part of their television watching routine.

Click by arthritis-flaring click, he flipped through the channels determined to find one of his favorite shows but to no avail. All his favorite shows were reruns from twenty years ago and beyond. Darryl with a *y*, as the residents called him to identify him from the other Darrell, could always count on watching *Sanford and Son* no matter what the day of the week was, but the young nurse with the round butt that gave him confirmation that he wasn't a candidate for the little blue pill, called out sick. She was the only nurse at the assisted living facility who knew how to access On Demand so he could watch the show on Starz. With no other option available, he settled for familiarity.

"Tick, tick, tick, tick . . ."

The gag order was put in place as the speeding ticks of the Aristo stopwatch on the magazine silenced their moans.

"They done switch the stopwatch up. I remember when it was diagonal on the magazine cover," a raspy woman's voice declared from the rear of the room.

"It sure was diagonal!" another woman confirmed, this time from the front. "I saw an episode a few years back when they made the flip, and they fooled around with them colors too. The reporter said it was diagonal for thirty-one years, but I can't remember why he said they changed it."

"Money!" shouted a man between sips of his tea and honey.

One speculation after another to the reasoning behind the change filled the room as Darryl turned his hearing aids up. He heard the foolishness of the rumors but chose to tune out the background chatter and focus on the rest of the show's opening that he hadn't missed due to volume.

"*And I'm Stacey Wilcox. Those stories and more, tonight on* 60 Minutes. *Tick, tick, tick.*"

"Hey, Betsy, I bet you them folks at *60 Minutes* have dozens of interviews from here in Chicago. I remember when all those police and organizations got together to try to get this crime stuff in order. Do you remember that? . . . Betsy!"

Betsy heard her, but what took over her eyes demanded her attention more than the chatter filling her ears. Mr. Ronald entered the room, and for the first time since he arrived four months ago, he joined them, taking a seat next to Darryl on the couch. For 67 years old, his trimmed, reddish brown Afro had only been touched with a business-card-size patch of gray, off-centered and starting at his front hairline length-wise back. Tall, handsome, and swinging if you'd ask Betsy to describe him, and she wouldn't mind telling you how she couldn't get enough of seeing him in his vast collection of windbreaker and velour sweat suits with solid-colored sneakers to match. His fawn complexion only enhanced the depth of his smoke-gray eyes, and although quite thin, his lips inveigled you to kiss them from the middle of his groomed goatee. No one was certain what career Mr. Ronald had retired from, but judging by his physic and his stylish apartment, they assumed he did something physical and was successful at it. There was an empty spot on the couch, and after wiping the coffee off her dentures with a napkin, Betsy filled it.

"Tonight, history will be made as all three segments tie into one another, but I must warn you, due to its graphic nature, viewer discretion is advised. Send the children to bed and prepare yourself as we take a trip to the barbecue-and-blues-filled streets of Memphis, Tennessee." The reporter's voice heightened as a picture of downtown Memphis displayed and leaving those who were watching with a cliffhanger as the commercial cut in.

"Home sweet home," Darryl mumbled, and Betsy used the indistinct utterance to spark up a conversation between those on the couch.

"I didn't know you were a country boy, Darryl. I thought country men had manners?"

"We do, but when my wife wanted to relocate to Chicago, I left my manners back there in Memphis. I knew better than to move to the Windy City with all that 'yes, ma'am' and 'no, sir' shit I grew up with. If I hadn't left it, these city slickers and wig hoarders like you would have blown me away."

She cut her eyes at him. Any other day, his remark about her wigs would have earned him a ten-minute tongue-lashing. However, her crush was in the room, and she'd bite her tongue until the porcelain caused it to bleed before she said anything unladylike.

"What about you, Mr. Ronald, where are you from?" she asked with a smile forcing herself to look unbothered by Darryl's words.

"South Side of Chicago born and raised." He inched to the edge of his cushion as the show returned from its commercial break. Ronald was sure Betsy was still talking, and he didn't care as he read the viewer advisory written on the screen. He didn't join the room to be social; he needed a break from the confinement of his four walls and with the snow covering his tires and rising by the minute, he wasn't in the mood to battle the weather to cruise. The task of making new friends wasn't pending on his things-to-do list, and with the lousy retirement package he received from the school board after forty years of service, the assisted living facility was the best he could afford on his budget. He didn't own not one complaint about the facility or the one-bedroom apartment he was given. It was the occupiers and the weekly unannounced visits from the staff that filled his mental safe with irritating events. But with his three-year losing battle against Alzheimer's, old age, and his son marrying and starting his own family, he'd rather pay a stranger for help every now and then than to burden those he loved most.

"Memphis, Tennessee, home of the legendary Stax Museum, and a tasty plate of barbecue seasoned in one of many famous Memphis rubs. It's the city that houses Elvis Presley's Graceland, Danny Thomas's St. Jude's Hospital, the Beale Street Blues Boy famously known as B. B. King, and, sadly, the historic Lorraine Motel where Dr. Martin Luther King Jr.'s life was taken in his fight for equal rights.

"You'd never think that a city worthy of its own history book would annually retain a spot on the list of cities with the highest homicide rate, ranking in the top ten for the past five years in a row. But before we take you on a bloody stroll through Memphis's crime- and drug-infested streets, I must take you back. Last March, I brought you a piece on the top five most notorious kingpins of all time, which turned out to be one of my most controversial pieces. Your emails in response to the episode crashed our servers, and we received 500 pounds of letters from all over the world within a week. Our producers outsourced help with reading the mail, and a few caught our attention, one, in particular, that we felt we had to follow up on. Besides voicing the lack of knowledge he felt I had on what a kingpin is and does, he said the information I reported wasn't accurate and gave gruesome details on acts authorities were able to validate as true. He is ready to spill his guts behind the safety of a blackened face and change in voice to help aid twelve U.S and international agencies arrest what could be the most notorious kingpin of all time, born and raised here, in the United States. In other words, take this episode as a retraction to my previous piece. This interview has me living in fear."

As the camera focused on the man hiding in the shadows fidgeting in his seat, uncomfortable by the situation, to say the least, Ronald shook his head and exited the room.

"There goes your *Jet* magazine hunk of the week, Betsy," Darryl shouted over the buzzing of his hearing aid. "Looks like the pretty boy couldn't handle the graphic nature. Viewer discretion of his manhood needs to be advised!"

Build It Up

Chapter One

Chicago, Illinois. Friday, January 18, 2019

The sound of plastic store bags being crumpled together ceased as Ronald stopped walking and fumbled with his keys at the door. It was arthritis in his hands that retired him from using snaps, buttons, and zippers. He missed the secure feel of denim surrounding his legs, however, not enough to endure the pain securing his britches caused. Elastic waistbands became his best friend.

His aging joints lacked the mobility to turn the key in the lock easily; yet, the shaking he was undergoing supplied the momentum he needed to conquer the task. He was in his condo, placing a call to his only saved contact in record time.

"Hello . . . RJ? Oh, hey, Ron-Ron, this is Grandpa. Where's your daddy at?"

A smile grew on his face as his grandson screamed, "Grandpa! It's Grandpa calling." Ronald would have said more to his heir's heir, but in his excitement, the little boy dropped the phone to continue announcing his call. To hear his grandson fill with joy at the sound of his voice was his slice of heaven on earth. How he once wished his own son would have done the same.

The thought of the unhealed wounds from the father-son relationship that never existed due to decisions he made aided him in getting back to the mission at hand.

He moved the books and magazines that were once neatly stacked in search of the remote control. He wasn't a habitual television watcher, and there was no telling where he set it down last. Placing the phone on top of a book titled *Any Idiot Can Learn Spanish*—and feeling like the only idiot that couldn't—he put the call on speakerphone. One by one, he recklessly tossed the couch cushions like a newspaper boy destined to lose his route, but the remote wasn't under there. Nor was it in the bedroom, bathroom, linen closet, on the kitchen table, or on top of the refrigerator where he normally found his missing keys. He'd already missed five minutes of the show waiting for the elevator to arrive and ride up to the eighteenth floor. He was willing to risk another five minutes riding it back down before settling for missing the show.

"Come on, now, Ronald, think. When was the last time you remember seeing the remote?"

Surprisingly, the answer popped up with ease and made him want to kick his own ass for forgetting. The last time he had the remote was when he placed it on top of the cable box that sat next to his TV so he wouldn't forget where it was, and if he did, he'd find it when he stopped being lazy to turn the television on manually. Once he found the channel, his son picked up.

"Hey, Pops, what's up?" Sandpaper grinding against wood sounded less dry.

"I need you to bring me that white box with the blue lid out in your garage."

"When are you trying to have me do that? There are at least seven inches of snow on the ground."

"This is Chicago. There's *always* at least seven inches of snow on the ground in January." For someone who prides himself for not holding a grudge and believing in forgiveness, RJ couldn't apply either to his failed relationship with his father, and Ronald was tired of kissing his ass with apologies. "You know what? Never mind. I'll come out there in an hour or two to get it, if that's all right with you?"

"Man," RJ hissed. "You know you shouldn't be trying to drive, especially in this weather. Your memory is getting worse, and I thought the doctor told you to turn in your license after that incident with the fire hydrant. You ain't long for this world, Pops, with your mind deteriorating like it is. What you need to do is . . ."

And that was all Ronald heard. Whenever RJ decided to switch roles and become the father, Ronald would tune him out. It seemed like neither man wanted to be the other's son. He focused his attention on the computerized voice the show hid their special guest behind.

"I know what I know because I was there when the cat planned it out. Back then, I thought it was just some childish talk, and then I'm chilling on the couch with a beer watching international news, and there it was—crime and drugs in Memphis. There wasn't shit . . . I mean, nothing else on TV, so I decided to watch, and then the little pants, big shoe, German shepherd-faced dude start saying what was going down, and it all felt like I had heard it before. For a second or two, I thought I was drunk, but when I could finish telling the story before he did . . . I was sure someone had told me that story, or I had read it in one of those urban book stories."

The mystery man chuckled at his own words, and in the movement, showed the identifying mark Ronald hesitated to believe he saw. There had to be a large population of men with tattoos across their knuckles; however, there couldn't be too many with a tattoo in the middle of their palm. The producers had his hands blacked out completely but not his palms. Seeing that the tattoo of the word "Crip" had been scribbled over, making it unreadable, the producers must have felt there wasn't a need to focus on covering it. A palm of bubbly scribble scramble that Ronald paid to have done was the opening of a time capsule in his withering mind. He would never forget the day he first met the hidden man as a child, given that it was their encounter that led him to meet Ethan.

Chicago, Illinois. Monday, September 2, 1991

It was the first day of school, and Ronald sat at the head of the classroom with his stomach in knots. For a 39-year-old, six foot, 200-pound man, you'd think he was entering the tenth grade instead of teaching it. His bout of jitters wasn't uncommon for first-time teachers; however, this wasn't Ronald's first stab at teaching. After graduating from the University of Georgia, he had a stint at a few schools in Metro Atlanta as a substitute. Nothing permanent or full-time; nevertheless, he had experience commanding a class. Though in truth, nothing could prepare him for teaching at his alma mater, South Side Heights High.

The halls he once walked proudly in his letterman jacket were now covered in letters belonging to gangs that made their home on the South Side of Chicago. Ronald had yet to travel outside of the United States, but oddly, seeing the Bloods', Crips', and Gangsta Disciples' graffiti on the white walls made him feel like he was in South Korea. The destruction of the walls inside of the school he loved and held dear to his heart mirrored the colors in that country's flag. To see its decline caused by the generations that followed him pissed him off and that anger made him susceptible to the attack he endured.

"What are those kids out there doing?" Ronald asked after joining the principal, peeking through the blinds at the parking lot.

"Looks like they are breaking into Mr. Johnson's car or are about to steal it. It's hard to tell from here."

"What? Why are you just standing here watching? Did you tell Mr. Johnson or call the police?"

He laughed as he removed his finger from the blinds, and they closed.

"Call the police for what? By the time they arrive, the boys will be gone, and why would I send Mr. Johnson out there knowing those boys would beat him to death if they didn't have the heart to the pull the trigger, and I highly doubt they know what fear is. We'll handle it whenever they get done like we always do."

"No. I'm going out there to handle it now!" Ronald yelled, storming toward the exit doors.

"Go ahead and try to be a hero. Don't say I didn't try to warn you, though!"

Ronald could have sprained his wrist with the force he used to push open the double doors leading to the staff parking lot. His pace matched the aggression of the wind blowing around him as he reached the first parking spot from the building.

"What in the hell are you out here doing?" he screamed as the wind turned his voice into a roar. All three of the boys looked up from their current task at him and then continued as if he weren't standing there.

"Get away from that car now, or I'm calling the police."

The shortest and youngest-looking boy stopped his raid of the glove compartment and got out of the car.

"Man, take your dumbest ass back into the school-house. You know you can't stop this shit. Mr. Johnson upstairs standing in the window like a mannequin watching us rob his shit, and so is the faggot-ass princi-pal, Mr. Pierce. Don't let them send you out here to get your ass whooped a new booty."

"He new?" asked the taller of the three who was carefully unwiring the radio from the dashboard.

"Yeah, cuz; he was supposed to be the new basketball coach, but the nigga lucked up and gets to teach history too since that ho got pregnant and quit. I got this nigga for third period," he announced as he looked back at Ronald who was about a yard away. "Ain't you Mr. Hill?"

"You go here?" he asked, snapping his neck toward the window he was sure Principal Pierce was peeking out of and gave him a shameful head nod.

"Yep, and that bitch-ass nigga Mr. Johnson failed me and my niggas last semester. I told him he'd better let me pass when I retook it for summer school, and he didn't, so we're hitting his ass up!"

"Not on my watch, you aren't. Put everything back and walk away from the car while you still have your freedom." The boys laughed; the makeshift electrical engineer was almost in tears. "This isn't a joke! Get out of Mr. Johnson's car or all three of you are going to regret it. I'll not only call the police; I'll attend every court hearing and testify against you. This is wrong!"

"Aye, you probably want to shut the fuck up and go back in the building," his future student warned and even gave a head nod toward the boy who would most have an issue with the threat.

"I'm not a fucking mannequin, and I'm not scared of a group of lost-ass little boys who need the protection of a gang to feel worthy. I'm the new gang buster!"

"Yo, Mimic, if you smash his bitch ass right now, I'll tell the big homies that me and Crook put you down." The third and obviously the one in charge said, finally breaking his silence, "Beat his ass little home, and I'm gon' bless your name with cuz on the end. That's on the set!"

Ronald didn't know what to expect next and wasn't given time to think about it. Before he could get his footing together to prepare for his student to hit him, he was put on his ass. Molly-whopped, boo bopped, or whatever fly term that meant he was ass-whoopin' worthy and received it, left him bloody on the asphalt parking lot. Of course, no one called the police or came to his rescue, but once the trio was out of sight, Mr. Johnson was nice enough to help him off the ground and to his car.

He hadn't stepped foot on the school grounds since and battled if he were going to quit before he started, but after Principal Pierce called ready to accept his letter of resignation, his ego stepped in, and he confirmed he'd be in his classroom ready to teach on the first day of school. He spent the last seventy-two hours praying that Mimic had been arrested or was on the run and he would never have to see him again. However, with his history of misfortune, Mimic was the first to walk in class.

"Aye, cuz, I hope you ain't salty about that little shit that happened in the parking lot. I tried to tell you to shut the fuck up . . . I mean, be quiet, but you weren't trying to hear me. I don't know where you come from, but that Superman shit only works in Metropolis. This here is the Chi. You got to get it how you live it. I hope you understand."

"What's your name, son, and don't give me that 'Mimic' bullshit. I want the name that's on my roster." Ronald was determined to sound fearless.

"Martin, but if you refuse to call me Mimic, I'm only answering to Marty. That Martin shit will get you ignored."

"Martin?" he repeated as he ran his finger down the paper he was holding. "Martin Boyce. You live off Garfield Boulevard in Fuller Park? I know a few Boyces from Fuller. Let's get an understanding so we won't

have another mishap. No grudges held about the parking lot incident. That's what I get for trying to defend a man who was too scared to defend himself, but if you decide to fuck with me directly, I'll forget that you are a student and treat you like the scared little boy I see in front of me. I didn't beat yo' ass to prevent getting jumped, but the next time your little 15-year-old ass decides to show your ass, I'm going to take off my belt and beat it. You might take that shit in the parking lot as a victory, but what's a victory to a battle, young street soldier? I'm a war vet, and Ms. Shirley, your grandmother, used to babysit me. Does she still sit on the porch rolling a baseball bat with her feet? Don't make me call her!"

"Aw, you want to be tough, now?" his voice shook as he spoke. "And my grandmama old and sick. Don't bring her in our beef."

"So, we got beef?" quizzically, Ronald looked into his eyes in search of an answer as he waited for his response.

"Nah, we straight but stop getting in shit that don't have shit to do with you, and we'll stay straight. Where's my desk at?"

"Right here. Right in front of mine. Pull those pants up and have a seat, young man. When you're in my class, that gang shit stays in the hallway for Ms. Shirley's sake, right, Martin?"

"Yeah, that's right but only for my granny sake."

Students began to pile in and introduce themselves. Ronald could instantly tell the crews and cliques and tried to separate them with assigned seating. There were a few hard heads, but none held a candle to Martin, and the only problem he could foresee himself having the school year was the chatty Cathys and the children's choice of almost naked or baggy clothing. Everyone was wearing something bright or had their clothes on back-

ward. If those were his biggest problems, he was ready
for the challenge.

"Excuse me, are you Mr. Hill? They switched my class-
es this morning, and I'm supposed to be in history with
Mr. Hill right now."

The boy was built for a 15-year-old. In comparison to
his peers, he was average besides the bulk of his body.
No flashy colored clothing, his sneakers didn't display
a known brand, and he didn't have the look of a trou-
blemaker; yet, something about him sent a chill down
Ronald's spine as he answered.

"Yes, I'm Mr. Hill. You must be Ethan; I was just about
to mark you absent. Take a seat in the back of the class
by the window."

"I prefer the front. If you don't mind, I'm willing to
swap seats with Martin."

"Hell yeah!" Martin responded scooping up his belong-
ings, and the class lit up in laughter.

"I mind. Your desk is in the back of the class by the
window. There's no division in this classroom. I teach
those in the back of the room in equal quality as those in
the front. Take your seat, young man, and welcome to
Mr. Ronald's U.S. History."

"Mr. Ronald, why don't you go by Hill?" Ethan questioned while the kids whispered and pointed at his shoes.
They identified that the shoes were purchased at Payless,
a shoe vendor that catered to those battling poverty and
that sent poor jokes headed in his direction.

"Yeah, why do I have to go by Martin, but you get to go
by Ronald?" Mimic added.

"That's Mr. Ronald, and if your grandmother ap-
proves the name Mimic, I'll use it." He stared at Ethan,
wanting to see a sign of discomfort as the jokes about
his shoes got louder.

"I bet you his toes musty as hell," a girl seated closest to him said as the boy seated in front of her chimed in.

"Nah, look at his ashy ankles. That boy powered up his stankin'-ass feet. He got more baking soda in his shoe than the crack house. Call that boy Arm and Hammer!"

You would have thought Ethan would've at the very minimum blinked or cringed in acknowledgment of the insults being shot at him, but on the contrary, the only look on the boy's face was of a young man waiting for his question to be answered.

"My father is Mr. Hill."

"Which makes you Mr. Hill too. You and your father got issues? I'm only asking because I can understand you not wanting to represent his legacy if there's resent-ment."

The class went silent as shock rearranged the muscles in Mr. Ronald's face. They weren't sure what Ethan was talking about, but they knew a child wasn't supposed to say it to an adult.

"No resentment. I prefer my first name, that's all."

"But why is that? Do you have a fear of getting old, and holding on to your first name makes you feel young?"

"Is he always like this?" Mr. Ronald asked, scanning the class for help.

Those who knew Ethan nodded, and those who didn't shrugged and turned to see the other responses.

"Is it a problem if I am? Does that remind you of your pops?"

Ronald shook his head to release the memory, but the image of the inquisitive poverty-stricken young man wouldn't go away. In twenty-eight years, Ethan's image had never gone away.

Chapter Two

Memphis, Tennessee. Friday, January 18, 2019

The bus depot was packed, and the sign that read *Standing Room Only* had to have been a deceptive attempt to bring comfort, considering there wasn't a single space of standing room available. If you were to cross over the Arkansas Bridge into Tennessee and had the misfortune of passing the bus depot during the morning hours of the workweek, your first impression of Memphis would be that no one in the city drove.

Crowds of assorted blue-collared workers, families struggling to normalize life without a vehicle, early-morning panhandlers, and those willing to entertain for pocket change waited outside instead of the crammed conditions. However, fresh air and the lack of climate control was the only difference in the two waiting areas. The poor, almost savagelike feel of the atmosphere and the hungry array of hustles and bustles must have been the reason why the bus depot was nicknamed the "Shelter."

Stacey didn't mind the five-block walk minutes before sunrise nor the slow, bumpy ride she endured to the bus depot for her connecting route. They were the hurdles she had to jump to provide for her family. Each one gave her a sense of purpose and made her feel like a superhero instead of a certified nursing assistant. However, what she did mind was traveling two hours a day to work her five, twelve-hour shifts to return home to a pigsty and seeing the king pig playing his video games and smoking his weed as if he were oblivious to his surroundings. How could he not see or hear the kids jumping and flipping over the shit she worked hard to pay the Rent-A-Room on time for? She was sick of walking through the door with sore feet and not being greeted with affection but by obnoxious questions.

"Aye, what'cha cooking for dinner? We're starving!" Tim's eyes never left the game. His team had finally made him proud by intercepting the ball and running for a 60-yard touchdown to tie the score. There was no way he'd let the computer win the Super Bowl he'd invested the last eight hours preparing for with his created player made in his likeness. Although his 287 pounds weren't molded by muscle in his six-foot-three frame like the lineman he created, it was the way he saw himself, and so did everyone else in North Memphis. Brick was the only name Tim answered to outside of his four walls, and if his visual wasn't enough to persuade those to do what he said when he said it, he didn't have a problem using his solid width and strength to get the respect he felt he deserved. "Damn, I know I'm not talking to myself!" he bellowed, pissed that his quarterback was sacked.

Stacey planned on responding when he first asked, but the empty juice pouches box on the floor next to his foot that was covered in blunt guts caught her attention. The box could have easily lasted until her payday as planned, but that was no longer the case.

"I know you didn't sit your big fat funky ass on my new couch drinking up all the baby's juices and playing this dumb-ass game all fucking day!" she spat before snatching the power cord out of the wall. In the five years the couple had been dating, she'd never raised her voice at him. Unlike the way Brick was viewed in the streets by those who feared him, Stacey only saw him as Tim, her life-size teddy bear and savior. They met at her lowest point; yet, she couldn't recall a moment where she had more strength. She walked away from the man who was bringing her down with their 2-year-old son in tote and didn't look back, not even for one last glance from over her shoulder. Without a dollar or food stamps to her name, thanks to her small possession charge for stashing her baby daddy's dope, she didn't let go of hope. The prayers she sent up increased, and she was determined to make her dream of becoming a nurse materialize. That's when she met Brick.

Stacey heard of the havoc the living black giant was causing in the streets long before they met, but he'd never shown her that side of him. He bought her a house from one of his smoked out customers, paid for her to go to nursing school, and made sure to heavily compensate anyone willing to help his queen along the way. Brick was a lover and provider. It wasn't until her missed period which made him move in to become a family that she saw her teddy bear as a lazy, sloppy, fat ass who wouldn't clean up after himself even if he was paid for it. Being sick and tired of his shit had their relationship on life support. He paid the bills with the income he earned in the streets, which she didn't complain about. However, she put her nurse certification to work to secure her own income just in case their love flatlined. She told Tim she was working as a front for his drug dealing. He'd upgraded from selling nickel-and-dime valued rocks of cocaine to managing the distribution of heroin for Big Joe. The promotion meant he'd never have to carry drugs on his person again; yet, carrying, storing, and hiding the money became a bigger task. He ate up Stacey's words as a result of his ego forcing him to believe she couldn't make it without him, and he didn't have a reason to question her loyalty. Tim knew he was number one on both of their lists, and she'd do anything to protect and keep him free. As his queen, she kept his crown polished on his head, his throne comfy under his tail, and catered to all of his needs. Her mouth could get under his skin at times, but she kept it filled with his dick, which, in Tim's eyes, was an equal trade. "I'm so tired of coming home to the same bullshit every day!"

"Then stop working! You're supposed to be home taking care of me and the boys anyway. If that job got you neglecting us, fuck it. I take care of you and the bills anyway," Tim countered, coaxing himself to stay calm about her killing the power seconds before he received his Super Bowl ring. He didn't say shit about the aggression she was showing in their arguments for the last two months, but he noticed it. Instead, he kept his fingers crossed, hoping pregnancy wasn't the cause for her mood swings. The way he saw it, they already had one kid too many.

"So, besides paying bills, how are you taking care of me?"

"What-u-mean how am I taking care of you?"

"I'm saying what I'm asking! Besides paying bills, what else are you good for? You don't watch the kids when I'm gone, my mama does, and I don't remember the last time you fucked me and did all the work. I gotta suck it to get it hard and then hurry up and sit on it before you nut. Hell, I gotta put my clit to your lips if I want it licked, so tell me why I should keep putting up with your shit? I'm better off leaving your ass for a bitch."

Tim was on his feet, hovering over her before she could blink. She'd be snoring on the floor with undies full of shit if she were a man. He promised to conceal Brick and his violent tendencies when he was certain she was the one, but she was begging for an introduction.

"Aye, you need to calm the fuck down and remember who you're talking to."

"I don't have to remember you're Big Brick. A big fish in the drug game that all these little guppies fear. How could I forget?" her acknowledgment slightly put him at ease, and he was glad that the introduction wouldn't be necessary.

"Damn right, baby!"

"Yeah . . . but I'm not fucking Brick, though. I got stuck with Tim's dirty ass, and that nigga ain't shit!"

Glass shattered, and the entire room shook. Stacey's world shifted and then flipped upside down. Of course, she knew about the three domestic violence charges Tim racked up over the years, but she never thought she'd fall victim to his hands—and she hadn't.

"Get down!"

The demand echoed off the walls, which was a waste of words as the DEA officer dropped Stacey where she stood in chase of Brick. Brick broke through the back door with his forearm and a soldier drop like a linebacker. His backyard was crawling with agents, some holding shovels and others had their guns pointed at the door prepared for his escape. Brick only had a second to decide his fate. Would it be jail or hell? Jail meant the possibility of re-uniting with his family in his old age, and hell meant no jail time at all. He wasn't sure what the DEA had on him but seeing the shovels, he knew they knew more than he would want them to. Never being one to make a quick decision under pressure, he opted out and let fate decide.

Right, left, left, left, right, spin, and then another quick right. Brick moved like he was pressing the button on his game's controller. He shot straight for fifteen yards to the vine-covered gate that connected to his neighbor's yard, and after jumping once to reach the top, his face met the flat backside of a shovel. He fell back, knocked out cold like a tree cut in the forests. Brick woke up with his arms and feet shackled in the back of a van.

"What's that?" he shouted, still woozy from his dirt nap. He was certain that every bone in his face was broken. His head was throbbing, but that wasn't the sound that woke him up. It was gunshots.

"We'll ask all the questions, big guy. Where else are you stashing drug money?"

There wasn't a face for him to lie to. He was staring at the side of a pair of black steel toe boots. Looking past the boots, he could see the dirty bags he stuffed with money and buried over a year ago. It was emergency cash that he hid just in case shit went sour, and no one knew about it, not even Stacey. He wanted to be able to point the finger at a snitch, but for the first time ever, he was the only person who could have snitched on him, unless . . .

"Fuck you. I ain't telling your crooked ass shit." Two quick kicks were placed to his face. One landed in his mouth and took out four of his teeth. "Is that the best you got? Joe sent you out here to rob me, and you think you're straight with him for doing it too, don't you? Look at this shit. If he's cleaning out his bosses, that means he's closing shop, dumb ass. When you're done knocking us out, he'll have somebody waiting to handle you next." He laughed, and to his surprise, the man joined in.

"Is that what you think?" the DEA agent asked, snatching Brick by his clothes and sitting him up right. "You see all the police movement on Joe's ass, and you think it's cleanup time. And you know what? It might be that time for those that are worth throwing away, but do you see this?" He held his badge that dangled on its silver beaded chain up to Brick's face. "This means he needs me a lot more than you think. He's not shutting down shop because some rat-ass-ho nigga from his past snitched to a bitch that runs her mouth too much on TV. He's a mastermind; he has to make it *look* that way."

"Do you polish his shoes and hum on his nuts too while you kiss the shitty tissue crumbs out of the crack of his ass?" Brick chuckled and then spat blood at his feet.

"Killing you, yo' bitch, and those raggedy-ass kids is just the beginning. There isn't an agency or organization big enough to stop Joe!" He wiped the spit on his shoe across Brick's cheek with force and then imitated his chuckle. He took a few steps backward toward the sliding door and shot himself in the thigh with the gun still in the holster, and then he freed it to put one right between Brick's eyes.

"Officer down! I repeat, officer down. I've been shot!"

He leaned against the door until he was in a perfect angle from the corpse. He planned to say that he assumed Brick was still unconscious when he placed the bags in the van and when he passed him, there was a struggle between the two while the gun was in his holster. After being shot in the thigh and pushed to the ground, he was able to remove his gun and give off a single shot. In the house, his partner was to stage a double suicide-homicide which would paint the picture that Stacey killed both of her children and then took her own life in love. She couldn't live with Brick doing life in jail, so she decided none of them should have to. The plan was perfect, which was expected, seeing that Joe was over the blueprint of it, or so the officers had been told because neither had ever met the man that gave them a $20,000 monthly bonus for their service. Orders always came by a call or text, and it was becoming evident that no one who worked for Joe had ever met him, and if the money stayed good, no one wanted to.

Agent Murray's rescue team was taking longer than expected. An officer down call was always the priority of anyone with a shield. He wanted to look out the back window to see what the delay was but didn't want to risk not being in the staged position when the doors opened. He waited another minute or so and then said it again.

"Officer down, I repeat, Officer down. I'm in the back of the van with the suspect," he added.

"Copy that; what's your 20?"

"I just gave you my 20. I'm shot in the back of the van with the suspect. Hurry, I'm losing a lot of blood!"

"10-4," the male voice responded emotionless.

Another five minutes went by, and still no backup or ambulance. The great loss of blood replaced the pain in his thigh and caused his leg to go numb. He didn't understand the delay.

"Officer down!" he yelled into his handheld transceiver.

"10-4."

"No fucking 10-4. I've been shot, and I'm going numb. Send help now!"

"What's your 20?"

"You already know my fucking 20. I'm in the back of the fucking van with the suspect."

"10-4."

Frustrated, he slid open the van's door—and there stood at least a dozen officers. To his right was a stretcher with a body being zipped into a bag, and on the left, the woman and her two boys were being placed into the back of a black-and-white squad car. A look of disgust was plastered on everyone's face.

"Derrick Murray, put the gun down and put your hands up."

Derrick looked back at the corpse and grinned as he shot at the crowd of agents in front of him. As the bullets ripped his flesh to shreds, he found peace in the foolish decision he made.

The crime scene had been taped off, and the neighborhood was buzzing with lies and speculations. Everyone knew Brick sold drugs; after all, he was their favorite pharmacist. From his herbal medicine, marijuana, to his pain-relieving crack cocaine, he serviced the likes of them, but not one of them knew who he worked for, nor did they think of him as a big fish. He wasn't flashy, he didn't own a car, and when you did catch him behind the steering wheel, it was in a car he rented from a junkie in exchange for a fix. The kids looked like the other kids in the area and each year received the bulk of their Christmas gifts at the community center like everyone else. His woman wasn't much of a looker and kept it all natural besides an occasional full acrylic nail set. The house was decorated in the Dollar General's best and garnished in Walmart-brand appliances. For the police to find $200,000 in the house and over a million dollars buried in the backyard was unbelievable.

The news reporters on the scene didn't care who had the facts or knew Brick's history. Anyone who lived within a mile of him and his makeshift family was interview worthy.

"He knocked my baby brother out for five punk-ass dollars during a dice game. I tried to tell Brick then that you can't do foul shit and think the shit you are dishing out don't leave a stain."

You could hear a man say nonchalantly into the camera, "If you want my opinion, that money they found wasn't his. Somebody was using him to hide their stash. When you're done doing your investigating and find out I'm right, come see me outside the liquor store on the corner of Chelsea and Hollywood for some more advice. That fool was all muscle. Cats like me got the brains."

Story after story filled the air, and each news reporter was hungrier than the previous one and was determined to be the first to report information the other hadn't learned. Though they all had seen two agents being carried out by the coroners, the general assumption was that the victims were causalities of Brick's wrath. Outside of the FBI and the other federal-based agencies involved, the only local law enforcement aware of the conspired bust on the compromised agents was the Memphis's DEA task force, the Tennessee Bureau of Investigation, and now, the heads of homicide.

"Looks like Murray and Jefferson followed through with Joe's plan," Detective Rawlings said, pointing at the bullet wound in Agent Murray's thigh.

"Yep, which means—" his Asian counterpart, Detective Ryu, began, but he stopped.

"Which means the Feds are going to pull their power card, kick us off the case we've invested our careers into cracking, and label our city their jurisdiction."

"Which means?"

"Which means they can kiss my barbecue-eating ass from Beale Street to Graceland. I'd lose my badge before I sit back and let them steal our fucking case."

"My sentiments exactly, partner. Go home and get some rest. Tomorrow, we're going to kick over some trash cans and barge through a few doors. They're guests in our city; they'll still be in the offices strategizing on where they should start."

Rawlings took another look at the young black man dead on the metal slab. He shook, not from the cold temperature of the morgue but from revulsion he felt about dirty cops. Rawlings would have whooped Murry's ass if he weren't already dead. Disgusted and annoyed that the body was on ice in the morgue instead of being torn to pieces by a pack of ruthless male tigers, he mumbled, "You's a dumb muthafucka" before dropping the sheet over the corpse's face.

Chapter Three

Chicago, Illinois. Friday, January 18, 2019, cont.

The nurses' station called to inform Ronald that his son delivered the box he requested. There weren't any visiting restrictions preventing RJ from delivering the box to his father. He simply restricted himself. It didn't bother Ronald that he passed on the visit, nor did he care to see him after the sermon RJ gave him twenty-five minutes earlier on the phone. Ronald wanted him to deliver the box to his door, not so he could see him; he just didn't want to miss any more of the show. By the time it would take him to make it to the first floor and back up, he'd miss the show and would be lucky to catch the closing credits. Defeated by the lack of having that option, he entered the elevator and watched the doors close. Instantly, he forgot where he was.

"What's going on?"

His voice echoed around the small, square room and sent chills up his curving spine. He was trapped in a dimly lit sealed box. There were no windows, vents, nor were there any emergency exits. Mirrors covered three of the walls. He turned to investigate the one at his right and knew he was being watched. Someone was on the other side, or maybe even a small group of people, watching and laughing at his fear. As one of the few people to have watched the 1962 movie adaption of Richard Condon's 1959 novel, *The Manchurian Candidate,* a thousand times or more, and then obsessed over comparing the 2004 adaption to its predecessor, he believed some people had been trapped in situations like his current one. All that time spent in watching seemed like time wasted after he'd confirmed neither was better than the book. Government-hidden agendas and secret organizations and brotherhoods were the reason he grew a passion for teaching. The only downfall of researching the tabooed history was there wasn't a platform he would be allowed to teach it on. That too made his list of conspiracy theories.

Ronald was doing his best not to panic, but one of the white round spots on the far right of the wall in front of him had lit up, and the room began to move. He screamed, "Let me out of here! Someone help me. They're trying to hurt me! Help!"

The air was tapering like oxygen had become a master barber, and his body temperature began to rise. It was becoming hard for him to breathe. Sweat glistened his forehead and secreted from every pore of his body. In seconds, he was drenched. A bell sounded and repeated seventeen times in five-second intervals. By the fourth chime, his eyes found the location of the noise. Above his head on the wall in front of him was a strip of small boxes and with each chime, another box lit up. It was a neurological brain synthesizer that private armies used to implant neurological diseases like dementia into their enemies. Once that last box lit up, Ronald knew his brain would be fried.

"They are coming for me. Somebody help me. I'm trapped in the elevator!"

Five seconds before reaching the first floor, he remembered where he was, but it was five seconds too late. Nurse Deena was on her way to do her nightly rounds, and at the sight of him, she screamed for help.

"I'm OK; just got shaken up for a bit. I think that PCP I tried in college came back to haunt me for a second," he snickered.

"No, you're not OK, Mr. Ronald. You're covered in sweat and standing a puddle of urine. I'm calling the doctor," she said and then continued to scream for help.

"I didn't know I pee'd on myself. I didn't even feel it," he acknowledged, speaking more to himself than the nurse.

Two years earlier, Ronald noticed that he was having some problems with his cognitive skills. It seemed to be a task to think, read, learn, remember, rhyme, reason, and pay attention. He couldn't find the right words during conversations to make his case, and it was easier to use titles with those around him, like "sir" or "ma'am" instead of names, which was a red flag due to the fact he only had a few acquaintances' names to remember.

Once he started frequently losing personal possessions and valuables, he grabbed his son and went to the doctor.

"Your performance on the memory tests detect impaired cognitive functioning. I'm sorry to have to say this, but your concerns are valid. You have Alzheimer's, and my professional opinion would be that you are at the end of stage three of the disease or early stage four."

"How many stages are there?" RJ asked, gripping his father's shoulder in concern. He quickly let go of his grasp when he realized he was wearing his emotions on his sleeve.

"Generally speaking, there's three. Early, moderate, and severe; however, each of those stages can be broken down into smaller stages, so in total, there's seven."

"Well, can you tell me about the other three or four? I'd like to know what to expect," Ronald asked in an

even tone. He could feel his son staring a hole into the side of his head, and that's what gave him the strength to remain emotionless. RJ called him heartless and self-centered for putting his wants and goals before being a father. Allowing his son to see him disheartened by the news was walking that thin line of selfishness again. He'd let RJ bear the hurt for him.

The doctor used his legs to push the stool he sat on across the room to the computer, and then he paraphrased what he was reading. "Stage four symptoms include difficulty with reciting, computing, and identifying numbers. A decline in short-term memory. You may not recall the simple things like your favorite foods or drinks. You may even forget the important details about your past, like where you are from or parents' and siblings' names. Stage five has more moderately severe symptoms, and you will need help with your daily activities like dressing. However, you may be able to still bathe and use the restroom on your own, but at this stage, doing so becomes confusing. When you progress to stage six, you will need constant supervision and require care from a professional. You'll become unaware of your surroundings. It will be a task to recognize faces outside of your closest friends and relatives. You will lose control over your bladder and bowels. Wandering may become common, and behavioral issues may arise. Think of an unruly child that doesn't like hearing the word no."

"So, let me get this straight. Are your saying my pops is going to become a grown child?"

"Technically, I can't think of a better comparison. Your father will remind you of a 5- or 6-year-old child, but the kicker is that he will still see himself as the elder and defy you. The two of you will basically switch roles."

"How long do we have between stages? I mean, how long does it normally take for it to progress?"

"For a man in your father's health, it could take him fifteen or twenty years to go through the stages. He's in perfect health besides the attack on his mind. For people with other aging issues, like heart disease, diabetes, and history of blood clots, they can fly through them. That doesn't mean your father can't experience the change in stages rapidly; it just means he has a better shot at—"

"And what happens at stage seven?" Ronald interrupted. The look on his doctor's face said he wasn't ready to go there yet, but he knew he wouldn't be able to avoid it now that RJ looked interested in knowing too.

"Stage seven is the final stage. Alzheimer's is a terminal illness, and at this stage, you will be nearing death. You might be able to utter words and a few phrases, but you won't be able to communicate. The brain has finally burnt out and can't send messages to the body to keep going. Your brain won't tell you to swallow, eat, relieve yourself, and it won't tell your heart to continue to beat. They will call your death a natural cause, but there won't be anything natural about the misery you die in. Hopefully, at that stage, you won't be able to remember what misery is."

"Well, I'll be" was all Ronald could say.

Diagnosing himself from the incident in the elevator and the urine covering his shoes, he'd say that he had progressed from stage five into six in less than three months. Today's golden shower wasn't the first. It was the third in four weeks. The elevator incident was new, but he'd gotten lost in his condo twice and spent half the day reading a book in the bathroom on account he had mistaken it for the living room. It wasn't until he complained about how hard his couch had gotten that he realized it was the cover over the toilet seat giving his ass the blues.

"Excuse me, young lady, can I tell you a joke?" he asked as the male nurse secured him in the wheelchair. Ronald was a lady's man by birthright and had his fair share of lovers throughout the years. Some lasted months, others days, but none ever made it a year. He'd get rid of them the moment they felt comfortable to question his past.

"What's the dumbest way to die?"

"Let's not joke about death, Mr. Ronald. I don't—"

"Can you please humor me, just this once, and I promise you the next joke I tell will be about an old man who marries a beautiful young nurse that came to his rescue in an elevator." His smile was more contagious than a yawn in the middle of a packed conference room. Defeated, she softened and gave an approving nod.

"What's the dumbest way to die, Mr. Ronald?"

"That's an easy one . . . when you die because you forgot to live."

She gave him a somber smile, then nodded at the orderly to transport Ronald to the medical van waiting to take him to the hospital for evaluation.

Ronald fell asleep on the ride to Chicago Memorial. Unbeknownst to him, his mind was exhausted. It didn't seem like a struggle for him to recall those days of his past. Yet, the action drained him. His goal wasn't to put in detective work when he sat down to watch the show. It was fate, and the job chose him. Out of all the memories he's lost in battling the disease, his days of teaching Mimic and Ethan were completely intact.

Chicago, Illinois. Friday, October 18, 1991

"Yo, Mr. Ronald. You sound country as hell to be saying you're born and raised in the Chi," Mimic announced

as he walked into the class. Ethan lagged not too far behind him and responded before Mimic.

"He's from Chicago, but he's definitely lived down South for a while. My guess would be a major city in Georgia or Tennessee."

"And why would that be your guess? I'm sure you planned on sharing your thoughts whether or not I asked you to," Ronald said, making his annoyance with Ethan evident. The boy found a way to get under his skin every day for the past month and made the third period his most hated time of day. He wouldn't call Ethan smart, but he dubbed him the King Supreme of Being Inquisitive and Overly Opinionated.

"I've been researching both places, and it's common for people living in Nashville, Memphis, Atlanta, and its suburbs to drop their last name and put a Ms. or Mr. in front of it. You don't have that TN hospitality, and judging by the way you dress, I'd say Atlanta. A lot of old people living there think they're hip."

"Take your seat, Ethan."

"Dang, what happened to you in Atlanta? Your eyes bucked when I said it. I got it right, huh? So, you got daddy issues and a secret past you're hiding in Georgia. You're way cooler than I thought."

The few kids that beat the tardy bell laughed like they always did. Ethan's antics were becoming a daily distraction, and the time it took to get the class back in order took away from his lesson plan. He had to put a stop to it before it got worse.

"Ethan, change in plans. I need to see you outside in the hallway for a second."

"Those sound like fighting words to me," Mimic chimed in, and the class made their instigating oohs and aahs.

"And, Martin, I need you to join us."

"What did I do?" he spat as Ethan walked out of the room without an objection.

"You'll find out when you step out of the room."

"Oooh!" the class harmonized after his statement. Ronald followed Ethan's lead, knowing if he continued the back and forth, Mimic would feel provoked to show out.

"What's the problem?" Mimic asked when he joined the private meeting.

"You two are becoming the problem. You both are leaders, and the class lives for your daily outburst. Although you both snap back to task quickly, the others don't. I need you both to refrain from . . ."

Ronald stopped talking, seeing that no one was listening. Both boys' attentions were locked on the five-person posse in red, making their way down the hallway. It was obvious that they weren't students. They looked too old, and it was clear the only agenda they were following was one given to them from their gang. Remembering the multiple times he had to correct Mimic for calling him cuz, he shot his eyes at him.

"Go in the class and lock the door behind you. Under no circumstances do you come back out. Do you understand me?"

That question was left unanswered as Mimic slammed and locked the door behind him. Although his attention was on the safety of the Crip standing next to him, he assumed Ethan was smart enough to go with him.

"Why didn't you go with Martin?" he whispered, and the group stopped in front of him.

"Because they want me," he said, stepping in front of Ronald and extending his hand. "What's up, Bones, Slick, B-Town, and what are your names? I don't think I've seen you two around. Did you just get initiated and affiliated?"

Slick stepped up and knocked Ethan's hand out of the way. His duck-shaped lips were centimeters from touching the top of Ethan's head as he hovered over him.

"Where's my money?" Slick asked, stabbing Ethan in his chest with his index finger.

"This is a schoolhouse, young man!" Ronald interjected.

"And this is a gun," Bones said as he flashed the pistol that rested on his six-pack under his shirt. "Take yo' old ass in the classroom. We got business with little dude."

"No, you have business with my dad. Stop fronting him dope, knowing he doesn't have a job and then expecting me to pay for it. I'm a kid, for Christ's sake!" He turned to Ronald. "Go into the classroom, Mr. Hill. I do have business to discuss with them."

"I'm not going anywhere. Until that bell rings, you are my business."

"Why don't you like being called Mr. Hill?" Ethan's eyes begged Ronald to do as he said while the question threw the crowd off.

"Ethan . . ." he started, but the boy's look worsened and caused him to shut up.

"We all got secrets and daddy issues, Mr. Ronald. Maybe one day we will both stop dealing with them on our own and share them." He smiled and then turned to the impatient, aggressive faces in front of him and said, "I got your money. We can go get it now."

The confidence in the boy's eyes would have been perfectly suited in a man whose age was doubled. Ethan wasn't old enough to vote. Yet, he mastered the art of nonverbal communication. With only the glossy look in his whiskey-brown eyes, he assured Ronald everything would be all right and told him he had a plan for the interaction that couldn't fail.

Feeling persuaded, Ronald pulled out his key to the classroom and locked the door behind him.

Chapter Four

Memphis, Tennessee. Monday, January 21, 2019

The words, *"I am a man"* were the focal point in the mural painted on the wall a block north of the historical Lorraine Motel. The motel famously known as the home of the National Civil Rights Museum told the history of its founding by being the site for the ninetieth birthday celebration of Martin Luther King Jr. There's wasn't a place more suitable to gather in celebration of the civil rights leader's life than the place where he met death, and judging by the masses walking the streets in front of it, everyone held the same sentiments.

"Can we please have ice cream after this, Daddy? You said we were going to get ice cream after we left the museum." The 10-year-old boy whined, tired from all the walking and standing he and his family had done in the last three hours.

"Ice cream, ice cream, ice cream . . ." the two 3-year-old twin boys swinging from the big brother's hands chanted excitedly.

"Ice cream and then home to Mama, I promise. Let me find someone to take a group picture of us, A'Chance, and then we're gone!"

"We don't mind taking it for you, do we, partner?" Detective Rawlings said, smiling as the man turned to face the familiar voice.

"Of course, we don't mind, partner. We go out of our way for the stand-up residents of Memphis, Tennessee. You're still a stand-up guy, right, Demarcus?"

The ex-high school football star-alleged rapist-criminal drug lord-turned businessman and now leading candidate in the city council race couldn't catch a break from the duo. He knew why they were there and what they planned to harass him about before they started.

"I don't know anything about this Joe cat besides what's been on the news all month. Never heard of him, never worked for him, and when I was trapped in the Dog Food game, he and I never crossed paths."

"Quick answer, but it sounds like something is missing, doesn't it, Rawlings?" Detective Ryu asked.

"Sounds like Demarcus is full of shit, that's what it sounds like to me. He might have the people of Memphis fooled with his 'make the city great again' speeches, but I don't trust him anymore than I trust that orange-hair muthafucka who claims to be making America great again. I think Demarcus knows a lot more than what he's saying. He was the largest distributor of heroin in the city. He had to have been getting it from Joe . . . weren't you?"

"So, y'all really about to do this shit in front of my kids?"

Demarcus was livid. He'd battled leaving Tennessee after he got closure on his past, but his fiancée at the time was pregnant, and his son A'Chance's doctors were here. He didn't want the progress he was making to decline as a result of the relocation. Being born addicted to heroin caused Chance to have learning disabilities, behavioral issues, and he was sick a lot with horrible asthma. It was times like these that made Demarcus regret his choice to stay.

"We don't have to. We can call Child and Protective Services to babysit them while we book you for suspicion," Ryu countered. "Or you can call that pretty district attorney you married and have her meet you downtown so we can talk this out without taking your freedom away."

"Yeah, let's grant him option two, partner. I don't want to screw up his chances at being elected if he's innocent. I voted early for his lying ass," Rawlings said, turning his back to Demarcus to head to his car. He took two steps and then hit the ground. No one heard the shot fired nor saw a gunman fleeing . . . but there lay Detective Rawlings, dead with blood oozing from a wound above his forehead. Demarcus's and Detective Ryu's cell phones rang at the same time as both men dived to protect the children. After the third simultaneous call, they looked at each other, and they both answered the unknown number.

"I am a man, like the wall says. I am not an animal you can hunt down to strip away my life from me, Detective Ryu. How many years were you hunting me down without coming up with a name for your files? You thought I was that handsome Pettus boy working for the Mexican Mafia, and once you learned you were wrong, I became the right-hand man to Lord King, or was it Gutta? You've never had a handle on me until recently, and even now, I'm a hot pot burning in your little Asian American hand. And you, Demarcus, poor misled Demarcus. You're married to a lawyer who knew her worth and became the DA of Memphis, but you still haven't learned your rights," the voice started high-pitched like a man who inhaled helium, but with each sentence, the voice transformed. Next was a Southern accent, followed by New York swag, and now the man on the phone sounded German. When he spoke again, it was in a heavy Australian accent. "Look here, mate, the police can't question you whenever the spirit moves them to. At this point, you should be suing the Memphis police department for harassment, but I guess the bitch in you everyone around you sees won't let you."

"Fuck you. You don't know me, nigga!"

"On the contrary, I do, and I knew your brother Omar too. He was quite the pit bull, but I liked his viciousness," he said in a British voice. "He was true to himself up until you killed him, but I guess that's a secret that was supposed to stay between you, Rawlings, and Ryu, huh?"

"So why kill R-Rawlings?" Ryu stumbled over his name as he continued to watch their surroundings and take quick glances at his dead partner.

"To save him the heartbreak of coming home to find his only son dead. You didn't know it, but Rawlings forced that badge onto his son so he could send him undercover to get close to me. It didn't work, and I planned on pretending I didn't know about it, but then those idiot DEA agents I hired tried to bring him in on a task I gave them to make their workload easier. If it's time to shut down shop, then I must clean it up before I put up the for sale sign on my entire operation. Let Demarcus go and leave that grown-ass boy alone. He and his wife are pawns for the Haitians now. The only reason the ho is running for city councilman is that his wife made him do it. My case doesn't belong to you anymore, Detective. The government is shutting down my operations from coast to coast as I enjoy the show. If you value your life, Ryu, saddle up and ride into the sunset. I'm double backboned, and this here ain't my first rodeo." His last words were in a heavy Texas drawl before the call ended.

Chicago, Illinois. Friday, October 18, 1991, cont.

Ethan didn't return to class, and the thought of something fatal happening to him began to play with Ronald's emotions. It was obvious that Ethan irked the hell out of him; still and all, the thought of the young man left for dead while under his care didn't sit right on Ronald's heart. He decided he would check on Ethan after lunch once he got his mind right.

Like a track star ready to break his 100-yard dash record, Ronald shot to his Regal, cranked the engine, and listened to his pipes roar as he sped out of the parking lot. He had fifteen minutes to smoke his joint, fifteen minutes to enjoy his high, and twenty-eight minutes to sleep it off. The extra two minutes were allotted for him to make it from the parking lot to his classroom. His date with "Mary" had become a daily reoccurrence after meeting Mimic and Ethan. Ronald was thankful that lunch came after the third period because he didn't know how he'd manage to get through the rest of the day after spending ninety minutes in class with those two. Mimic was a menace, and Ethan was more subtle yet sinister. It was both amazing and spine-chilling to see such a young boy master the art of making people think the opposite of him. The two boys together made teaching a nightmare.

Ronald was in full inhale by the time he reached the second stop sign from the school. Weed had always made up for the bullshit he stomached throughout his life. A bad job . . . A puff or two during his shift could fix it. An ugly girl with plentiful parts and willing to give it up without question . . . Two joints chased with a shot of something strong, and even that dilemma could be fixed. Weed also helped him push the thoughts away of the little boy in Atlanta with his strand of DNA.

Ronald was high and feeling relaxed. Some pussy would be nice, but with none around and too much pride to pull his dick out like a pervert and beat it in the car, he'd settle for music. As he reached toward his dashboard to turn on his radio, he caught a glimpse of a familiar shape. He wasn't sure that his vision was serv-

ing him truth considering Mary had just opened her legs to lure him in, but he could have sworn he saw Ethan running through the projects. From what he could tell, the boy wasn't being chased, but at the speed he was throttling at, it was fair to assume that he needed to get away from where he was . . . fast.

"Fuck them badass little boys, I'm off shit," Ronald said, relighting and pulling on his joint again in an attempt to convince himself not to turn back. His nerves caused him to pull a little too hard on the joint to inhale the smoke, and the tip of his joint went out.

"Ugh!" he moaned and grabbed his lighter as a series of shots went off a block behind him. It sounded like a war had erupted, a combination of a steady car back-firing sound mixed with the noise a string of fireworks lit at once would make. There was loud knocking, but it wasn't the bullets ripping the sound barrier. It was his heart beating against his chest cavity. Out of fear of being seen and perceived as a witness, he pulled over to the right and slouched down in his seat.

"Why didn't I keep going?" he asked, but he knew why. It wasn't his fears; it was Ethan. Ronald didn't have his gun on him but decided once the shooting stopped, he'd ride back past the entrance to the projects to see if he saw him, hopefully, still alive.

The director of the latest Hollywood blockbuster couldn't have set the scene up better. Two SUVs filled with black men covered in blue rags and white T-shirts shot past his Buick, running the stop sign. Ronald was sure that they had been the shooters since he could almost touch the adrenaline that was flowing from the cars. Once the SUVs burned rubber and disappeared from making sharp left turns, Ronald eased back up and his car door opened. Immediately, his heart stopped beating.

"I knew *that was you. What are you doing rolling through here smoking a joint on your lunch break? This is Crip territory, and let me tell you, those fools are crazy!" Ethan reached for the joint, but Ronald beat him to it.*

"Why does it feel like you had something to do with that shooting?" Ronald asked while starting the car to head back to school. There was a long silence, and the muscles in the boy's face tightened. He looked as if he placed the youth in him on hold to answer Ronald's question. A cold chill filled the car as he spoke.

"I did what you wouldn't do, Mr. Hill. I'm handling my daddy issues for good."

Ronald almost ran the red light as the boy's words shattered any innocence he hoped the boy had left. There was no doubt in Ronald's mind that Ethan wasn't telling the truth. He didn't need the details to know all five of the Bloods he stood in the hallway with an hour ago could be found in those projects dead.

"This ain't your first rodeo, is it, Ethan?"

The boy shook his head.

"I don't know about the rodeo part, but if you're asking if this is the first time I had to handle my daddy issues, no, it's not. Not with crackheads for parents, but it's becoming one of the last."

Ronald didn't want to seem uncomfortable with Ethan's participation in his murder confession and didn't have enough information to know his involvement, so he cracked his window and lit his joint.

"I used to mess with a girl from Texas when I lived in Atlanta. She was pretty as they come, but dumb. Not dumb to the world, just in the books and everything I liked back then. Anyway, I was trying to talk quick and hoping she was listening slow, but she picked up on the game I was trying to run on her fast. I knew she wasn't

girlfriend material, but I had to see what making love to her felt like. I spent more money than I had on getting us a nice hotel room that night with room service and the extra, unnecessary stuff you see on TV, and when she got there, she walked in wearing this ugly, ankle-length dress. All the curves I wanted to run my hands over were covered like she converted to an Amish lifestyle. Staring at her, I couldn't remember why I went out of my way to get with her. Her face wasn't as pretty as I remembered without her titties showing. She saw the look on my face, but once I closed the hotel room's door, she came out of the dress and stood there in front of me, stark naked. I wanted to play shy and shocked, but she didn't let me. She walked up on me and rubbed on my little big man and said, "I'm double backboned, and this here ain't my first rodeo. Get what you want from me, and I'll be on my way."

"Did you get it?" he asked excitedly.

"Yeah, I got it all night long and woke up with her gone. I tried to hunt her down for months because I had changed my mind about her after that night, but I couldn't find her." He smoked a little more of his joint before putting it out. "She had more experience in the shit I tried to dish out than I did, and I was wrong for thinking she couldn't handle my arrangement. Hell, she handled it better than me."

"So, what does that have to do with me?"

"Nothing; nothing at all. I said all of that to say that you're double backboned, and you know it. You got confidence built from a strength you shouldn't have so early in life. I don't think I've said this to anyone and ever truly meant it, but, you, Ethan, you can be anything you want to be. I'm just scared of what that will ultimately be."

Ethan leaned back in his seat, nodding his head.

***

Ronald was snatched out of the memory as the door of his hospital room slammed.

"I'm sorry to wake you, Ronald. I heard bits and pieces of what happened to you the other day and wanted to check in on you. I baked you a cake. I hope you like caramel."

"That was sweet of you, but I'm OK. It's called old age."

"But that's the thing," Betsy said, inviting herself to the available bedside seat. She was hoping to catch him sleeping to steal a peek at his front or back end, depending on where the hospital grown opened. However, seeing him in bed, knowing there weren't any drawers covering him seemed to suffice. "You're not all that old. Did you use to box?" she asked, smiling like she was envisioning him floating around the ring in knee-length shorts.

"No, but for a while, I wanted to. No head injuries; just rotten luck."

"That's more than rotten luck. I believe old age reveals the secrets of our youth, and the way we go out reflects our character."

"Is that what you think?" he grunted.

"Yes, I do, and if your memory is the problem, I'd say there was a lot of stuff in your past you tried hard to forget!"

"Now, I'll agree with you on that!"

"Well, good. I also grabbed that box of books you had your son bring. They didn't know when you'd be coming back, so I thought it would be nice if I brought you something to help the time go by."

"What box of books? My son came by?"

"Yes, he said you asked him to bring them. I was standing at the desk when he came. Don't you remember asking him?"

"No, I don't. I can't remember the last time I spoke with the boy. Honestly, he hates me."

"No, he doesn't!"

"That's one thing I can't forget. He hates me for not being there for him when he was growing up. You know, I was young and selfish and thought I was doing the boy a favor by staying away, but I was wrong. Didn't realize that until he said it."

"Oh, Ronald."

"No, ma'am, don't feel sorry for me. I enjoyed fucking up in the past. What books are in that box anyway?"

Betsy stood up and made sure she put a shake in her walk to bring attention to her ass. As she felt her pants bunch and release with each shake, she wondered if he remembered the effects a phat ass would normally do to a man. She glanced back and was reassured by Ronald's eyes locked on her butt.

"Let's see what you got. There's *Think and Grow Rich, The Book of Life*, a Quran, and a Bible. There're a few Iceberg Slim books in the box. Did you know that Iceberg Slim is from Chicago? My daddy used to read his books religiously, and you have this folder," she said, flipping through a three-ring binder, "with newspaper clippings on Frank Lucas, 'Bumpy' Johnson, the Miami drug war, and a lot of stuff on the Mexican and Columbian drug cartels. The last few pages are on Memphis. Oh wait, there are a few maps of Memphis in here too and a couple of articles on the city."

"Why in the hell would I have any of that?"

"Your guess is better than mine. There's a yearbook in here from 1992 too and a few sealed envelopes. Wait a minute. I think your son brought you the wrong box. This box says *Ethan Wade Carruthers* on the side of it." With the sound of that name, his memory came back.

"The yearbook . . . Pass me that yearbook."

Ronald flipped through the pages knowing the page he was looking for and who he would find on it. Before kicking Betsy out so he could take another trip down memory lane, he had to ask, "That episode of *60 Minutes* we were watching, did anything come of that? Like, did you see anything on the news after it aired?"

"Are you kidding me? It was on the news before and after that show aired. They have been playing it once a day. I take it the show was taped months before it aired because the FBI and those other agencies have been finding and shutting down that kingpin's operations all over the U.S., and they said that boy even has a few going outside the country. They don't know who he is, but they know he's black, from Chicago, and that he isn't working for nobody but himself. They think his operation might be bigger than Escobar's. They've arrested more law enforcement than they have drug dealers, and they're shutting down different pharmaceutical companies too. They don't know how many different sources this Joe was using, and I saw one report on CNN that said he has been dead for years, but his operation is so large that it's still running without him. Nobody knows what's true and what's not, but I can promise you this. When all of this is over, the smoke is going to linger for years. There are a lot of people locked up and serving hard time behind these dirty cops and agents. The government is going to have to investigate this stuff, and you know like I know, they are going to take their time because they hate admitting when their people do wrong."

"Sounds like a lot of corruption is going on. I haven't been able to catch none of it with my illness flared up. I only saw a small piece of the show."

"You can watch that episode whenever you want. It's on, On Demand. You know, if it weren't for that *60 Minutes* piece, none of this would have been uncovered."

"I'm sure it wouldn't."

"Give me the remote, and I can put it on for you before I go. I'll try to check on you tomorrow if I get this way. Don't you forget me. We're *special* friends," she added, playing on his memory and hoping he'd think they were more serious than what they were.

"How could I forget all that ass," he flirted as he remembered thinking he'd love to be able to bend her over from time to time when he first moved into the assisted living facility, but her mouth made it easy for him to forget about her horselike backside.

"Oh, Ronald, stop it. I'll see you around this time tomorrow."

The show was on, but this time without the commercials. In less than five minutes, Ronald was at the point of the show where he had left off days before. The man with the blackened face was talking.

"I didn't think none of the moves he was telling me about could really happen. It all sounded like it would work, but it would take armored truckloads of money to get the corporations to do what he needed them to do, and even more money to persuade law enforcement to join him. His plan couldn't work without dirty cops, hungry bankers, and greedy politicians. Think about Frank Lucas in the 1970s and who he had ties with, and then five times his connections. You'd have to have enough backup and money to cut out the middleman, which is like causing a civil war in the drug game, and unlike Frank, you'd eventually have to take out the supplier and become him. I'm not smart, but even a dummy knows that kind of money could buy small countries and maybe even a few low-budget planets around Earth. My boo Oprah don't even got bread that can stretch like that, and she's the bakery." He blew a kiss to the camera that wouldn't be seen behind his disguise. *"I love you, baby, and it should be you interviewing me with yo'*

sexy self. That security guard ain't hitting you right. Let a real nigga get in there, and I'll give your articulated ass something to talk about."

"I think we all love Oprah, but can you please continue?" the reporter demanded in the tone of a request.

"Yeah, no problem. I just wanted my lady to know what it is with me. But, yeah, I really thought dude was tripping because he stayed dirty and always had on a pair of busted shoes. Everybody knew he was broke. He was a crack baby, and his people were on that pipe hard."

"You're speaking about the pipe used to freebase cocaine, which is how the drug can be smoked once it has been separated from the chemical impurities. Is that right?"

"Shit, you tell me. I'm not a chemist. I just know that's how the addicts around me liked to smoke it—you trying to add too much science and math to this interview. You're doing too much, baby girl. You need to watch some of Oprah's throwback shows. You got to let it flow!"

"Continue," she countered visibly annoyed.

"Like I was saying, dude was a charity case, so I asked him how did his broke ass plan on getting the bread. The nigga looked me in the eyes and said, 'First, I'll get the numbers I need from the stock market, and then I'll walk into the bank and shake a few hands for the rest.'"

"Wait a minute; let me get this right. You're saying a poor, underprivileged, South Side of Chicago inner-city youth with drug addicts for parents told you he'd create and fund the biggest drug empire in the world with money he'd invest in the extremely risky stock market, and you sit here today, confirming the almost fictional plan worked?"

"I thought that's what I said a minute ago. Weren't you listening? To be a good reporter, you've got to listen and pay attention." He reprimanded her and shook his head in disbelief before continuing. "Dude flashed a few books at me when he was breaking it down. I didn't read the titles; reading wasn't really my thing back then, but I knew by his crooked smile he had done his research on the shit. Yes, his plan worked. Little dirty cuz pulled the impossible off."

Chapter Five

Memphis, Tennessee. Wednesday, January 23, 2019

"This is harassment, and the slander surrounding this investigation is absurd. This is a classic case of discrimination, and we will file suit against the federal government over this unlawful intrusion. Why aren't there any white-owned financial firms in Memphis under investigation? That's easy. This Joe or whatever pseudonym this criminal elected to go by that the FBI is on a losing manhunt for is black, and the perception of the black community is that we stand together through everything, including criminal activity, which couldn't be further from the truth. Everything I have, I earned legally, and I would never tie myself to the sickening antics of a drug dealer and murderer, nor would I take part in them. Take a fine-tooth comb and a microscope . . . Hell, you can throw in a bloodhound too and dig through whatever financial records of mine you choose. Please note, once I am found innocent, use this same platform you have me under suspicion on as the stage you stand on to give me a public apology and restitution for defamation of my character."

"That was a piece of the statement Dwayne Hollingswell of Zion Venture Capital requested his new CEO, Heather Rodgers, to release on his behalf shortly after federal agents entered their building and began their formal federal investigation just days ago," Zack Til-

man of WNOB Memphis radio said over the airways.
He threw that same bone out to his panelists of certified
guests, and he knew exactly which vicious dog would go
after it.

  *"I don't know much about brother Dwayne besides the
little research I did after being invited to the show, but
as a black Afro male choosing to reside in this color-di-
vided country, I agree. This is a discrimination case.
Here, we have a successful black male born and raised
here in Memphis who saved every nickel he earned to
invest in his dreams, and as soon as this imaginary
black villain is invented, he gets dragged into this mad-
ness. Now, everything he worked hard to obtain is in
question."* Dr. Uthman, the doctor of International Black
and Afro Studies at Memphis State University and author
of *Black in My White Coffee Mug* was only getting started, but Wanda Steel, of *Financial Wave* magazine, wasn't
in the mood to hear his black empowerment speech. She
cleared her throat obnoxiously and cut the doctor off in
midsentence.

  *"It wouldn't please me more to label this a discrimina-
tion case, but once you've done more than a short spell
of research to earn a chair on a popular radio show,
you'll uncover this raid and investigation are warranted. Dwayne Hollingswell's historical relationship in
finance is book worthy, but what about his past over a
dozen arrests, or, case in point, his current open investigation with the SEC for insider trading? Millions, if
not billions, of dollars are under question as to if it was
traded and earned legally, and from the vast hours of
research I've invested on my own, I'm leaning toward
him being guilty."*

  *"With a father who is only an eighth black, I'm sure
you would act as the judge and juror in Mr. Holling-
sworth's conviction,"* Dr. Uthman said, returning the
favor of shutting her up before she could finish.

"His name is Hollingswell, and you're so primitive. This has nothing to do with race, nor how many authentic black strands are in my DNA makeup. I'm sharing the facts which are, Mr. Hollingswell has a tie to both firms involved. He just fathered a child with Nivea Bowen of Bowen Capital Management, and Nivea admitted to having a past sexual relationship with the owner of the other firm mentioned in the investigation."

"That sounds like this Nivea is taking information from one firm and sending it to the next if she has a sexual relationship with both. I don't know too many men that would be ecstatic to work together knowing they've shared the same woman." Pam Dagger, life coach and reoccurring guest of the show, chimed in.

"Right!" Dr. Uthman grunted as Wanda Steel spoke.

"I agree if this was a bar brawl, but when it comes to millions of dollars of profits, normal rules don't apply. Before the media could wrap their hands around it, Mr. Hollingswell fled the country with the money, so there were no accounts to freeze; he stepped down as CEO of his company, and a few months later, sent for Nivea Bowen to be with him. The innocent does not flee, nor do they step down from the company they invested their lives into building, and that's not the kicker. Edward, an employee and best friend of Dwayne Hollingswell, was arrested and found guilty of insider trading in this same incident. A little investigation into him, and I learned he's been arrested and convicted of this before. He had his rights to trade in any format taken from him. Yet, he continued under his girlfriend's account, and what bothers me the most is Mr. Hollingswell found him valuable to hire with knowledge of his illegal acts. He just had the new CEO state, the perception of the black community is that we stand together through everything, including criminal activity, which couldn't be further from the

truth, but his actions show the perception in this situation is, indeed, true. The toxin in Mr. Hollingwell's venom can't be hidden!"

Feeling defeated with nothing left of substance to say without doing more research on the case, Dr. Uthman leaned over his chair toward Wanda Steel and said, "If you have that much time to research someone's business for free, you need to secure your own dick and stop focusing on Mr. Hollingswell's."

"Is that what you do?" she snapped. "Focus on securing dick in your free time?"

"Whoa whoa whoa. We aren't even ten minutes into the show, and gloves are already off. Let's take a few calls and let this heated pot simmer," Zack announced, loving the hostility in the room. "John Ryan Smethwick the Third, you're on. What're your thoughts?"

The name alone raised every panelist's brow. It wasn't forbidden for white listeners to call in, though it was rare.

"Hello, Zack, and guest panelists. How are all of you doing?" There wasn't any other way to describe the voice they heard besides white. Not country white; yet, it was American. It was that educated and rich voice you'd hear in an attorney's office in California.

"We're doing great; thanks for calling. What are your thoughts on this Dwayne Hollingswell investigation? Do you think he's Joe or tied to him?"

"Honestly, I've done my research on Dwayne like Wanda has, and I know for a fact he's not Joe. Those dozens of arrests she mentioned were for domestic violence and violation of the restraint orders placed on him. All of his arrests involve one woman, and from what I can tell, she's rich, crazy as hell, and is still giving him the blues."

"We had a show not too long ago about the high domestic violence arrest in Memphis and how easy it is

to be found guilty of DV without evidence. Men and women are both being convicted of it off hearsay. I'm not saying Mr. Hollingswell is innocent, but that does straighten out Wanda's arrest argument against him. What about the insider trading pending investigation and what information, if any, did you run across that has you convinced Joe and Dwayne aren't the same?" Zack questioned.

"That insider trading stuff doesn't matter to a man like Dwayne. He'll beat it, but even if he didn't, it couldn't stop his drive. He's a wrecking ball with momentum; he's unstoppable. He'll die being the most successful black man in finance history, but by the way he moves, no one will ever know. They'll have access the information to prove it. I understand why people would think he and Joe are the same person. His moves are exactly like Joe's."

"And how do you know how Joe moves?" Wanda Steel *shouted, not liking the feelings that being outshined brought her.*

"Simple. I know because I am Joe."

"I knew Joe wasn't black!" Dr. Uthman *yelled in relief.*

"Wrong. I'm 100 percent black and have traced my bloodline back to a small tribe in Kubuta, an inkhundla of Eswatini, located in the Shiselweni District. In other words, a place where your black enlightenment hasn't reached, but you are awakened, my brother. I'm dying to know if your enlightenment leads you into kissing white women in their mouths when you pass up our strong black sisters to make love to them," he asked through chuckles.

Wanda looked at Dr. Uthman, ready to hear him tear this Joe in half with his words. However, he sat there silently with his hands in his lap, awaiting Joe's next words.

"Instead of debating over my race or if Dwayne and I are one and the same, how about stating the obvious. Dwayne and I both are incredibly successful men who played the game and won. It doesn't matter who created the playing field or set the rules. We learned the game, made it our own, and we both are victorious."

Zack had his hands in the air waving them frantically, trying to get the show's manager Wayne's attention. He was asleep over the station's switchboard like usual. The alcohol had him in a sedative state, and the quickie he had in the maintenance closet with the 23-year-old, big-breasted security guard who needed help getting her bills caught up this month had him drained. Wayne hadn't shot two loads off in one session in years, but the excitement of his 55-year-old dick being inside of a beauty so youthful reset the libido he thought he outgrew.

"How do we know you're the real Joe?" Pam spoke up to buy more time with the caller once she caught on to what Zack was doing. "Any nutcase with a phone and who has been watching the news could be calling in."

"No one is listening to the show but me. Everyone that's tuned in is listening to last year's Christmas show. Don't believe me; turn on the radio. I was a fan of the show. Most of it is propaganda and twisted facts to raise the ratings, but I dig it, and that's why I own the station to make sure the show never gets cut. I was thrilled when I heard I'd made the topic of today's show. Yesterday, I decided to give Zack an opportunity for an exclusive one-on-one interview with me. However, he seems to be disappointing me right now. What are you doing, Zack?"

"I'm listening and wondering what I could have done to disappoint you," he lied as Wayne finally moved around for comfort and glanced at him. He mouthed, *"Joe is on the phone; listen,"* and used his own version of sign language to act out what he said.

"You're sick!" Wanda couldn't bite her tongue any longer in fear that it would bleed. "How can you compare yourself to the achievements of Mr. Hollingswell? You're a murderer with multiple killing methods ranging from guns to drugs. You poison our streets and destroy our people. Misfortune is your fortune, and you disgust me!"

"And your fortune comes differently? Whether you invest on the up or downside of a company's growth, there's always someone left with the misfortune. I didn't compare myself with him. I pointed out similarities. This show wanted us to be one and the same. You wanted to be the bitch that had the inside scoop on Dwayne, and you wanted your information to link us. You were trying to gain on his misfortune. Shame on you, and I looked at your trading history. You're a bear trader. You only profit off losses."

"And no one dies because of it!"

"Shut your mouth when I'm speaking!"

Wanda roared in laughter. She could barely catch her breath. Her laughter forced Wayne to join the room. Although he heard what she said loud and clear, he couldn't believe how Joe's words had tickled her.

"Did you call the police?" Zack whispered to Wayne.

"And what do you think you're doing, Zack?"

"I'm—"

"He doesn't owe you an answer, nor do you have any control over my mouth. You're an egotistical psychopath. Let me guess what led you to this life . . . daddy issues?"

"Wayne, I'm tired of hearing her voice!"

There wasn't time for anyone to digest Joe's words to the show manager. In a flash, he pulled a gun from his waistband and shot Wanda in her forehead, an inch from her hairline and then in her face. Pam jumped up to run . . . and received two shots, one in her chest and the other in her neck on her way down. Zack and Dr. Uthman were frozen in their seats.

"I asked you a question, Zack, and if I were you, I'd answer it truthfully!" the voice blared through the studio.

"I was . . . was trying to get Wayne to call the police." He stammered over his words.

"Call them for what?"

"To inform them that we had you on the phone."

"And what was that supposed to do? I allowed you to interview me in private, but you decided it should be public. So, let's make it public."

Wayne reached over the switchboard and flipped a button.

"Go ahead, Zack. Introduce yourself and today's topic. Make sure you mention me and your studio guest."

Zack looked at Wayne for help, but his boss and friend of the past ten years wore a blank expression. Wayne was a punk that feared his own shadow. Zack could only imagine what Joe had done to turn him into a killer. After a second more of pleading with his eyes, Wayne pressed the gun to the side of Zack's head, and he immediately spoke.

"Welcome to Say It with Your Chest radio with me, your boy Zack Tilman on 95.1 WNOB Memphis radio. I have a special guest joining us today, and you're never going to believe me when I say who it is, and I also have the president of black America, Dr. Uthman, up in here ready to assist with this historic interview. We have . . . Um, we have the man that has the city buzzing and all twelve U.S government agencies bugging. The man of the hour, every hour, of the past three months . . . Jooooooooooe."

"Wow, thanks for the warm welcome, Zack. I liked that throwback Arsenio Hall show opening at the end, but I changed my mind. I don't need you for this interview."

Wayne emptied the remaining bullets of his Beretta into Zack. Blood and brain matter flew everywhere, including on Dr. Uthman who had his first response in minutes. Although silent, his frantic breathing spoke volumes.

"I won't keep you long seeing most of you will need time to grieve your favorite radio personality as will I. I just wanted to clear up this rumor that's spreading about this fancy dressing hedge fund manager possibly being me. It is so disheartening that we live in a world that strives to take the easy way out. It took no thought or strategizing to pin the only successful black stock trader to my moves.

"From what I heard from the late Wanda Steel of Financial Wave magazine is that Mr. Hollingswell has a few criminal arrests and an open insider trading investigation. That's not enough to make him me. He's a stock guy, and rumor has it, I'm from Chicago. Isn't that the home of the Chicago Board of Trade, or for those that don't know, the commodities version of what they have in New York on Wall Street? Why did I have to get it through stocks? You took the words of a Crip in need of retirement for face value and put no thought in your investigation. Did anyone take a second to see what color the person managing the electric company's fund was? What about the police or fire departments? How about the surrounding cities? It's been assumed Memphis is the home of my operations, but it's known my operations run coast to coast and in many countries. Did anyone check to see if there is or was a black man tearing a hole in the foreign markets? Watching the moves Dwayne is making in the world of finance is as amazing as watching a unicorn drink rainbow-colored water out of a rambling stream flowing peacefully through the hood, but I am not your average Joe. Leave the billionaire alone and get back on task. I'm still free. Isn't taking my freedom your objective?"

A clicking sound followed. Wayne ended the live feed and sprinted for the exit like there was a time restraint on his next move. After waiting a few minutes, Dr. Uthman stood up under the assumption the coast was clear. Even if it weren't, he could no longer keep his cool keeping company with the dead.

"Do you know why I didn't kill you, Dr. Uthman?" The voice caused him to jump. In the silence of the room, he felt like he was trapped in the center of the sound.

"Yeah, I know why."

"Why?" Joe asked with a slight chuckle.

"Because I know when to shut the fuck up!"

"Exactly!"

Hysterical laughter filled the building as Dr. Uthman's feet turned into wheels. He was gone in less than sixty seconds.

Ronald watched the show, and Ethan's photo owned his attention. The innocence in the boy's smile did nothing to hide the pain planted deeply in his eyes. If the eyes are truly the window to the soul, any Peeping Tom would run from the damage they would see within.

Rubbing his shaky finger across the boy's face, Ronald smiled as he remembered the bond they grew after the shooting incident. It was funny how their ten-minute ride back to the school caused him to see Ethan and his annoying behavior as small previews of the boy's wit and wisdom. The only time Ethan's actions irritated him was when he acted on behalf of Mimic.

The smile on his face demilitarized as his finger made his way down to Mimic's tight-lipped mean mug. He was trying too hard to invoke fear in others by use of the muscles in his face. The picture spoke a thousand words and said, *"This boy is not to be fucked with"* to those who didn't know him, but Ronald knew him, and the only word he heard spoken from looking at the picture was, *wannabe*. It was obvious that those he gangbanged with agreed. They nicknamed him Mimic. At Ronald's best guess, they chose the name thinking it sounded a lot cooler than calling him "Baby Imitation" or "OG Copycat." It's not that he didn't like the boy. The issue was he knew he couldn't trust him, and that made him uncomfortable. Mimic would pretend to be anything and do whatever was asked of him to be accepted by the Crips, and once he was officially initiated, he longed to be ranked amongst the most loyal to the gang. It was sickening to watch the boy give up so much of himself to pretend to be something he wasn't and to play such a deadly game. In fact, it was astonishing to see that he was still alive.

The show blinked twice marking another commercial break, and though Ronald had grown accustomed to the way the show played on On Demand, it still caught his attention.

"The interview you were watching was filmed over three months ago. I really wish we could show you more, but that is all the footage we managed to tape. During our break, my guest went to the restroom, and he never returned. He was found in a stall in the men's restroom with four feet of electrical wires tightly coiled around his neck, and his mouth stuffed with a bundle of hundred-dollar bills—the exact amount he had been offered to do the show. His murder could have been written in a paranormal horror movie seeing that there was no evidence left behind from his killer. The restroom had been searched before his use, and there was an armed guard at the outer door during the murder. The restroom has no windows, and the vents to the air and heating unit open no more than twelve inches. The coroner's office

labeled it a suicide, but if you were in the building at the time of his death and could see the fear in his eyes, you'd know different!"

"No!" Ronald yelled as those in the building gave accounts of what they saw. Seconds later, his room's door flew open, and he hit the power button on the remote.

"Are you in pain, Mr. Hill?"

"It's Ronald. My father was Mr. Hill, and, no, I'm fine. I was getting into a movie, and it turned out to be a horror flick. The director of the show had one of his writers kill off my favorite costar."

"Aw, man, I hate when that happens," the nurse whined and then sucked her teeth.

"Yeah," Ronald agreed, pacing his words so she wouldn't hear him sob. "It's heartbreaking."

"It is, but they have to keep you interested and give you a reason to keep watching, or, like all my favorite shows that aren't on, they kill off a star so they can end the show. Maybe it's the last season it'll be on the air," she suggested.

"It's the last season for the actors, but for the director, I'm sure the show must go on."

She sighed. "That's the truth. The actors are out of a job while the director is busy working on his next project. Well, I was due to come in here and check your vitals in thirty minutes. I might as well do it now and make sure that heartbreaking news didn't really break your heart," she giggled.

While the nurse pressed different buttons on the machines Ronald was connected to, a slide show of Mimic flashed through his mind until the memory that made him identifiable on the show resonated.

Chapter Six

Chicago, Illinois. Wednesday, December 18, 1991

It was a rare occasion not to see snow blanketing Chicago a week before Christmas. It was cold out; however, the weather was picture-perfect for the last day of school. Christmas had always been Ronald's most hated holiday. His father didn't allow the celebration of holidays under his roof—or the celebration of anything else, for that matter. It wasn't a religious rebellion; he didn't allow it celebrated because he thought it was a clever distraction used to take the focus off the reality of life. After years of watching his friends floss their new items after the holiday, it turned his jealousy into hate. This Christmas season, Ronald was in the spirit to receive and accept every gift the holiday sent his way. His first gift of the season was unwrapping the chick who had been eye fucking him for weeks at the gym. She gifted him with a B+ grade pussy and some dynamite head. Kim, Kimmie, or whatever her name was had never said a word to him, but that quickly changed when he took his shirt off to wipe the sweat from his face, and she got a good look at the print embossed in his gray sweatpants.

"Looks like another great workout," she noted with a sexy smirk.

"Nah, it could have been better. I still have a lot more energy I need to burn off."

"Sounds like you need to hit something." She lifted her brow and gave Ronald a head nod toward the men's room. "I'm sure you'll get a better workout in if you beat something up."

"Is that right?"

She didn't respond. Instead, she about-faced and strutted to the men's restroom. The man walking out snapped his neck as she passed him and walked in shamelessly. His curiosity disappeared when he saw Ronald throw his T-shirt over his shoulder and follow her lead. The guy had seen them both at the gym and knew they weren't together. He gave Ronald a mischievous smile and approving head nod. Ronald returned the sentiment.

"Where did you go?" Ronald asked after looking under the stall doors for a pair of woman's legs. There wasn't an answer; yet, the echo of a running shower at the rear of the room called out to him. He continued his search for a pair of sexy legs and couldn't find any. The shower was running in the handicapped stall, and unless the person could hover like a genie, he knew he found her.

Ronald opened the door slowly, and there she was . . . completely naked, sitting on the accessibility bench with her legs gapped open with her index finger over her lips. Her labia were swollen, and her clit enlarged like a porn star that had been in the industry for a while. The sight was disappointing. He hadn't had sex outside of the intimacy he shared within his hand in a few weeks, and he knew from the looks of her gapped leg peace offering that she couldn't say the same. He pumped body wash in his hands and emerged his balls into it to do away with the scent of sweat and then rubbed the remaining soap down his shaft. The motion made him stiff, and he sent his dick straight to her mouth. As if she had a strange fetish for an active chemical in the soap, she forced him *down her esophagus. With his balls now resting on her soapy chin, she looked up at him with her eyes fully open. She looked like a begging dog, but Ronald had no sympathy for beggars. He placed his palms on both sides of her face and fucked her mouth like it was the pussy he was forced to bypass. Soap suds covered her face completely in seconds. It was the sexiest shit Ronald had ever seen and caused him to crave to get inside of her. He glanced around the room at her clothes hanging on the hook on the back of the door and hoped she had a purse on it with a condom large enough to fit him inside. There wasn't any. He'd have to suffice for the use of his imagination and her mouth. When he tilted his head back to visit his own version of the land of make-believe, a gold square flew over him and hit the wall.*

"Just in case."

The voice startled Ms. Soapy Face, but Ronald knew who it was.

"You just saved my life."

"I already know!"

That fly, thank you, and you're welcome exchange gave Ronald the opening he needed to retrieve his second gift of the season. He slid out of her mouth, into the condom, and then into her from the back. Gripping her breasts to keep his balance on the slippery floor, he jingled her bells until his balls were drained.

Feeling renewed, he skipped his breakfast of Champions, a joint followed by a large bowl of honey-flavored cereal, and got ready for his third and most favorite gift, the last day of school with early dismissal.

"How about we watch a movie since this is the last period of the day?" he asked, rolling the TV and VCR in the room. He received a response from most of the class, but the two voices he waited to hear from were absent. He looked toward Ethan's desk, and Ethan nodded his head toward Mimic's seat on the front row.

Mimic had a hoodie over his head and face lying on the desk unseen behind the folding of his arms.

"Are you all right, Martin?"

"Yeah, I'm good; just hella tired."

"That's a desk, not a bed. You're in class. There's no sleeping in here."

"This is a school, not a movie theater but we're about to watch a movie. What's the difference?"

Ronald charged at him to snatch the hood from his head, but once Mimic looked up, he stopped in his tracks.

"I'm good, Mr. Ronald, play your movie." Mimic could tell by Ronald's concerned facial expression that his answer fell on deaf ears. He battled coming to school after his initiation last night, but out of fear of what he'd be asked to do next, school was his excuse for why he couldn't do it. He knew he wouldn't be able to avoid answering the question for long, although it was obvious what occurred.

"We'll talk after class."

"Yes, we will!" Ethan said disappointingly and gave Ronald a sympathetic look and quietly begged him to let it go temporarily.

"Okay, well, I hope you like historical documentaries." The class moaned in disgust, and some students decided to join Mimic in his ninety-minute nap. That didn't last long. Once he hit play, *the class was alive. "Wow, how did my bootleg copy of* House Party *get in there?"*

Cheers filled the room, and even Mimic slightly lifted his head to watch. "If the principal comes in here, I need you to press stop *on the remote. Can you handle that, Candice?"*

The girl nodded her head. She was excited to have been chosen. The only sound that could be heard in the class was laughter.

The bell rang, and Mimic tried to slide out the door with those fleeing the room, but he was pulled back in by the back of his hoodie. Ronald locked the door when the last student stepped out.

"So, you're a real Crip now?" The question shot out of Ethan's mouth before Ronald could say a word.

"No, I been a Crip. Crips aren't made, homie; we're born."

"That doesn't even make sense. You joined a gang that gassed you up to believe shit that don't make sense?"

Ronald knew he should have intervened; however, curiosity of the outcome of Ethan's peer-to-peer mediation stopped him. He didn't know how far back the boys' relationship went, but he recognized their tie months back.

"It wouldn't make sense to you because you're not a Crip, and you don't understand our history."

"What's there to understand? Hate those in red, do illegal shit, and lie and say you're uplifting those in your hood while doing it. It's the same for Bloods. The hardest decision to make in gangbanging is birthed in a box of crayons, Red or Blue," he said with a shrug.

"Damn, nigga, you sound like you're the new recruitment officer for the Gangsta Disciples. Don't speak on shit you don't know shit about."

"Never that. I'm Ethan, my nigga. I don't need a gang or organization to back me or stand with me. I'm my own gang, cuz, Blood." He threw up a fake gang sign with his fingers and then pointed at Mimic's hand. "Was busting your hand open really worth it?"

Ronald hadn't noticed Mimic's right hand was bandaged up until that moment.

"I didn't bust my hand open, dumb ass!" he snapped, unwrapping his hand and removing the gauze from his palm and knuckles. He revealed the word Mimic tattooed across his knuckles and the word Crip tattooed

in the palm of his hand. Both Ethan and Ronald stepped closer to read it.

"Are you crazy?" Ronald yelled. "You just painted a target on your back!"

"Man, ain't nobody gon' run up on me. They ain't stupid."

"They don't have to be stupid; you are," Ethan countered. "You don't even want the tattoo. Look at where you got it."

"I got it where everybody I hit up can see it."

"You mean when you use gangbanging sign language," Ethan chuckled. "You won't ever get a job with that in your hand. I hope you're good at robbing and stealing."

"Like your daddy?" Mimic chuckled, giving him a scoop of what he dished out.

"More like your daddy. He's still facing those federal drug charges, right? If he got caught, he wasn't too good at it."

"My daddy is the coldest cat in the game, and you know it, so stop it. Your daddy is praying my daddy gets released, but since you call yourself checking me, tell your daddy mine is no longer accepting change. Cash those pennies in for dollars before he rolls up."

"Both of you shut the fuck up, please. Neither one of your daddies is worth shit, and neither is mine. Pack your shit and let's go."

"Go where?" Mimic questioned.

"One of two places. Your choice. Place one, to your grandmother's house to see what she thinks of this Crip tattoo, or place two, the tattoo parlor to get the shit covered up."

"Who does this cat think he is?" Mimic asked, looking at Ethan but didn't get the response he was looking for.

"I know who he thinks he is, but let's keep it all the way real. Mr. Ronald is the only nigga in both of our

lives that gives a fuck. Are we going to the tattoo shop or your granny's house? I know she's in there cooking something."

The tattoo parlor had music blasting, and the occupants were covered in piercings and a variety of meaningless yet colorful tattoos. The boys had never been in a parlor before, and their dropped jaws told on them. Everything they looked at amazed them, and they took turns pointing in different directions and telling each other to look. They kept the game going until Ronald joined them in the waiting area.

"I'm your uncle, and you live with me. You have a caseworker that's trying to get my custody taken away. If they see that tattoo in the palm of your hand, that's it. You go to foster care out of state, and I'll never see you again."

"Dang, you lie good!" Ethan acknowledged. He shook his head, wondering what else shady Ronald was good at.

"Yeah, only when necessary."

"When do you feel lying is necessary?" he shot back quizzically.

"When it saves a life."

Ethan accepted the answer and sat there thinking of situations that he would agree with it.

"Fuck you. There wasn't a Mexican, Cuban, Columbian, or Italian kingpin on Pablo Escobar's level. That fool made the blueprints for the prison he agreed to let the government put him in and forced them to set up shop at his shit to guard him. He's number one; you're fucking tripping!" a tall Latino biker covered in tattoos, including his face, said to the guys he'd been sitting with. The group had been talking since Ronald and the boys had arrived, but it was the first time any of them could hear their debate loud and clear.

"Are you fucking kidding me? How do you not give Frank Lucas the title? He was black and American. He had way more restrictions to get around than Escobar, and he was shipping that shit in using military coffins. To this day, nobody has pushed a purer heroin than him, especially not at that price. You better calculate what he could have made if he wasn't showing the hood love with discounts," the fattest and darkest-skinned biker said as he filled out the consent form for his upcoming needle work.

"I don't know, Nick; I think both of y'all are forgetting about La Madrina. That chick was coldhearted. She went against her woman nature and a man's too with her heartless moves. Anybody that crossed her could get it—babies, drug heads, and her husband. That chick was ruthless. My kinda lady!"

"You need to stop drinking, fool; you're tripping out. That woman scares me, and did you forget about the Ochoas? I'm not saying they were harder than Escobar, but they are my number two."

The other men agreed and chimed in on their favorite Ochoa brothers' story, and, of course, a battle over the Don, Fabio Ochoa, which broke out. Opinions on Fabio's involvement in the scheme of things sent the debate in a circle. After hearing names like Rafael, Noriega, and Carlos Lehder being dropped, an unexpected referee stepped in.

"You guys are crazy. You can't compare kingpins. There are too many factors you'd have to consider. First and foremost, is the person really a kingpin, or are they a drug lord, gangster, trafficker, mobster, or bandit? They have different names because they aren't the same. A kingpin is supposed to be essential to the success of the organization or the success of an operation, and depending on the moves that are being made, your king-

pin might really be a drug lord. You said, La Madrina, right? But Griselda Blanco was a member of the Medellin Cartel. That's the organization Pablo put together. You aren't a kingpin if you are a boss under someone else's organization. She was a drug lord and don't try to debate me. That's a fact.

"One of you mentioned Frank Lucas. He's one of my top five favorites, but truthfully, he wasn't a kingpin; he was a drug trafficker. Yeah, he knocked out the middleman, but he still had to re-up with somebody else. He never manufactured his product. He bought it, trafficked to the U.S, and made it his own by renaming it. If he would have bought a piece of the Golden Triangle or partnered with those running it instead of being a customer, I'd label him a kingpin, but when the war stopped, it cut off his transportation. If he wouldn't have been snitched on, his time was coming to an end.

"I'm surprised none of you mentioned 'Freeway Rick' Ross since he's been on the news lately. He was making 2 million a day moving weight. He's not a kingpin by my definition, but he's definitely an honorable mention trafficker. So are the Ochoa brothers. They were labeled as traffickers, but I beg to differ. They produced, manufactured, and distributed their cocaine. Yeah, they were in the Medellin Cartel with Pablo but were looked at as founders of the organization, not members. I'd label them kingpin bandits. Noriega and many more earned honorable mentions, but y'all were killing me with the way you were throwing that kingpin title around." He shook his head and sat back quietly like he'd never spoken. No one in the room made a sound. They couldn't; they were too amazed for words. It took two minutes before the man they called Nick spoke up.

"Hey, kid, so, Escobar is your all-time favorite?"

"I guess you can say that for now because there will never be another Escobar. Times have changed, and so has the image of a kingpin. There's no trust amongst thieves, and loyalty is fading away. By 2010, the snakes around you won't slither anymore. They will be rocking high top sneakers and flashy jewelry. The next generation of kingpins in the future will be ghost."

"Shit, don't stop now, youngster. Break that down. What do you mean they will be ghost?" the darker one in the group asked.

"Virtual, like that computerized talking thing on the Jetsons' cartoon. Technology is going to take over, and it's going to be easier to hide your face."

"Yeah, but drugs aren't virtue . . . virtual or whatever the fuck you said. These fools getting high and fucked up every day would sell their souls to get high. All that electronic shit will be in a pawn shop window. The hand-to-hand sells will never disappear."

"Why would you think a kingpin would care about the little fish who has to touch the product if he knows that the little fish doesn't know whose product he's moving or who he's really working for?"

"Huh?" the room hummed in unison.

"It's not that complicated if you listen to what I'm saying; it's simple. All you have to do is create a complicated pipeline that leads back to a throwaway corporation or maybe a midcap business. Be sure that the throwaway company is under the umbrella of a corporation that's too big to fail, and most importantly, make sure those with the longest lines of money back the standing of that corporation. If you can do that, it'll buy you political power which grants you protection from the corrupted branches of government." He stuck his index finger out to count off his list.

"The money that will be made from hand-to-hand transactions is the crumbs. Distribution will be the green veggies." With three fingers out, he said, *"Manufacturing the product is the meat and potatoes. The server of the meal is the big corporation covering you, and the chief is the political power protecting you."* With his free hand, he folded his fingers down until they were balled into a fist and then covered his closed hand with it. *"The restaurant is the corrupted officials protecting the chief, and I'm the restaurant owner. I mean, the kingpin is."* He removed the hand that covered his fist and then placed his fist in his pocket. *"That's all profit for the kingpin."*

"But how does anyone get higher than the politicians and government to be in a position to hire them?"

"Money . . . Lots of it and proof you can keep it rolling in. Money is a universal language. You can't just understand it; you have to know how to speak it fluently."

"Seems like you gave this a lot of thought," Ronald managed to say in his speechless state.

"Hell nah; it sounds like the little homie has put some shit in motion. Can I get a job?"

Everyone in earshot laughed except for Ronald and Ethan.

"Ronald and nephew Martin, you're up," the artist shouted, and Mimic shot his eyes at Ethan.

"Aye, can you break down what you were just saying while I'm getting my cover-up done?" His fear was deciphered through his meaningless words.

"Yeah, I got you."

As the artist set up shop, Ethan gave a step-by-step heavily detailed plan to achieving kingpin status in the next ten to fifteen years. His plan was so detailed that the artist forgot what they all had gathered for.

"What are we doing again?" he asked with tattoo gun buzzing away, but it seemed he wasn't the only one who had forgotten.

"Cover up the boy's hand," Ronald said as he read the titles of the books Ethan was pulling out of his backpack and stacking on the table.

"Cover it with what?"

"Just cover it. Black it out . . . I don't care."

Ronald's tone of voice made Ethan stop what he was doing to look at him. For the first time since Ethan began talking, he realized that maybe he had been talking too much.

Break It Down

Chapter Seven

Memphis, Tennessee. Thursday, January 31, 2019

Rain on a funeral procession is believed to mean the decease's soul escaped the confinement of the flesh and was in the process of traveling to heaven. The only indication that the soul was welcomed at its final resting place is the sound of thunder after the burial. If this belief were true, than heaven's gatekeepers were throwing Detective Rawlings a welcome-home party; hence, the reason for the thunder and lightning acting as garnishment to the storm.

The soggy weather made for stale moods as those attending the funeral dodged sinkholes and puddles to cross the muddy grass. The area of Memorial Park Cemetery was reserved for those of Rawlings's bloodline and, coincidentally, the chosen starting point of the lawn replacement service. The grass was removed the same day Rawlings was murdered. It was scheduled to be replaced the day of his funeral, but the rain postponed the installation, and to make the muddy situation worse, the funeral home didn't lay out a path for the attendees to follow to get to the tent where final words were to be said as his coffin was placed in the ground.

The star of the event's family, friends, coworkers, and even a few criminals whose lives changed from their arrest fought the thought of turning around and leaving when they realized the tent wasn't shielding them from the rain. The swampy hike they would have to endure to get back to the service road where their vehicles were parked would cause a higher level of grief than the gusty winds blowing water on their already tear-saturated face. As the pastor prayed to open the ceremony, the guests prayed that he'd make the burial service quick. With every head bowed, Detective Ryu took another shot of scotch from his flask. He seemed to be the only person unbothered by the weather, which might have had a lot to do with him being drunk.

The murder investigation of his partner was taken over by the Tennessee Bureau of Investigation, and his career case was stolen by every federal agency involved. With no wife or kids to shift his attention to, his purpose was in question, and the bottom of the bottle is where he decided to begin his search. Ryu gave absolutely no fucks that the mayor and his other superiors were in attendance and that any of them could potentially catch him drunk. He never liked any of them, especially not the asshole who was making his way up to the podium to speak.

"This is going to be harder to do than I foresaw, so please bear with me as I give it my best." The deputy director of the TBI, the agency formally investigating the murder of Rawlings, took an exaggerated deep breath, hoping the grief he created in his mind materialized as if it were coming from his heart. Ryu called his bluff before he ever made it to the stage. Hell, he knew there would be an Academy Award–winning performance when the deputy director took the podium days before the funeral because he knew Fredrick Davidson was full of shit.

"Mr. Perfect," as Ryu mockingly called him in conversation, was Rawlings's childhood friend and ex-partner. He proudly credited himself as the reason Rawlings made detective, and everyone agreed with him except for Rawlings. Hearing what really happened that night from his new partner's mouth, Ryu didn't agree with him either.

***

"How the hell would a kid get over that gate to climb up to the roof?" Rawlings asked, eyeing the abandoned commercial building in search of a way to get in to check it out. His resting partner was of no help.

"As I said, the old bitch was seeing things. This is an old service road, and there aren't any houses for miles. The question you should be asking is why the old bitch was driving down this dark-ass road this late at night, to begin with. I don't know why you wasted your time driving out here. I'm going back to sleep."

Fredrick pressed the button that locked his seat belt in place, and once it snapped back to its position along the side of the door frame, he turned to the right and sought some sleep facing the window. It never failed that when it came time to work, Fredrick went MIA. He'd been the same way since grad school. The teacher would give out an assignment and partner them up, and Fredrick did nothing but find excuses for why he shouldn't be doing anything. Rawlings had been carrying Fredrick's weight since the seventh grade and knew there would come a time when a grain of rice would be the reason he dropped him, but until then, he'd enjoy the perks of being good friends with someone popular.

"I take it you're staying in the car while I go check this one out?"

"Damn right, I am. One of us has to be the smart one. You're a fucking patrol officer, not a detective. Why do I have to remind you every day to leave the unsolved mystery cases to those who get paid for investigating that bogus shit? Go ahead and take your ass in there. I bet you get bit in the ass by a giant wood rat."

"Thanks for the words of encouragement," Rawlings said sarcastically, exiting the car. Fredrick's laziness irritated him to the core, but he couldn't deny when his partner was right. Rawlings did overdo what his posi-

tion required of him at times because he knew that his worth exceeded the position he was given. He was a detective at heart, like his father. It was in his blood to find the answers to questions that weren't asked. Something about the call and the building was suspicious, and until he had the evidence to clear the suspicion, there was a crime he needed to solve.

Barbed wire surrounded the gate, and it looked new in comparison to the building. It could have been added to keep trespassers out by the owner, but if the building meant that much to them, why had it been unoccupied for the last ten years? It was left abandoned on a service road least traveled. The longer Rawlings scanned over the gate with his flashlight racking his brain, the stronger he felt that something wasn't right. Looking back at the squad car only to see the back of his partner's head, he decided to walk the circumference of the property for an entrance.

Less than 300 feet into his inspection of the side of the building, something caught his eye. If you were passing by in the lit hours of the day, you'd think you were looking at a large pile of debris taken from the building. The scraps appeared to be a mound of carpet and miscellaneous structural items like doors, window frames, and Sheetrock. As he moved closer, he saw something that didn't belong and had been carefully blended in to give the impression that it was a part of the pile of trash. It was a tire, standing upright, attached to something. He moved a slab of Sheetrock to the side and found the hidden van. Calling backup immediately came to mind—until he thought of the hell he'd caught for calling in on his last self-appointed investigation . . . which turned out to be a large, black duffle bag filled with essential oils. He needed a solid piece of evidence before calling it in over the radio.

Quietly, he moved a folded office sectional aside and discovered a 3 cm in diameter cord that seemed to be running from the van to the dark back entrance of the building. He hurriedly moved a few more items, and when he uncovered the van's hinged double doors slightly cracked open, he opened them farther and found a 400-pound, 25,000-watt and gasoline-powered generator that could, at the very minimum, power that size of a building for eight hours at a time.

"Hey, partner, you might want to come see this," Rawlings whispered into his walkie-talkie, and, of course, he didn't receive a response. Fredrick slid down in his seat and was asleep. "Fuck it!" he announced, pulling his pistol and following the cord.

The cord led him to a stalemate. One dark room, one direction, and no upcoming doors to duck off to if he had indeed made the wrong decision in not calling for backup. He said a quick prayer for protection and took a step forward. Lights lit up along the corridor, and five seconds later, he heard a man yell, "The cops are here!"

Running down the hallway at top speed, he came to a padlocked door. It was the only door he could choose, and it was in the same direction he had heard the voice come from. He ran a yard back and then charged at the door with his booted foot. He fell on his ass, pulled his hamstring, and the door stood there completely intact. He had to get in that room before whoever was in it could escape.

Fredrick was abruptly woken out of his sleep by the sound of shots being fired in the distance.

"Partner!" he screamed as fear forced his adrenaline to follow. He wasn't a total dick with no emotions, especially not when it came to Rawlings. In all honesty, Rawlings was the only true friend he had managed to keep over the years, and he had grown a soft spot for his undying and unwavering loyalty. Yes, he used him for his own greater good and abused the friendship more than he nurtured it; however, he'd be first in line to take a bullet for him. Immediately, he called for backup and exited the vehicle with his gun and toe. He wasn't sure which direction his partner had taken, so he took the route less traveled, which was toward the shooting.

As he neared the turn he would take to get to the side of the building, he heard heavy panting and breathing headed in his direction. He kissed the mouth of his pistol and placed his back against the gate. He hoped the dim lighting would be enough to protect him from their line of sight. As the first man ran past him unaware of his presence, he peeked around the corner and shot the one approaching in his face before quickly turning his gun and shooting the other in the back of his head. Once he was sure neither man would be able to proceed with the bullets he dished out, he continued running in the direction from which he saw them come. There was a small exit door with no outside handle that was left ajar. Once he entered it, his jaw dropped. The individual office spaces had become miniprison cells with bars you would find protecting home windows as doors. The prisoners were children no younger than 5 and not greater than 12. Before Frederick could unlock and free one child from his situation, the children had already deemed him their newest favorite superhero.

When his backup arrived, he told them the excited, exaggerated version of the day's events without considering what Rawlings would write on paper. He was immediately perceived as the hardest-working patrol officer that the Memphis Police Department had on staff. And for Rawlings being found nowhere near the prison that housed the human trafficking operation, limping, with a torn hamstring and every bullet he had in his gun embedded in walls and a door that led to an unused pantry, he immediately became the laughingstock of his unit and deemed unworthy to have such an honorable person for a partner.

***

There were many opportunities for Frederick to come clean and give his partner the honor he deserved, but being the selfish prick that he was, he would not dim his own light to bring light to someone else. Rawlings attempted to speak with him about it once the jokes had become more than he could bear, but Frederick redirected him to the truth he created and in some sick way, convinced Rawlings that he, indeed, did all the work. If you focus your attention on the facts, it was Frederick who called for backup. It was Frederick who subdued both perpetrators, and it was Frederick who saved the children from their imprisonment. Rawlings might have been first on the scene, but he never solved the case. Frederick was immediately offered a position with the TBI, and throwing the dog a bone, he pulled some strings to have Rawlings promoted to homicide. Sad to say, over the years, Frederick began to believe his own story and even credit himself as the reason Rawlings accomplished so much as a homicide detective. He swears to have taught him everything he knows.

Detective Ryu knew the truth, and that's what prevented him from respecting anything Fredrick Davidson was a part of, including him being the guest speaker at Rawlings's funeral. It didn't surprise him in the least that Frederick opened with the story of that night years ago to steal from Rawlings even in death. His falsified story brought the attendees to tears, and Frederick was thankful for it. There was no way in hell he would be able to deliver a powerful speech on behalf of anyone except for himself. He had all intention of asking his wife to write his speech for the occasion, but knowing the man that she married, she had beaten him to the punch. He read over her words until they became his own and even went as far as to memorize them. He needed to sound as authentic as possible because he would use this platform to announce something no one foresaw coming. With the mayor, city councilman, and those in other higher-up positions giving him their full attention as he grieved the loss of his childhood friend and ex-partner, there wasn't a better time to gain their support.

"I am a man, and so was Detective Rawlings. We are not a two-legged breed of animal that can be hunted for slaughter; yet, so many good men die in that manner. As a law enforcement officer in this day and age, we fear when the right time is to pull our weapons in day-to-day situations. Not because we didn't receive proper training but because so many are using their weapons and their badge as the right to kill. As a black man, I fear being pulled over by those I work for and work with. Not because I'm involved in illegal activities but because I was born black. I have family who won't eat a meal with me, alone stand in the same room with me because I carry a badge. I have coworkers who walk by me as if I were invisible because my skin tone can store more melanin than theirs. I am a man who will not die by slaughter from the hands of a criminal with or without a badge, and I stand here today wishing that I could say the same about Rawlings. He was a man!"

Ryu wasn't listening, but he heard exactly what Frederick was saying. There was something in the tone of his voice when he said *I am a man* that was familiar. He was sure Frederick used the words to acknowledge the location Rawlings had taken his final breath; yet, there was something else hidden in his words. Pulling out his flask in plain sight, he took another sip and decided to pay attention. Frederick went into another spiel about his relationship with the deceased and told a story of him carrying Rawlings through school. It was so hard to listen without wondering how much of it was a pure fabrication and what percentage of it was fact. The moment he could no longer listen was when he heard the most.

"Last night, I couldn't sleep, dreading what I would have to do here today. To bury my closest friend and to bury his son two days later, it breaks my heart. I found myself lost in my thoughts, and then I asked myself if I died today, would I be happy with the life that I lived? Did I give all that I had to be a change in this world? Was I the change that was needed? I thought about Rawlings and all that he did, all that he had sacrificed to be that change, and it took me to the story in the Bible of Abraham. Abraham was willing to sacrifice the only son his wife Sarah could bear. Without thought, he was willing to sacrifice his son for the greater good. I am not saying that by any means can Detective Rawlings be compared to Abraham, but in similarity, he sent his son undercover as a sacrifice to help get this Joe out of our streets and into prison, but unlike Abraham, he wasn't given a lamb at the last second. His only child was killed."

"Huh?" Ryu said but not loud enough for anyone not sitting near him to hear. He knew that no agency could find proof of Rawlings sending his son undercover. The claim made by Joe was unverifiable, yet Frederick spoke of it as if he were sure that it was. He wondered if any updated information had been found since his last inquiry two days ago. The investigators working the case promised to keep him in the loop, but the Bureau and the police had never gotten along, so he wasn't surprised if they had lied. They were known for lying. If his partner did send his son, who was still a rookie, undercover on a case neither one of their experiences could solve, why would he keep it a secret from him? He didn't know Rawlings to withhold information from him, especially about a case they were working together. Frederick's words weren't sitting right and made him uncomfortable. It wasn't long before he understood why.

"I stand here before you today in front of my colleagues and my extended family by way of Detective Rawlings and say with no shame that if I died today, I did nothing to change this world. Neither did my good friend Detective Rawlings because we both have dedicated our lives to the great city of Memphis, Tennessee. Be that as it may, Detective Rawlings will not have died in vain, nor would his sacrifice be in vain. I must do more, and I will, so please accept this as my official announcement that I will be running for governor of the great state of Tennessee, and that is only the first election I will win of many. As governor, I will remove all the men like Joe or those who strive to be like him to jail cells and off our streets. I will be the change, and you can take my word for it because I'm double backboned, and this here ain't my first rodeo!"

Ryu pulled his gun from his holster and pointed it at the podium. "It's him; it's Joe!"

As guns were being pulled and pointed in Ryu's direction to mix with the screams and yells for him to put his gun down, he had a split decision to make. Would he allow Joe to be prosecuted in the court of law as his oath made him promise, or would he take justice in his own hands and become another officer to kill an unarmed black man? Ryu's decision was made before he could formulate the thought, and the smirk that grew on his face as he watched the bullet pierce through Frederick's left eye took the pain away from the multicaliber bullets being shot into his own body.

The funeral became a murder scene.

Chapter Eight

Chicago, Illinois. Friday, January 3, 1992

Christmas break was nearing its end, and with three days left before the start of the new school semester, everyone was reluctant to return. Ronald had thoughts of calling out with the excuse that he was battling the flu, but with teachers calling out like their position was optional, Principal Pierce mandated medical excuses be turned in with the return from absence and planned absences had to be submitted at least two weeks in advance for approval and scheduling of a substitute. Ronald didn't agree with the stipulations in the mandate; yet, he understood the necessity of them.

He couldn't furnish a reason for needing the extra time off, and he didn't have any plans pending. There wasn't anyone he wanted to spend time with, and there wasn't any pressing business he had to handle. Ronald wanted more days off simply to lie in his bed with his nuts out like he had been doing since the first day of vacation. Leaving the house hadn't crossed his mind. After dropping his two pain-in-the-ass students home from the tattoo parlor, he grabbed a stack of movies from Blockbuster rental and went grocery shopping. The thought of inviting the girl he fucked at the gym crossed his mind, but it was the holiday season. He assumed she'd be busy with her family . . . or worse, she'd expect a gift from him. He'd settle for drinking his spiked eggnog and beating his meat as the neighbor's Christmas lights flashed on his walls.

Briiing, briiing . . .

The phone was ringing off its hook. It had been doing so for the last three days, and that's why Ronald decided to leave it like that . . . off the hook. No one should have his number, nor should they know how to reach him. His parents were under the impression that he was in the military and stationed out of the country. That lie broke his heart to maintain it with his mother. He was her only living child, and she did a damn good job of raising him. She gave everything she had to ensure that he received every opportunity to excel. Lying to her felt like a betrayal, but so did her sleeping with the enemy. He saw his fabrication as a fair exchange.

Robert Eugene Hill was the misery, pain, and suffering described in hell and transformed into a human. He passed out samples of what living in hell would be like to his wife and son as if he were the devil's realtor. Besides mentally abusing his wife until he brainwashed her into thinking that it was love by keeping her laced in the finest of material things, he enjoyed spending his pastime tearing down Ronald. Nothing Ronald did was ever good enough, and sadly, this included his birth. Mr. Hill, which is the name he preferred Ronald to call him, took pride in telling his son the story behind his name whenever the opportunity presented itself.

"I knew from the moment you hit the air that you'd grow up to disappoint me. You were pretty like a little girl, and your eyes were soft. Up until that moment, I was excited about having a junior, but once I got wind of you, I changed my mind. No man serving his country in the Korean War would ever give a pansy with girly eyes his name." He slapped his knee, laughing before he finished the story. "I told your mother right then and there we'd be working on another son as soon as she healed."

As a child, the story would bring him to tears, though as he became of age, he used the story as a reason to respect his father. The man kept his word and always had. If he said it, you could take his words to the bank because his truth never bounced. Robert didn't waver, and he stood firm with any decision he made, even if it was done without a thought in hast. Robert Jr. was born eleven months after him, making them Irish twins. You'd think his father wouldn't have any leverage with God for his acts on earth; nevertheless, he was shown favor, and Robert Jr. was his spitting image. He was exactly like his father inside and out with only one exception . . . He loved Ronald dearly and would go to great lengths to protect him from their father. Although he appreciated his brother standing up to their father whenever he witnessed injustice, it wasn't enough to force their father to stop. Ronald left after a heated argument about him going into the military at 18 and never looked. He'd call and check in with his mother sporadically but never left her a method to do the same. His curiosity of who the caller was made him place the phone back on its cradle.

"Hello," he answered in a voice he made up in that second.

"Yo, can I speak with my teacher, Mr. Ronald, please? Tell him it's Mimic, and we got an emergency."

"What's wrong, Martin?"

"It's Ethan. You gotta come quickly. Do you know where the Robert Taylor homes are? We gotta go there, but you got to come get me from my house first and don't tell my granny shit."

He hung up the phone before Ronald could question him. Panicking, Ronald threw on a solid gray windbreaker jogging suit and dashed out the door. He made it to Mimic's house in what he was sure was record time and was stunned by what he was seeing. Mimic came out in a long sleeve, button-up dress shirt, and slacks with a peacoat in his hands and loafers on his feet. He looked like he was either coming from court or church.

"Why are you all dressed up?"

"Because that's GD and the MC's territory. I ain't trying to die going to check on this nigga."

There were so many things Ronald wanted to say to him, one being, you shouldn't be gangbanging if you're scared, but there was something more pressing he needed to ask.

"What's wrong with Ethan?"

"I don't know until we get there. Have you been watching the news?"

"No, not really."

"Well, they found a John Doe shot up and dumped in the dumpster behind Building 22 Christmas morning. They identified him today. It's cuz's dad."

Ronald's foot flattened on the gas, and they were weaving in and out of traffic to get to the other side in silence. He glanced over at Mimic and caught him staring at the scribble scrabble covering the word "Crip" on his palm and wondered what the boy thought as he looked at it. Now wasn't the time for him to try to persuade Mimic to let go of the gang and focus on his education, but the talk made his list of priorities. Mimic was screaming for help and refused to recognize the sound of his own voice. His call to Ronald confirmed it. He was too compassionate to be a coldhearted street figure.

Adrenaline was fueling Ronald and didn't leave any room for him to fear his surroundings. He left his car doors unlocked. They must have passed at least fifty people lingering about the building on their way to the eighth floor. On the sixth floor stairwell, he used his hand to cover Mimic's eyes as they walked up on an older woman blowing a boy that couldn't have been any more than 17 as he played with her pussy.

"This bitch owes me money. You feel me?"

There wasn't any shame in his voice and judging from the way he was moaning before Ronald could see him, he preferred her chosen method of payment over money anyway. By the time they made it to the eighth floor, Ronald was ready to leave.

"I said it's open!"

Mimic reached past Ronald in that very moment knowing better than to knock.

"Hey, Sug, is Ethan here?"

"Who the fuck is that?"

"Little Martin."

It was like watching a ventriloquist act because Ronald couldn't see anyone, and the voice sounded too damaged to be real.

"If he's here, then you know where he's at. Come here for a second, Martin."

He held up his hand, wanting Ronald to stay where he was and walked around the wall.

"Do you have any money, baby? I need to get a few things for the house and that sorry-ass husband of mine ain't no fucking where to be found. He's probably over there on your side of town smoking up all the damn money."

She wasn't told her husband was killed, Ronald thought, and his question was answered.

"Stop lying. I seen yo' ass on the news this morning. You found out he was dead like three days ago. They couldn't put his name on the news until you gave them the okay. I'm not giving yo' junkie ass shit!"

"Martin!" Ronald yelled, making his way around the wall. "Don't you speak to her like—"

His words went right back down his throat as he turned the corner to see a half-naked woman washing her ass in the sink with a tub behind her. However, in the condition the tub was in, Ronald wouldn't have climbed in it either.

"And who is you?" she asked with a smile growing on her cracked, ashy lips.

"That's Mr. Ronald, our teacher, and he don't buy pussy."

"Martin!"

"You don't. That's why she's smiling like that. Come on; his room is back here."

Mimic took off toward the open door at the end of the hallway, and Ronald followed. He looked back, and she was gripping what was left of her pussy with a dirty wash rag and waving at him as the hardened tips of her titty nipples resembled prunes.

"You all right?" Mimic asked, crossing the threshold.

The room was empty other than the stacks of books on the floor, balled up paper, a backpack, and the quote, "It is better to be feared than loved if you can't be both," written on the wall. Ronald wondered how Ethan learned of Niccolò Machiavelli's quote, but the boy knowing it didn't surprise him. There wasn't a bed or a window, and from what Ronald could see, there weren't any clothes. Ethan sat on the hard project floor with a Walkman in his right hand and a pencil in his left. He was writing something and bobbing his head to the music at the same time. Mimic snatched his headphones off.

"What are y'all doing here?"

Ethan's eyes never left his notepad besides to glance at the open book beside him. It was like their presence didn't matter to him.

"Shit, to check on you. I heard about your pops on the news and called Mr. Ronald so we could come through. Even put on the church clothes my granny got me to wear on Christmas."

Mimic did a few fly poses and stopped when he realized Ethan wasn't looking.

"Thanks for stopping by, but I'm straight. That nigga been dead to me and my moms. It's more of a loss for you and your pops than it is for us."

"Damn, nigga, you really ain't got no feelings behind this shit, do you?"

"Why should I? The nigga ain't never done nothing for me. Your granny has put more food in this bitch than he has. He probably fucked one of those MCs over on some money, and they got tired of givin' his smoked out ass passes."

The boys cussed like sailors, but so did Ronald, and they weren't in class, so he didn't reprimand them. Ethan talked about his father's death with no emotion to it. It wasn't until his mother walked in that he showed he had some.

"Yes," he replied to her calling his name and quickly jumped to his feet.

"You in some kinda trouble up at that school? Why is yo' teacher here?"

"No, ma'am. Little Martin told him about what happened to my daddy, and he wanted to check in on me."

"Why?" her suspicion was real. Her left eyebrow was raised.

"That's just how he is, Mama. He's from the South. That's how Georgia cats are. He's cool, though. I checked him out."

"Uh-huh. You always saying somebody is cool, and then Child Services are at my door trying to see if I'm taking care of you. After this year right here, you got two more years to go until you're 18. You gon' have to get out of my damn house after that!"

"Yes, ma'am, I know."

"Do you got any money? We need some bread."

"No, ma'am. I gave you everything I had last night."

"Then why you ain't out there getting some with Little Martin? You think sitting on yo' ass is going to take care of us?"

"Mrs. Carruthers—" Ethan stepped in his face before he could finish.

"I had daddy issues, Mr. Hill, not mama's. Don't say shit to my first lady unless I okay it first." The look in his eye was deadly, and he must have felt it because he blinked twice to clear it. "We straight, but let me handle my moms."

Ronald threw up his hands in defeat and took a few steps back.

"You right, Mama, I'm about to leave now and go make sure you eat tonight. What do you want me to grab from the store?"

"I didn't ask you to go to the store. I'm gon' buy some food stamps from that girl with all the kids upstairs. You just bring me the money!"

"Yes, ma'am. How much are you trying to buy?" The question didn't sound like he was asking the number of food stamps. His sober tone sounded like he knew it would be spent on drugs.

"At least twenty dollars, and make sure you get you something to eat because I don't know when I'm going to make it out to the store with this shit going on with yo' daddy. I'm sure those niggas that killed him will be knocking on our door next trying to get the money he owes them."

Ethan walked across the room and grabbed his backpack. When he turned around, Ronald was holding a twenty-dollar bill for him, and so was Mimic. He nodded his head in approval and took them both.

"Here you go, Mama. My friends looked out for us. Get the food stamps and hold on to the other twenty for later." He pecked her on the cheek as she took it.

"I will, but you still need to make something shake today. Forty dollars doesn't last long in this house."

"I know, Mama. I got you."

He headed out of the apartment and didn't say anything to either of them until he got to Ronald's car.

"I appreciate what you did upstairs, and I promise to pay both of y'all back tenfold. I can't tell you when, but know you two are the first people I'm blessing after I get my moms off that shit and in her own place."

"Nigga, all the tests you let me cheat on and the homework you turned in for me . . . We straight. We brothers in this shit."

"Nah, we ain't brothers. We don't think or move the same. We more like cousins in the struggle, and Mr. Ronald—"

"Save that soft shit for the first bitch you have to sweet-talk. Your words ain't gon' make my boxers wet."

The boys laughed as Ronald let his guard down in front of them, and he joined in with a broken chuckle.

Chapter Nine

Memphis, Tennessee. Thursday, January 31, 2019, cont.

The roar of the thunder camouflaged the sound of the gunshots from those traveling up and down Popular Avenue. Not that Roman would have heard the gunshots anyway with his earbuds submerged in his ears. Bobbing his head to a track he never heard before, he played the drums with his index fingers on the steering wheel. He never saw the change coming and would deny it if asked, but Neo Soul was now his favorite genre of music. Rap was nice, but the lyrics and beats all seemed to be the same lately was the lie he convinced himself to believe. But in truth, he was getting older and turning up at the club to stunt on his haters had gotten old. The thrill of bumping his music with the bass set on ten so the truck could rattle no longer appealed him, and at times, he wondered why it ever did. There was something about Neo Soul that made him relax and gave him a piece of peace while he was driving. He needed that comfort behind the wheel whenever he was scheduled for high mileage trips.

Roman couldn't believe that he loved his job, especially after being self-employed in the street; yet, he did, and if there were anything he could do to make those long hours on the road seem shorter, he would. With two felony convictions and no high school diploma, coming across employment was hard; however, as a first-time father, he had no choice. From the moment his daughter's head crowned from his favorite vacation destination on a woman's body and before her lungs were cleared for her to take her first breath, he vowed to let go of his fast life. He needed to find employment that required him to punch a time clock and receive a W-2 yearly that offered medical benefits, if possible. Going legit didn't feel like it was an optional choice for him. He had to do whatever was necessary to be there for her every day because there was no way he'd be content with his daughter feeling like he wasn't a part of her life. His baby mama didn't know, nor had she met her father, and the effects of it showed in the lack of respect she had for men, but more so in the lack of respect she had for herself. He wasn't the judge whose job was to throw the book at her for the choices she made throughout her life, nor did he have any qualifications to run a family therapy session. Neither was needed to see the real in the scheme of the things. Baby girl was fucked-up, and though he loved every second spent in between her mentally unstable legs, he couldn't fix her. He wasn't giving up on the thought of them being a family in the future, though he wasn't rushing it into fruition.

He was determined to never put himself in situations where he would have to accept a visit from his daughter through a glass window or to accept her visiting his grave to place fresh flowers on his tombstone because he fell victim to his own dirty moves in the streets. He didn't want her dealing with typical hood shit, and that would require him to do untypical things to ensure she wouldn't.

Finding employment wasn't hard because he was a convicted felon; it was hard because he had an empty space on his résumé where his employment history should be. In all his years on earth, at no time did he have a job. There weren't any lawns he cut during the summer as a teen that would allow him to list landscaping as past employment, nor did he pick up on any trades like changing brakes or painting houses that he could use. From the time his mama let him off the porch, trapping and hitting licks was the extent of the jobs he had done. Those around him who knew of his struggle convinced him to apply at fast-food franchises seeing that they hired people with no work experience, which is true, but it seemed they preferred to hire a 16-year-old high school student than a 31-year-old man who never had any proof of gainful employment. Now that the clock was ticking, he played with the thought of creating an employment history from his street credibility. He thought about finding a slick way to talk about the drugs he sold, the shipping and receiving of them, how he marketed and promoted his product, and called the hand-to-hand sells and order taking customer service. The only reason he didn't follow through with the thought was that he didn't think his supplier would like being listed as his employer and have his contact information included. Roman knew that cute shit like that could get him killed.

Still and all, he applied for every job he found online and in the local paper, and everyone denied him with the statement they found a more qualified candidate that matched the company's needs. Frustrated but not discouraged, Roman was on his way to a job interview when God decided to send him a helping hand in his time of distress.

"Mama, can I use your car to go check on this job? They're hiring immediately, and they are starting at eleven dollars an hour, with no experience needed."

"Yeah, you can use it, but it's almost on E, and I'll be looking for half a tank when it gets back, or you'll never drive my car again."

She gave him a look that said, test me if you want to, and then handed him her keys. She made sure there wasn't a dollar worth of change in the cup holder to teach him the importance of handling his own responsibilities without looking for handouts. He didn't know what lesson she was hoping to teach, but its effects were forcing his back against the wall. With selling drugs his only option of getting the gas money, he swallowed his pride and asked his father for a twenty-dollar loan until he received his first check. Watching his son man up and take fatherhood seriously, he gave him $100 and told him he didn't have to pay it back. Roman headed to the interview with his chin up and his chest out, feeling like the man he knew his father was.

The closest gas station to Roman's father's house was at a truck stop near the interstate in West Memphis, Arkansas. He was only supposed to be buying gas, and then he saw the sign that read sixty-nine cents for any size drinks. It was at the drink fountain where he met his angel.

"Damn, my bad, youngster. I didn't see you behind me. Did my drink get on your clothes?" The man had on a headset that had a small microphone extending from it. He wouldn't have heard Roman behind him with them covering his ears even with it off.

"Nah, you good, big bro. I snuck up on you. When I saw that sixty-nine cents for any size drink sign, I had to jump on it. When you ain't got no job, and you're out here on the hunt, these discounts be looking really good," he said and concluded with a laugh.

"You don't have to tell me about it. I remember those days. That's when those twenty-five-cent noodle packages tasted like steak and potatoes," he chuckled. "Then when the money first came in, I even got fancy and threw in some cheese and hot sauce with them. You learn a thing or two from being locked up, like survival. I thought that drug charge had sentenced me to a life of noodle eating, but those direct deposits that hit weekly from truck driving said I could go ahead and order me a steak."

"They let you drive 18-wheelers with felonies?"

"Hell yeah. Who you thought drove them . . . Harvard grads? My guess is that 90 percent of truck drivers either have a fucked-up background or a fucked-up past that they are running from, and driving their trucks makes them forget about it. You make too much bread to be stressing over your mistakes, you feel me?"

"That's what I need to be doing. I'm out here begging these folks to give me a job for crumbs because of this felony on my record."

"If you don't mind me asking, what type of felony you have?" he asked, removing his headset.

"Possession with the intent to sell, or so that's what my record says, but straight up, I got caught with about $200 worth of crack on me."

"If $200 worth of crack got you a felony, you must have had the worst lawyer on the planet, or you didn't have any business in the streets slanging anyway. Everybody moving weight knows if you get popped with something that small, you go ahead and lie and say you smoking it unless you get caught doing the sell. Ain't no way in hell I'm agreeing that I was selling something small anyway. You better off doing six to nine months in a drug rehab going through the program and taking all the steps then to let these folks put all these blemishes on your background."

He looked the guy in the eye and said, "It was a violation of my parole. I had been caught with a lot more than $200 worth on me six months before I got picked up and went back."

"I knew it was more than what you were saying, but I'm happy you lied. That means you don't take pride in the shit, and you shouldn't. I don't know how big the moves you used to make were, but I've made more money and kept my freedom driving. If you got a minute, you can come over here to this little food spot and sit down with me, and I'll tell you how to get on."

"Honestly, I'm supposed to be headed to an interview right now, but if you are going to give me all the information on getting started, I'm rolling with you."

"Then go pay for your big-ass drink and meet me in my office. That's the last booth on your left."

Two hours later, he was walking into DWR Logistics to enroll into their next class. By the time his daughter could hold up her head, he had finished school, and when she had mastered crawling, he was already manning his own truck and taking local and out-of-state routes. He worked as many hours as the company would allow him to drive, and he did it because of his love for her.

A familiar, old-school love ballad was blazing in Roman's ears, and he nodded and tapped his steering wheel to the rhythm. It had been years since he heard the song, but everything about it reminded him of the twisted relationship and love he felt for the mother of his child. She was crazy as hell, louder than cheap perfume, and Kool-Aid on a pickle stuffed with a peppermint hood, but she held their daughter down while he got his shit together. The thought of his ghetto queen brought a smile to his lips, a smile that was wiped off just as quickly as it appeared as he swerved to avoid hitting the Lexus that had run the light of the intersection he was crossing.

"Dumb-ass bitch!" he yelled, but he knew she hadn't heard him. Her chin was in her chest, and she focused on finishing composing her text.

"I'm on my way, baby, I'm stuck in traffic."

Sending those nine words had more value than the life she spent the last 47 years living. Had she not sent them, she'd be facing the same odds knowing that she might have run the red light as a subconscious attempt at suicide. She was given two tasks in order to receive her freedom from the dangerous web she was stuck in. The first task was to write the eulogy her husband had given honoring his childhood friend. Though she was told to compose it, most of the writing she had done came from dictation she took from Joe. Joe, the man with the heavy Texas drawl that she had never met, had been her boss for the last fifteen years, and he opted to take his profits and retire.

Tamica wanted nothing more than to be free from Joe's leadership. His retirement would do just that, so when he reached out to her for help with tying loose ends, she was all in. Besides ending their professional relationship on a high note, there would be a large monetary award given for her loyalty and years of dedicated service. Willingly, and most of the time, fearfully, she did whatever it was that Joe asked. Joe originally targeted her because of her title, Fredrick Davidson's wife. Unknown to her at the time, her husband was deeply rooted in a lot of illegal things and with a lot of deadly people. Fredrick's dirty dealings eventually caused him to cross Joe's path. For him to keep his name off the books in a money launder-ing case that involved retired cops' pensions, he needed the help of those higher up. Joe saw how Fredrick would do anything to keep rising to the top and wondered if that included putting his wife's life in danger. He got his answer and immediately informed her that she was sleeping with the enemy. The betrayal was unforgivable, and whenever the opportunity presented itself for her to avenge his actions against her, she would.

"I don't understand why you're telling me he'd screw

me and in the same breath, asking me to be a more sub-missive wife. He doesn't deserve me!"

"You're right, but you knew this before you said 'I do.' Money and power are what made you walk down that aisle in tears."

"Yeah, but let's not forget that I hold my doctorate in pharmacology, and that's what made Fredrick come after me. I can make it without him, and if it doesn't interfere with your plans or cause suspicion to what we're doing at MediTech, I'd like the okay to have him killed." Her words were cold, and there wasn't any doubt in Joe's mind that she was serious. However, it was too early in Joe's plan to cut the fat off.

"I've found more value in you than anyone under my umbrella. Do as I say, and I'll grant your request." He hung up abruptly as he always did. Joe telling her she was more valuable to him than her husband meant nothing to her. For all she knew, Joe was just a voice. She didn't trust him, but then again, who *did* she trust? She came from a family heavily involved in law enforcement, politics, and the government. She watched those who were noted as righteous in the public's eyes do the most wrong. She didn't trust anything or anyone, and sad to say, she no longer trusted herself.

In the beginning, Tamica did love her husband, but once he proved that he couldn't love anyone as much as he loved himself, she began to lose interest, and that's around the same time that Joe entered her life. She held on to the marriage only because there was no way out with Joe partnering with her husband.

Fredrick should have known better than to trust any-one's partnership. He was much older than Tamica, twenty years her senior to be exact, and he made mistakes like an unguided child. For years, she enjoyed being his younger woman and his prized possession, but as he aged, she saw the sickening pedophile behavior she experienced when meeting other men of the same age as he. On the hind side, she was given the opportunity to be the senior in a new relationship that was put together at Joe's request. Although the sex with the younger man was whack, she enjoyed him praising her. She enjoyed being looked at as a goddess and receiving the benefits from him that only a goddess would. At times, it was hard and felt cruel to play with the feelings of a man who really loved her, but the perks she received from Joe made playing with Harold's feelings worth it.

Harold praised her; he worshipped the ground she walked on, and he promised to give her the world. Yes, she was rich in her own right; nevertheless, she was greedy. If she continued to allow him to spend his money on her, her savings could only grow larger. Harold was clueless to her deception and with him being thirteen years younger than she, his understanding of what real love is mirrored the comprehension of love to a 12-year-old that yearned to be accepted by a group of new friends. His undying devotion to what he assumed they were building gave her the advantage she needed to complete the second task Joe demanded of her. It was the last and final task standing in the way of her new start. All she had to do was make it to Harold in the time frame she was given, and her life would be back in her control.

"Hurry up, baby, I'm ready to go!" Harold replied as he paced his office floor until the soles of his shoes suffered from carpet burn. He was fear stricken by the possible outcomes of the day, and that fear did away with the excitement he previously felt about receiving his freedom. Initially, he was involved in his company moves by choice. That changed when he found out who his true employer was.

Years ago, Harold's employment with MediTech Pharmaceuticals sounded like a modern Cinderella story without the falling in love with a prince part. It was a heartwarming story of a boy who grew up poor with dreams of having better, who worked hard to achieve the goal, and that made him worthy of becoming rich. He was young, hungry, and driven to make it to the top, and he'd do anything for a shot to show his worth. He began applying for biochemist positions months before he had his doctorate in hand with a résumé labeling him in the top 5 percent of his graduating class. Unlike most college grads that started at the bottom in hopes to earn their way into greater positions, Harold googled the top five largest pharmaceutical companies in the United States and applied first at the company that was listed as number one. With their corporate headquarters less than two hours away from the hole-in-the-wall city where he was raised in West Tennessee, he was destined to have a career at MediTech. Although quite cocky with an ego larger than the dick he had to offer, his nuts weren't big enough for him to confidently apply for a top-level position. He ended up applying as a chemical floor runner, which really shouldn't have required a degree to do. If he were hired, he'd take a chemical to point A at the plant and securely load it into a machine at point B. It sounds like something a child could do, but it was a start, and the bragging rights that came with working for the company fresh out of college was ultimately the reason he'd be thankful for the crappy position.

A week later, Harold interviewed in front of what he assumed was the board of chemists on a Tuesday and wasn't offered the position for which he applied when they invited him back that Thursday evening for a second interview. Instead, he was offered the lead chemist position, which was the high-dollar position, the position of plant operations manager. If accepted, he would be the boss of everybody who worked in the building—from the floor runners to the director of chemistry over the lab, and even the boss over the foreman in the distribution portion of the plant that oversees shipping and delivery.

To say he had impressed the board members was an understatement. When he read over his employment offer and saw that the salary was a little over $240,000 per year, plus bonuses and kickbacks, he wondered how he could have been chosen. He didn't have any managerial experience, no experience in pharmaceuticals besides running the cash register at a mom-and-pop pharmacy in high school, and MediTech would be his first job as a chemist. There had to be someone more qualified than a boy who witnessed his family celebrate $500 in the bank. It wasn't sitting right with him, but he accepted and signed his soul away.

Growing up in the comforts of small-town living, you could say he was naive to what was taking place around him, which made him susceptible to the deceit he received. After months of training, the first quarter of the pharmaceutical company functioning under his management was a success, and the board members threw him an official welcoming party. Although he had done his research before applying and knew he landed a job with the largest pharmaceutical company in North America, being in the same room with the bulk of Forbes top 100 Billionaires list felt surreal. He mingled and shook hands with people he'd never imagine sharing the same oxygen supply with. If judging bank statements, he was the smallest fish in the ocean; yet, his personality made him the biggest fish in the pond. For days on out, he relived his night in the spotlight, and when he could steal away to his office for a break, he'd kick his feet up on his desk and scroll through his contacts amazed by the names and personal cell phone numbers he had stored.

A little over a week later, he received an email inviting him to attend a board meeting the same day by private jet in the Yucatán Peninsula. The email said it was an invitation, but two hours later, a limo picked him up. The last-minute meeting did seem strange, but with vast amounts of money, he wasn't surprised by the urgency. Powerful people made things happen at the snap of their fingers whenever they needed to. He added learning to accept impulsive behavior to his list of things to do.

With only the clothes on his back and his phone, he sat in the back of the limo wondering what could be so important.

"Your phone, please," the flight attendant of the private jet asked before Harold could take his seat on the jet. She must have read his thoughts via his facial expression because she quickly answered his question. "It's for all of our safety, sir."

Not knowing the safety protocols for private jets as this was his first time on one, he smiled and gave it to her,

"Safety first!"

Harold slept the four-and-a-half hour ride. He hadn't realized how tired he was until the flight attendant woke him up. Still drowsy, he missed a step exiting the jet and came close to flipping down the stairs. Thank goodness for the flight attendant's compassion. She volunteered to help him exit and snatched him up before he could fall.

The first red flag waving in Harold's face is that armed guards surrounded him, and then he was placed in the back of a large SUV with blacked out windows. Once inside the vehicle, he couldn't see out, nor could he see who was driving. There was an armed guard to his left and his right, and neither said a word to him. He tried making light conversation but didn't receive a response. When the vehicle stopped, two familiar faces greeted him.

"Harold, my friend, it's great seeing you again. How was your flight?" The man extended his hand, and Harold shook it.

"How are you, Joseph? The flight was great; everything after that not so much."

"Yes, I must apologize for that, but due to the people involved and their privacy, we have to protect who they are. With time, you won't have to be drugged or blindfolded to meet with us."

"Drugged? Is that why I was so sleepy? Why in the hell would you drug me? I can understand them wanting privacy, but don't you think that's going a little too far?"

"No, not really. We don't think we went far enough."

That voice came from behind him. Two men were standing shoulder-to-shoulder. One of them Harold was sure he'd seen on TV but couldn't remember on what channel or why, and the other he was positive he had never seen.

"What's going on here? What is all of this about? It said invited, but none of this feels like an invitation!"

"All of this is about you, my friend, and once we get back to the villa we will be able to discuss it in more detail," Joseph answered, hoping his familiar face would bring Harold some comfort.

"I'm not sure if I even *want* to go to the villa or wherever you're planning on taking me. As a matter of fact, where is the international airport? I'm declining the invite."

"Come on now, Harold, calm down. We're your new friends. When we sit down and talk, you'll understand the need for us to go through all of this. Please, just come and hear us out."

Joseph gave him a pleading look, and Harold decided to give the men a chance. If the billionaire boys club poster child Joseph McLaren felt the men were trusted allies, he'd give them a shot.

The beauty of wherever the hell he was at had consumed his sight. He had never seen water as blue as this except on television. The trees were so vibrant in color, it was as if they were made from plastic and planted along their ride to maximize the scenery. Harold assumed that they would be driving for a while but judging by the downhill slope they were traveling, the airport was up the hill from the villa on the same property. Another perk of being in the company of billionaires.

They arrived at the house and filed into the meeting room. Instantly, he noticed that he seemed to be the only person who had just arrived. The other members of the board who he met previously were dressed in a relaxed look. Some even had their golfing bags with them. Joseph stood at the front of the room, and everyone in attendance took their seats. Harold had been directed to take a seat across from the two men that met him with Joseph at the airport.

"Once again, we meet to honor the man of the hour," Joseph humbly bowed toward Harold. "But this time, we are here to give him an open invitation to our private club within the board. Some of these faces may be familiar to you, Harold, and others you may never see again after today. Let me start by introducing you to the men who were so kind as to join me in welcoming you at the airport, Señor Carlos Valdez and the godfather, Frankie Romano."

Harold could have shit his pants. Carlos Valdez's face wasn't familiar to him, or to anyone else for that matter, but his name was legendary. He was Mr. Mexico, so legend had it. The notorious leader of the Valdez Cartel was sitting across the room from him, staring at him eye to eye with a smile on his face that said, *Yes, motherfucker, it's me!*

Frankie Romano, on the other hand, was a face he knew all too well. He was legendary in his own right. He was the head of the Italian mob. Less than a year ago, his face was plastered on every news outlet there was. After twenty years of running a crime syndicate and drug trafficking empire, he had made a mistake that landed him facing hundreds of life sentences. Harold couldn't remember if the case ever made it to trial, but before he could get into it, the United States government was dropping the charges against Romano, and once again, he was a free man. Seeing the two of them in the room, he turned his focus to everyone else and stared into their faces. The names and faces that he remembered from his welcoming party he ran background checks on in his mind to see if he could remember them being affiliated with any crime or illegal activity. Sad to say, one by one, he remembered almost 50 percent of the room was involved at one point in time with an illegal act or accused of contributing to it. Immediately, he felt like a confidential informant being the only person with clean hands in the room. After seeing their faces, he knew whatever they said to him in that meeting he was going to agree to. If he didn't, he was dead meat. They didn't have to tell him that. He already knew, and if this was the board of the company he was working for, more likely than not, he was already a major part of whatever was going on with the company anyway.

He spent the next three days in Mexico learning the ins and outs of MediTech's underground operations, and when he boarded the jet headed back to Tennessee, he accepted the truth that his real title was Kingpin of a Legal and Illegal Drug Operation. The money he made thus far was crumbs compared to the money he would be making now, and he was ready to see the deposits stack up.

Harold let go of his cocky ego. It was replaced with confidence. There was nothing that he felt he couldn't do, and there was nothing his money couldn't buy. Most men in his situation bought cars, houses, and clothes . . . maybe even a home for their mother, but not Harold. With his first off-the-record payroll check, he purchased a married woman. From the moment he was introduced to Tamica, he knew he had to have her. She was smart, beautiful, and the director of chemistry and overseer of the lab. In other words, she was the smartest person in the building. He could list her assets for hours and take only a second to list her one flaw, which was, she was married to the deputy director of the TBI. The Tennessee Bureau of Investigation wasn't a friend in his line of business. In truth, he was a modernized drug lord, manufacturer, and distributor. Hate for law enforcement came with his title. He'd do whatever was necessary to get her out of the bed of his enemy. What he didn't understand was why the Mexican Cartel, the Italian mob, and a plethora of other criminal-minded billionaires employed someone whose husband could show up to the company picnic and shut down their whole operation. He assumed that his question had to be the answer for the reason why they did it. Why would Frederick Davidson investigate and shut down the company his wife spearheaded? It made sense, but then again, it didn't.

Tamica's last name was a mistake, and the ring on her finger was an oversight. To prove it, he bought her, her dream car, flew her to one of the board members' private island for the weekend, and placed a ring eighty times the value of the one she wore in her belly button, and he sucked on her pussy in twenty-minute intervals. He wanted her to fall in love with his dick to help his character and personality aid her in leaving her husband but didn't have what it took to do so. He was given a thin five inches to work with and hadn't quite mastered how to work with what he was given. Honestly, she was only his third sex partner, the first being his childhood sweetheart that left Tennessee for college and finished two years at Arizona State before getting pregnant and dropping out. His second partner was a woman Señor Carlos Valdez sent to his room as a gift for joining the team. She did everything. All he had to do was pull it out, and she handled all the rest. Tamica was different, and maybe it was because she was older, but she expected him to do everything in bed. She only took him down her throat or rode him if she wanted to ask for something. Her pussy was good; better yet, it was magical. Every time he slid inside of her, it broke him down to mush. If she wanted it, it was hers, no matter what it was.

Harold couldn't have asked for a better life, and then after eight years, he learned the truth that brought his world spiraling down. He learned that everyone he looked at as his superiors were under someone else's umbrella. They were pulled together to become richer by a ghost named Joe.

"So, you're telling me I have a meeting with a man none of you have met, but you report to because this is his operation?"

"Yeah, I know it sounds crazy, but that's exactly what I'm telling you. We don't know who he is besides the fact that he goes by Joe, and he's made all of us filthy rich. We had a board member attempt to find out who he was . . . and no one has seen or heard from him since."

"Then how do you know we can trust him, Joseph? How do you know he's not a government agent put in place to bust all of you at the same time?"

"You mean all of *us,* right? Even though you're not a founding board member, you are on the board, and you're the face of this whole operation. You *do* know that, right?"

Knowing it and hearing it were apparently two different things. Harold knew his position in the scheme of things but to hear it spoken out of the mouth of someone he respected made his stomach quiver. Joseph said it in a way that made him feel like if it ever blew up, they already had him in a position to be the fall guy.

"You said that as if you have me set up and ready to accept a prison sentence for the whole thing," he said with a chuckle.

"That's *exactly* how we have you set up. Why else would a group of billionaires, mob bosses, cartel leaders, government agents, and government officials place a little boy fresh out of college over their drug empire? Do you think we're dumb or just outright stupid?"

"Neither. I thought you were trustworthy entrepreneurs that knew how to work together to have more and a fresh mind could take you further than you'd ever been."

"Then you are more naive than what we originally thought of you. That ego cocky shit you pulled during your interview let us know you were wet behind the ears. But, wow, looks like we got our money's worth," he laughed hysterically until his voice turned sinister. "If this operation goes to shit, no one goes to jail but you and those working in the lab for you."

"Do you think I'm dumb enough not to be recording your messages? Do you think I'm that foolish not to keep a record of what you asked me to do and how much I am paid for doing it? If I fry, we *all* fry, so get your fucking plate of spaghetti ready and get ready for the fish fry." Harold grabbed his keys off the table and began to make his way to the door.

"Your niece Kendra is such a beautiful little girl," he mentioned, causing Harold to freeze in his tracks. "Oh, but, of course, she is. She's as gorgeous as her mother, your youngest sister Kenya who works odd jobs through the local temp. agency. In my opinion, all the girls in your family look just like your mom. Speaking of your mom, I wonder if she hit at bingo last night. She's been doing pretty good lately. It's like her luck finally changed, and how's your grandfather? Did his crops come in?"

Harold's laugh topped Joseph's on the sinister scale. He could barely stop laughing to catch his breath so he could say what was on his heart.

"Man, fuck them broke-ass people! Do you think threatening to kill those that you *assume* I love and care for is going to make me do whatever you say? Do you *really* think I would risk everything that I've accomplished here and my freedom to save the lives of some people who still get excited when they win twenty dollars on a fucking scratch off? You can start killing them now. I don't give a damn about anything except my freedom and my money. That's a lesson I learned from all of you, so kill them. As a matter of fact, I'll save you the trouble and do it before you get the chance to!"

"Wait," Joseph requested as he took a deep breath to take their conversation down a notch, "this has gotten out of hand. This is ridiculous!" he added with a chuckle. "We are taking a what-if scenario and giving it life. We're not going to be caught or popped by the Feds. We have too many of them on board. This is the end of the operation because we're shutting it down, but not because our hands were forced to close it."

"Well, how about I don't believe you or anything you have to say? And from now on, how about you let somebody else do the communication between the board and me? I don't got shit else to say to you. Oh yeah, make sure you set up that meeting with Joe and me. I think I'm interested in speaking to the man in charge." Joseph laughed as Harold walked out the door, but if Harold had turned around and walked back into the room, he would have seen the deathly look Joseph had on his face.

Of course, his meeting with Joe never came into fruition, and with no way to track down a ghost, there was nothing in his power he could do to speak with him. However, Joseph never said another word to him after that day, which, in his eyes, was still a victory on his part.

That day, his life changed, and yearning for his freedom began. He thought he'd have to come up with a plan to escape, and then Joe announced his retirement. The illegal operations would be leaving MediTech for good, and from what the board said, his salary would go back to where it was when he was first hired. Everyone on the board would be selling their stock and shares in the company, and by his calculation, in less than five years, the company would be filing bankruptcy. Harold would never let that happen. With all the hell he went through, he still loved the company and would save it, even if it took his last dollar. The only money he spent over the past eight years was money he used to put and keep a smile on Tamica's face. When the smoke cleared and the company started to crumble, he'd save it, and he wouldn't take on any partners besides his future wife. He'd even go as far as to change the name of the company and its location. All he had to do was make it through the day. However, that seemed to be his hardest task.

Once the news and social media outlets started shedding light on who this "Joe" was, he lost all faith in everything. He couldn't believe that it was possible he was under a black man's umbrella nor that the people he worked side by side with would have been open to being under a black man's leadership. Harold didn't know how it would turn out in the end, but he knew the Italian mafia was hot and cold when it came to black men in power. They didn't mind having black men work for them, but there has been a strong history of them having a problem with working for a black man. He wasn't sure if Romano would seek to kill Joe now that the new information was out. Valdez, well, Valdez was Mexican. And it was no secret that Mexicans and blacks looked at each other like they were family. There might not be any smoke in the air when it came to the Valdez Cartel with Joe being black, but you never know when it comes to these types of things.

Harold lay awake at night wondering what if Joe was more sinister than all of them combined. What if Joe were more powerful than all the government agencies tracking him down? And what if he set up his operation to never be known or traceable? Who is to say that Joe didn't plan on killing everybody involved when all was said and done? These questions kept Harold up all last night. He had mentioned to Joseph two years ago that he would snitch. He said he would turn in everything and everybody if the operation fell upon his head. What if he shared that information with Joe? What if *that* was the reason Joe never reached out to him to schedule the meeting? What if he hadn't thought about the right *what-ifs?*

Harold didn't know what to do. He didn't give a shit about his family being killed. In his eyes, none of them had a future anyway. Although his niece had found a soft spot in his heart and nested there, she was too young for him to see any value in her anyway. Tamica, on the other hand, that was a different story. He knew if any of them truly wanted to hurt him, they would go after her, and he would die protecting her.

Where the hell was Tamica?

Chapter Ten

Something had changed about Ethan. Ronald didn't know exactly what it was, but he was determined to get to the bottom of it. An unexpected loss had a way of changing people. Sometimes for the better; other times for the worst. He hadn't been around Ethan long enough to decide which was the latter of the two. Trying his damnedest to keep the mood light, he decided to take the boys out for a steak dinner. Mimic was all dressed up, and he and Ethan . . . Well, they both were wearing sweats and a T-shirt. He thought it would be best if they stopped at a department store on the way.

"Go ahead, Ethan; get whatever you want and try it on. If you like it, leave it on and wait for me at the register. I'll pay for it there."

"And what about me? I don't get nothing because my granny already bought me some clothes? That ain't fair, Mr. Ronald."

"Stop whining all the damn time, boy, and go get you something. It better be of the same caliber of what you got on, or I'm not buying it."

"Aw, then, that's okay. Only one monkey suit per year; that's law. I'll just help Ethan find him something."

As a child, Ronald's mama used to tease him about being a backward shopper. He would go straight to the shoe department scanning the racks for a pair of shoes that called out to him. After finding those shoes, he'd look for clothing that matched. Seven out of ten times, he would find something that matched perfectly, but those three failed times, he'd settle for walking around looking like a damn clown before he'd exchanged those shoes. It seemed when it came to the way he shopped, nothing about it had changed. He walked straight to the shoe department, took off his left shoe because, for some odd reason, his last two toes always seemed to swell, and, as always, he started trying on shoes. He spent more time in the shoe department then he had looking for clothes. By the time he had his outfit on and was ready to go, the boys had made no progress.

"What's wrong? You couldn't find nothing you liked?"

"This stuff is expensive. Who pays thirty-five dollars for a shirt? I saw some similar at Goodwill in the business section for fifty cents apiece. The markup in here is crazy. Let's just swing by Goodwill."

"Hell no, don't take him to Goodwill! I'm not going out for steak in the white people neighborhood with you in some damn mothball-smelling clothes. Man, you be tripping. You ain't paying for it. Mr. Ronald is. Ball out, nigga!"

"I don't know about the 'ball out' part, but Martin is right. Ethan, pick what you like. Don't worry about the price. Let me worry about it."

"I see how you come to work, Mr. Ronald; you don't never worry about it. You wear all those fancy clothes to teach at a school in the hood. Do you know if you cut back on your shopping expenses by ten dollars, what your savings account can look like in the next ten years?"

"No, Ethan, I don't. And I don't want you to tell me. Another ten years of life isn't promised to you or me. So, I'ma enjoy living my life at the moment."

"I can see why you would think that was something smart to say. But what happens if you don't instantly die, and your arms and legs are severed off? You're left with your brain and the midsection of your body. Living in the moment don't help you live the rest of your life as an amputee. You got to have something to put up, something that guarantees that you can always live the way you want to live no matter what health situation you're in. And I know ten years ain't promised to any of us. I'ma have to bury my daddy next week. I thought he'd live forever."

The reality of why they were all gathered together outside of school hours kicked in, and no one said a word. Ronald was horrible when it came to dealing with emotions and feelings. He liked to pretend neither existed. However, once in a blue moon, he played the wolf and growled at it.

"Hey, Ethan, if this is too soon, we can call it a day. I can take you to a drive-thru to get something to eat and drop you off back at the house. I know this must be hard for you to deal with."

"Why do you think that? Because I mentioned that I have to bury my dad next week? Come on, Mr. Ronald, do you think that junky-ass nigga had burial insurance?" He chuckled. "And if anybody gave my mom money to have him cremated, he would never make it to the fire, but her pipe would." He laughed and laughed so hard and so loud that it made Ronald uncomfortable.

"How about we pretend that I'm your son, and you get me dressed for a nice dinner at the steakhouse? Let's see how you have me walking around looking." He smiled at Ronald. He knew his curtness sometimes caused Ronald to be uncomfortable, and instead of apologizing for actions he meant to make, he would shoot a smile at him to let him know that everything was still all good.

They walked into the steakhouse in the predominantly white neighborhood, and every head turned in their direction. It wasn't because they were black. It was merely because all three were extremely handsome. While they ate, Ronald taught the boys a few table manners, and he gave them the game on dating and women. The first lesson was knowing which caliber of woman they should take to places like this.

"Nah, son, this isn't the type of place you take Kim-Kim with the big booty and golds in her mouth. This is a place you bring Sharlene with the long legs, upbeat conversation, and beautiful vocabulary to."

"Why not Kim-Kim? She gotta have steak too," Mimic interrupted.

"Because Kim-Kim wasn't raised to appreciate fine art. You see those paintings on the wall over there?"

"Yeah, I see them. They look like a bunch of spilt paint and scribble scrabble," Mimic laughed.

"Turn around but don't make it obvious. Do you see the girl in the rear of the building toward the bathroom?"

Slowly, both boys peeked at the girl. Ronald said, "Do you see what she is looking at?"

"She's staring at the pictures," Mimic said. "Dude she's with must be boring as hell," he laughed.

"She's a Sharlene. She doesn't care if he's boring or not because she's too busy appreciating the fine art."

"Everybody got their own taste. Y'all can date the chicks who used to sniff the magic markers in elementary, and I'm going to date the chick that used to steal them from those girls, threaten to beat them up if they snitched on her, and then try to sell the markers back to them with a bag of candy. Those are the loyal chicks that are willing to catch a charge for her man. Sharlenes are law-abiding citizens. I'll pass!"

"I see you weren't listening to nothing I was saying to you earlier about different displays of loyalty. Some women will love you so much that they show their loyalty by stopping you from making dumb decisions. Others show it by loving you so much that they participate in the foolishness. If you're not going to listen to anything, I'm saying, just remember this. AIDS and HIV are a real thing. Choose your woman wisely."

"I've been listening," Ethan said with his eyes locked on the girl. *"So, these Sharlenes you're mentioning, I want to talk about them."*

"OK, shoot," Ronald egged on.

"Smart, loyal, and safe is what I gathered from your talk. Are you also saying that Sharlenes couldn't give you AIDS and HIV because they are educated and might have grown up in a two-parent, morale-filled home?"

"No, I'm not. Sharlenes are human and can make mistakes too. For the record, you make sure you use a condom whether you with a Sharlene or a Kim-Kim."

"Then if I have to wear a rubber with both, I'm going after the big booty. Kim-Kim wins again."

Mimic laughed, and Ethan stood up and walked over to the girl. Ronald couldn't tell what he was saying to her; however, he knew the look of when a flirt was accepted. She pushed a lock of her hair behind her ear, batted her eyes, and then blushed. She had to be in her mid- to late twenties, which meant absolutely nothing because Ethan had her where he wanted her.

"Again, I didn't mean to stare at you, but you looked like you had questions about that painting on the wall. That's not the original, but the artist painted it while he was battling starvation. The cattle were dying and unsafe to eat in Wyoming at the time. He was forced to live on a green vegetable diet made up of mostly tall grass, and that picture was supposed to represent what his

*large intestines looked like free of meat. What a cliché to
have it in a steakhouse." He smiled, and she smiled back.*

*"That's exactly what I was thinking. Do you think it's
an oversight by the owner?" she asked, intrigued by the
young man standing in front of her.*

*"No, I think he added it for surrealism. To question
its presence would be to question the owner's loyalty to
himself."*

"Explain."

*"I will another time. I don't want to take your atten-
tion away from your date." He handed her a pen and
placed a napkin in front of her. She hesitated and then
took it. She wrote down two numbers for Ethan to reach
her at. He nodded at her date and gave her a wink. He
rejoined the table, and all eyes were on him.*

*"Well, what happened over there?" Mimic asked ea-
gerly.*

*"I verified what Mr. Ronald said, and I'm dating noth-
ing but Sharlenes when I go on the hunt for my wife." He
flashed her number at them and pointed out the heart
she dotted the lowercase i in her name with. Ronald
smiled like a proud father.*

*The steaks were cooked to perfection, and they all
enjoyed their time together. Ronald drove them through
the residential blocks so they could see how beautiful the
houses on this side of town were under Christmas lights.*

*"Okay, you got all the money in the world. Which one
of these houses are you moving into, Mr. Ronald? I got
the one on the left with all the lights and big windows."*

*Ronald looked around, but he didn't see a house that
fit.*

*"I don't think I'd buy any of these if I had all the money
in the world. I want one of those houses in California
with the pool that runs over into the ocean and where it
has forty bathrooms and eight bedrooms," he laughed.*

"I'm into movie star-type homes. This is more like an area for families like people with five or six kids. I'm not going to have any." Ronald stumbled over his words, and Ethan caught it and didn't say a thing, but there was something up with Mr. Ronald's answer. He decided to wait for another time to bring it up.

"Okay, your turn, Ethan. Which one of these houses is yours? Watch he say the cheapest looking one on the block," Mimic laughed.

"Watch I say none! They are family homes like he said, and I don't want a house, mansion, or condo, either. I want a commercial space."

"I'm talking a place to live in, not work." Mimic shook his head.

"Me too. I want to live in a warehouse."

"A warehouse?"

Ronald was curious too, but Martin beat him to the question.

"Yes, a huge warehouse with a for lease or sale by owner sign in front of it. I want it gutted before I move in so I can map it out how I want it."

"Why? That's sounds stupid. Just get a mansion."

"I don't want a mansion; I want commercial property. If I have all the money in the world, I'ma buy what I want and what impresses me, that's why."

"You can't never act like a normal nigga, can you? Blah blah blah! That's all I ever hear when you talk."

"I don't force you to listen," Ethan mumbled.

"Damn, be a kid. Stop spending every fucking second planning out your life. You can't control shit!"

"Why can't I? Who said?"

"All right, Martin, that's enough," Ronald intervened.

"Life said, nigga."

"Says who, you?" Ethan was growing irritated, and for the first time that he could remember, he couldn't control his growing temper.

"Boys!" Ronald yelled into the rearview mirror. They were closer than he'd like to be while talking shit to each other.

"If you're in control of your life, why was your daddy found in a fucking dumpster dead?"

The impact of Ethan's punch sent Mimic's head into the back window. Instantly, the glass cracked. By the time Ronald found a safe place to pull over, Ethan's new shirt was covered in blood, and Mimic failed to keep up with the punches. For every two he threw, Ethan gave him five. The boys looked like two heavyweight boxers with even score cards hoping for the win, but it was obvious who won this fight. When Ronald opened the back door to break it up, Mimic took off running. He wasn't far from home at that point, but Ronald felt obligated to try to track him down. From half a block away, he watched Mimic go in the house as Ethan continued to huff and puff in the backseat.

"What has gotten into you?"

"Why does it have to be me? Oh, I know. It's my fault because I'm always the bigger person, or is it my fault because my mind is mature, and his isn't? Why can't I be fed up with always getting picked on? Why must I always accept it?"

There wasn't an answer Ronald could give that trumped Ethan's questions, and he knew the answer before he asked. He lost his father, and though he tried hard to pretend like it didn't bother him, it was tearing him up.

"You're staying with me for a few days, you hear? I'll go by and let your mother know tomorrow."

"You don't have to. She doesn't care."

The ride was quiet, and after checking his rearview mirror every other minute, he saw that Ethan had fallen asleep. The boy didn't have a cut or scratch on his face, but his hand was swollen. He debated carrying him in *the house, but Ethan was almost his height and already built solid. Ronald was bony in comparison.*

"Come on, champ. Let's get you in some pajamas and into bed."

With his arm wrapped around his shoulder, he escorted Ethan to the guest bedroom. Seconds later, the boy was snoring. Ronald wondered how long it had been since he slept in a bed. He didn't even have a mat in his room in the projects.

"Hello." The phone rang at two in the morning. He already knew who it was.

"Want me to come keep you wet and warm?"

It was Corinna better known by the students as Ms. Lawson, the evil English teacher. None of the kids liked her because she pushed them to be their best, and slang wasn't welcomed in her class. She was heavyset, at least 245 pounds naked, and five foot five with short hair. Her face was beautiful contrary to the big and ugly jokes made about her. If the rolls under her chin didn't steal the attention, everyone would agree. Her size didn't bother him one bit. He secretly preferred a big woman. Not thick, chubby, or fat. He liked them big. Double his width with huge breasts. Fucking big women made him work harder to please them, which maximized the nut he'd get. And though it may sound shallow, he counted on the meal he'd get when they were done. Lying on a big chick inside of some big pussy was like relaxing in a Jacuzzi lined in feather-filled pillows. It was his version of heaven on earth.

Corinna was the first teacher to make him feel welcomed, and she brought him lunch every day. She liked him but assumed he'd never give her a shot judging by his looks, so imagine the shock she was in when he reached out to her first.

"That meat loaf with the mashed potatoes and broccoli last week, you put your foot in . . . I almost licked the plate," he joked as he returned all the Tupperware she packed his lunch in the previous week.

"Good, I'm glad you liked it, Mr. Ronald. I'm glad you're here. You give me a reason to cook. I love doing my thing in the kitchen, but I need a taste tester." She giggled. *"I kinda hired you for the job."*

"Well, I'm glad you did." He grabbed her hand, and she dropped her head. With the shit she talked to the students, he didn't think she'd be shy. Gripping her chin, he forced her into eye contact. *"Would it be asking too much of you if I asked you to come cook that same meal at my house tonight? I'll give you the money for the groceries and whatever else you need."* He stepped closer to her. *"And if you're not tied to anybody else, maybe you can cook us some breakfast too."*

She nodded, pulled away from him, and headed out the door.

"Corinna, this is your classroom, baby. You stay, I'll leave," he said, fighting back his laugh.

She was nervous and fucking up, which made him want to be inside of her even more. Dinner and breakfast lasted for two days, and they slept through lunch. She picked up a job at the community college on the weekends which landed her in his neighborhood Friday and Saturday nights. Normally, she'd come straight there, but his fear of commitment kicked in, and he set boundaries. They went from hooking up three and four times a week to once a month, and Corinna treated him exactly like she always had. It seemed she went out of her way to feed him more.

Fucking the chick at the gym was supposed to help him with the feelings he was growing for his phatty cake, as he called her behind her back, and it hadn't.

"I wish you could, baby, but my son is here."

"Your son? But I thought you didn't have any kids."

"Yeah, my work son," he chuckled.

"Ethan?"

"Yeah, the boy is going through some stuff, and since I'm not qualified to help him, I'm helping."

She giggled. "That's so sweet of you. You know how I feel about him, so if there's anything I can do to help, let me know."

Ethan was awakened by the sound of Ronald's phone ringing. The unfamiliar sound didn't mix with the unfamiliar place. He got out of bed in hopes that Ronald was up watching TV, and he could join him, and by chance, caught wind of his conversation.

"I sure will. I wish I could lick on that pussy right now and then bite into a piece of your buttermilk and honey corn bread . . . Ethan?" He looked up and saw the boy standing at the foot of his bed.

"Hi, Ms. Lawson," the boy shouted. "Don't let me stop you from coming over."

"Let me call you back. Okay, baby? Bye."

"She said hello, and why didn't you make your presence known?"

"I'm your work, son. What's a work son?" he asked, taking a seat at the foot of Ronald's bed. Ronald turned on his nightstand lamp and sat up, deciding not to waste his time probing the prober.

"It means I've taken a liking to you, and if I viewed those at the school as my family, you'd be my son."

"And what about Mimic? Would he be your son too?"

"No, I only have one work child. He'd be my son's best friend. Are you ready to talk about what happened in the car?"

"I thought we already did," he said quizzically. "I'll get with him later and apologize that I let my frustrations out on him."

"I was hoping you would."

Ethan got up and moved to the head of the bed. He stacked the extra pillows and then lay on the bed on top of the covers.

"Ms. Lawson is a Sharlene. Why isn't she your woman?"

"Whoa. She is a subject we won't be discussing."

"Why not? It's obvious y'all are getting down. You always have her Tupperware on your desk, and she goes out of her way to be nice to me. Whenever she talks to me, she brings you up even when it has nothing to do with you."

Ronald smirked and at the confirmation that he wasn't the only one smitten, he said, "She's your teacher, and I don't have the right to speak her business without her consent, that's why."

"Well, can you invite her over tomorrow? I'd like to try her corn bread before she cuts you your piece."

Ronald popped the boy across his face with a pillow and laughed. "I think I can do that."

Chapter Eleven

Memphis, Tennessee. Thursday, January 31, 2019, cont.

Today was the last time MediTech would make and distribute illegal drugs. Harold's pace around the office was warranted. Today had to go by smoothly. It felt as if he were a living cliché as he thought about how he loved watching movies about gangsters and drug dealers. While watching them, he'd think about becoming one. It seemed like the life for him, but the consequences scared him because he couldn't recall any of them successfully leaving the game without going to jail or being killed. If he could make it through the day without a snag, he would become his new favorite movie character.

"Oh my God, are you still in here tripping?" Alejandro, his best friend and third in the line of command, entered his office without knocking. He never knocked.

"Hell yeah, I'm still tripping. Not everyone has an uncle who runs the cartel."

Harold and Alejandro didn't have the same worries. While Harold was stressing, Alejandro was at peace. He was originally a plant placed there by the Valdez Cartel to keep an eye on Harold, but his genius and degree in biochemistry got him a salaried position as well. Being Carlos Valdez's last living nephew had its perks. One of them being, he was considered untouchable. If Joe decided to kill everyone in the building, you can be sure Alejandro would walk out without a scratch.

"Nothing is going to happen, man; just chill. After this, we are going to own this fucking company. We are still going to be partners, right?"

"Of course, we are," Harold lied. "Where would I be without my right-hand man?"

"I don't know where you would be. Judging by how you look now, probably on top of a building debating jumping or in some bar drunk as hell singing karaoke style to an empty bottle. You got to stop stressing so much, man!"

"I'll put it on my things-to-do list. What do you want, anyway?"

"I came in here to tell you that the truck just arrived. When he takes off, we are on a five-hour countdown to our freedom."

"Did everything seem normal?"

"Damn," Alejandro said, shaking his head. "Yes, everything seems normal. It's exactly the way it always is."

"Good, now let's go get this day over with. I need some pussy and a drink."

"Me too," Alejandro mumbled as he thought about bending over something thick and pretty before Saturday's sunrise.

Harold led the way with Alejandro on his heels. They entered the corridor and walked at least a quarter mile before entering the lab. The first thing Harold noticed was that Tamica's office was still dark, which meant she still hadn't made it in. Before he said a word to any of the chemists in the room, he pulled out his phone and sent a text message.

"Where are you, baby? I'm starting to get worried."

Alejandro knew the look he saw on Harold's face. He didn't know exactly what it was, but he knew it involved Tamica.

"What's up, bro? What's wrong with Tamica?"

"I don't know, but she should have been here minutes ago. She said she was running late, but she still should have been here by now."

"Well, after you get this shit straight here, go ahead and leave, and I'll close out the rest of the day for you. You can thank me later," he chuckled.

"Thanks, bro, I appreciate it."

Turning his body back to face the room full of waiting chemists, Harold cleared his throat and stood in the center of the room.

"Today is the last day I will ever ask you to mix or make any of the compounds that you have been pressing for the last ten years. Today, we turn over a new leaf, and we can only grow upward from here. Yes, we will all miss the extra bonus checks we had coming in weekly. However, there will be no more paranoia or fear of having the government run in on us, shut us down, or take away our freedom. Today is the first day of our lives as chemists creating compounds to heal, treat, and, hopefully, cure diseases that are plaguing the world. We are no longer poisoners; we are the lifesavers."

The room roared in cheers, and Alejandro nodded at Harold in agreement. Everyone was ecstatic about turning over a new leaf. The chemists, just like Harold, were thrilled about creating medications that would change the world for the better. They had been forced into the drug world and threatened to stay in it. The few chemists who stood their ground and walked out of the company didn't make it home to their families. Each died in some "accidental" death. Each one of their mates died in some "accidental" manner following the deaths of their loved ones, just in case they confided in them. After witnessing that, none of the chemists objected to what they were doing. Now, they would be free, and everybody likes their freedom.

"In honor of today being the first day that we all are merely chemists at MediTech Pharmaceuticals, I'm giving all of you the rest of the day off. Once you get home, you should check your bank accounts. I believe Joe left all of you a nice-size parting gift for your years of dedicated service."

He didn't have to say it twice; the room was empty before he could remember what it was that he was to do next.

"How do you think Joe will kill them? That's a lot of chemists dying at once."

"Why does it matter?" Alejandro shrugged. "That's fewer people who can run their mouths about us. Fuck them."

It was times like these that he reminded Harold he was a cold-blooded killer from a long line of killers. There was no way he'd continue to work side-by-side with him, and he wouldn't have to. The board told him that Señor Carlos Valdez found no use for his nephew, and when the operation was over, instead of watching him mingle with the wrong people and lose his life, he'd kill him. Harold didn't want him dead, but he didn't get involved in family issues either.

The men left the room using a different door than the one they entered. The empty room they were in led to a bulletproof security office and safe place. At least two armed security guards manned the room at all times, including overnight.

"How's everything looking?" Harold asked the stockier of the two men.

"Nice and peaceful, just the way I like it."

"Good. I'm going to be heading out a little bit earlier than usual today. Make sure you do a walk-through with Alejandro at the end of the night to change all the security codes in the building. There's going to be a lot of changes around here starting next week."

"Actually, sir, Señor Valdez wants us back by the end of the day. He said we would no longer be needed here as of next week. He won't be tied to this company after then. I'm sorry, sir, I wish I would have known to give you more warning, but you're going to have to hire your own security. We were part of the package deal." His words and demeanor were sincere. He didn't enjoy giving Harold the last-minute update; however, he was given orders not to mention it until the end of the day.

"No problem, no problem at all. You, my friend, will be missed."

Harold shook his hand firmly as he reminisced about the many times he watched Roberto risk his own life to save his. He would be missed, but he would be lying if he said he wasn't relieved that as of Monday, everything that reminded him of the last ten years besides the building would be gone. Each one of the chemists would be murdered over the weekend and, sadly, so would their spouses. The men had been interviewing and hiring chemists for the last three months. They opened a temporary location in Nashville to house and train the new staff as they cleaned up the old trash.

Exiting the security office, Harold and Alejandro took a series of steps and right turns until he made it to another hallway a quarter of a mile long. When he made it to the end of this hallway, there was a three-way. If he continued straight, he would be in the break room. If he went to the left, he would be in the restroom, and when he walked through the doors on the right, it was like he entered a new world. The warehouse portion of the building had two sides of it—one for shipping and the other for receiving. Glancing at the receiving side, he smiled. All the new equipment had arrived and would be installed over the weekend. Alejandro picked up his pace and made it to the shipping area, leaving Herald behind.

"What's up, bro? Why did you get out of the truck?"

Roman was holding the shipping slips and flipped through each one, one at a time, before responding.

"There seems to be a problem with the paperwork. It says I'm supposed to pick up eight refrigerators and deliver each to a different location, but your boys just loaded ten of them on the back of my rig. What's up with the two extra refrigerators?"

Harold had walked up in time to hear his question, and instantly, worry removed the smile he had on his face. He made it a priority to meet every driver over the last ten years as they picked up their loads. He didn't take it as a coincidence that the company sent someone new on the last day of production.

"Where's Dave?" Harold questioned.

"Who?"

"Dave. Dave, the guy who always comes on Thursdays to pick up our deliveries. Where is he?"

"Oh, you're talking about David. He quit yesterday, saved up enough money to buy his own dump truck and is going into business for himself. He's a real cool dude!"

"So why would they send someone new?" Alejandro asked, knowing what Harold was thinking.

"I'm not new. I'm just on the opposite route this time. This is my first time picking up your shipments, but I normally run your routes on the receiving end. I pick up the empty refrigerators and drop them back off here. They didn't have anybody familiar with how y'all get down, so they sent me instead. Is there a problem?"

Harold took a deep breath. He didn't like the fact that there had been any changes today. However, he did find comfort in knowing that the driver was familiar with the process.

***

"This stupid car is doing it again. Can you pick me up on Fifth and Madison?"

Tamika was officially stressed to the max. She had two tasks to complete, and the second task was timed. She had to get Harold back to his apartment so that she could stage his suicide. Joe had gotten wind of Harold's outbursts two years ago and decided it was best never to exchange words with the man he once admired. The board did hire Harold as a fall guy as Joe requested, but he excelled in his role. No one thought a college grad, fresh off the boat, would last that long. No one thought he would dive headfirst into the world of drug trafficking. No one thought he would create new pipelines that brought the money in tenfold. No one thought Harold was a winner except for Harold, and he was right.

Joe had every intention of letting Harold live because he knew the young man would do great things. There weren't too many people Joe had soft spots for, but Harold had earned one. Though their stories were day and night apart, there was a similarity in them he couldn't deny. It was the theme song of that television show *The Jeffersons,* where the broke prevailed and became the rich, and though it was only a jingle of the show, it was Joe's favorite song. Having Frederick murdered or placed under investigation so his dirty moves could be uncovered so he could be fired was not only a gift for Tamica, it was supposed to be a gift for Harold as well. Unlike everyone else involved, Joe didn't believe the hype about Tamica not having feelings for Harold. They were in a nine-year relationship, and he showed her love, he made her feel youthful, and he spoiled the shit out of her. Nine years is a long time to fake something, and Joe didn't believe she was that stone hearted to be up for the task. With them both being free, Joe wondered what choices they would make in the end, but Harold ruined that. The same cocky ego that had gotten him hired was the same cocky ego that sentenced him to death.

He partially blamed Tamica for not taming the young man. He thought that she should have taken some time to talk to him about the golden rule, no snitching, but she hadn't. Luckily for her, she owned one of those special spots in Joe's heart too. She was the first to show extreme loyalty to him, and she seemed to be the only person who wasn't scared of him. Something about her turned him on. He fought it because it wasn't a part of his plan, but if he had room for a woman, it would be her. He knew she only slept with Harold because he asked her to. He monitored everything she did, and besides the friendly flirt with men outside of her job, she was faithful to her husband. What Joe liked most about her was her background. Nothing she was experiencing was new. She either lived it or watched someone she was related to go through it. He could refrain from threatening her because she knew the game and the consequences of betrayal. Joe was smitten, to say the least.

As punishment for what Harold had done, he made her executioner, and she was given the opportunity to dictate how he would die. Precisely as Joe thought, Tamica chose a method that would cause him the least pain. She mixed up a concoction that would make his heart instantly stop while looking to the world like an undercover drug addiction from the year spent at MediTech.

Calling emergency roadside assistance and waiting for a tow truck to rescue her could take two hours or more, and Tamica didn't have that time to give. If she had a way to contact Joe, she could tell him her problems and ask for more time. She hoped Joe monitored her text messages, and he did, but he assumed the SOS text was a part of her plan. He didn't need to threaten her when he told her it had to be done during normal business hours. He knew she would get it done.

"No, there's no problem. My boss just likes for shit to run smoothly and for people to read directions." Alejandro snatched the shipping slips out of Roman's hands. "Do you see that little star-looking thing at the end of the order number? It's called an asterisk. If you look at the bottom of the page, there's another one. It says this location has two deliveries. If you go through your papers, you'll find another page that has an asterisk on it." He handed Roman the slips and then walked over to Harold. "Are you sure you're OK?"

"Tamica's car broke down on her again, and she needs me to get her. Think you can handle the rest?"

"I know I can. Go get your lady."

They bumped fists and walked off in separate directions.

"I'm on my way, beautiful," Harold texted as he grabbed his suit coat and keys from his office. He made it to the parking lot and found glass everywhere. None of his windows were broken; yet, both rear tires were flat.

"Fuck!" he yelled.

"Now what's wrong?" Alejandro asked, turning the corner from the side of the building. "Two flats, no spares. Can this day get any worse?"

"Yeah, it can, but you don't want it to. Neither do I."

"What am I supposed to do now? Tamica's waiting on me."

"There you go stressing again. Look, leave your car. I'll get the tires fixed after I take you to snatch up Tamica."

"You'll drop us off in Bartlett?"

"Hell no," Alejandro corrected.

"Why not?"

"Because it's rush hour, and my boss just left me a shit-load of Friday shit to do on a Thursday. We have people coming in and out tomorrow and Saturday to install all this state-of-the-art equipment you ordered. I can't make that long-ass trip there and back. One of us has to close out this day." Alejandro placed his hands on Harold's shoulder. "I'm sure Joe is watching to make sure everything gets done. We don't need him to think we abandoned the plan. I'm not trying to become trash like the chemists."

"You're right," Harold said, defeated.

"How about I take you to that hotel that I dropped you off at downtown, and when your car is fixed, I'll pick you up?"

The idea was perfect. Harold needed a nut to free his mind, and Tamica loved that hotel because there was a Jacuzzi in the room. He booked the hotel in seconds while Alejandro went back inside to grab his keys.

His uncle had given him two tasks to regain his respect. One was to make sure nothing is tying him to MediTech after the board pulled out, and the second task was to kill Harold and set it up to look like the Italians had done it. Señor Carlos Valdez never liked Romano and wanted the mob boss dead. However, he'd save the bullets and let the pancreatic cancer finish taking him out. It was a general consensus that Harold was liked and would keep his life when it came to an end, but his nephew gave him some disturbing news.

"*Tío*, I think that boy is going to snitch."

"What boy? Harold?" Señor Carlos Valdez was consuming his breakfast of a line of coke up the nose. He started his day the same way for the last fifteen years. It was the only time he'd use the drug, but his lines were becoming thicker. The cancer diagnosis had him numb to everything, and the increase of the amount of coke he snorted aided it.

"Yes, he's been saying shit for the past week or so that's made me want to pull out my gun and put a bullet through his head."

"So why haven't you?"

"What?"

"Why haven't you put a bullet in his head?" His uncle added bass to his already-baritone voice.

"Because you said we'd close up shop the way Joe and the board want us to."

"I know what I said. Do you think I'm too old to remember my own words?" The question went unanswered as he continued. "I asked you, *why* didn't you put a bullet in his head?"

"I wanted your blessings to do so."

"Right answer. You've gotten close to that black asshole. I had to be sure you weren't catching feelings for him or Joe."

"Joe? I don't know anything about Joe. I work for him because you told me to. My loyalty is with my blood."

"Save the Scout's honor bullshit, Robin Hood. Your loyalty means nothing to me. I will send orders on the manner Harold will die, and you will make sure it goes as planned or you and your black boyfriend will share a coffin, understand?"

"Yes, it's understood!"

When the order came in to make the Italian mob the fall guys, and for the orders to look like they came from Joe, another thought overtook him . . . comforting Tamica. He had never slept with a black woman, and though he spent a lot of time daydreaming of sucking on her huge titties while his swimmers made his meat deflate inside of her, Alejandro wanted more than a nut. She was older than him by seven years, but he was older and more experienced than Harold. Most importantly, they were close friends. She trusted Alejandro with her secrets, and in exchange, he provided a listening ear and a shut mouth. He'd never share her private thoughts with anyone, not even if his uncle asked him. He knew Tamica trusted him by the information she shared.

"I mean little, like a middle school student's dick. I tried sucking it so it would swell up, and the only thing that got swollen were my lips. Just once in my life, I'd like to be fucked by a big dick and don't let me get started on my husband's two-minute shooter." She kept rambling on and on until she realized what she had been saying. *"I'm sorry, Alej, baby. I'm sure you don't want to hear about my dick problems,"* she giggled, pretending to be shy.

"It's all good, mama. I know they got you stressed out. If we weren't best friends, I'd offer to help you out," he teased.

"Is that right? Sounds like you're saying you're blessed down there."

"I'm not trying to say it. I did. Maybe when I finally get a woman I like enough to meet you, she'll tell you about it."

"Pull it out; let me be the judge."

He chuckled nervously. He knew there was no telling what she would let out of her mouth, and he also knew she was dead-ass serious.

"Right here? Just pull it out, and then what?"

"And then I will be the judge. You knew better than to tease me. Now, I need you to show and tell!"

At first thought, he needed to touch and prep it for show, but her words had gotten his full attention, and it was ready to stand tall and salute her.

"Okay, but don't say I didn't try to warn you," he laughed. As he began to undo his belt, she walked over to his office door and locked it.

"I don't want you to scare anybody with that 'monster' you claim you gots," she giggled.

"Yeah, I don't want to have to pay off any life insurance policies."

His nine rock-hard inches were doing a balancing act over his balls. She walked over and grabbed it.

"OK, I see that you're half horse. This is one of the biggest and prettiest dicks I've seen in years. Well maintained too."

"You sound like a beauty pageant judge," he said, hoping she missed the small fluid that came out of the eye of it as she caressed it.

"I prefer taste tester." She took him greedily in her mouth and sucked on him like bobbing and weaving were her only goals in life. She did all the tongue-and-throat tricks she used to make men nut in seconds, but they did not affect him. He softly held the side of her face with his palms and fucked her pretty little mouth to his own rhythm. He wished her head could make him nut after seeing her yearn to swallow him, but he was a pussy man. He could get his dick sucked for hours, and all the sucker would receive was prenut.

"My turn," he moaned.

Tamica slid her heels, pants, and G-string off, all the while keeping him in her mouth. She didn't release him from her throat until she was undressed from the waist down.

He smiled at her, then lifted her onto his desk and licked her pussy just the way she liked it, wet and sloppy with speedy tongue slaps on her clit. He softly rubbed his hands up her stomach and around her back to unsnap her bra. When her breasts were freed, he took a break from the fruit of her body to suck on her titties. His dick throbbed against her wetness, and she opened her legs wider to let him in.

"Ain't no turning back once I'm inside of you, you know that, right?"

"Yeah, but what does that mean?"

"It means when this shit is over with, you're mines. Until then, I'll give you this dick as a reminder of what you're waiting for from time to time. Is that cool?"

"It's better than cool."

They kissed passionately as Alejandro extended his calf muscles to gain better entrance—and suddenly, Harold banged on the door.

"Go find Tamica and meet me in the lab. We've got a problem with Eric. Just caught him on surveillance stealing."

They hastily dressed. Harold was supposed to be at the airport waiting to fly out to Detroit but must've turned around because security called. Neither Alejandro nor Tamica ever talked about their close encounter or followed through with it. They pretended like it never happened. It was time for Alejandro to turn in his rain check.

The car bomb would be installed once Harold was gone, but Alejandro needed at least an hour and twenty minutes to install the timer. It had to be triggered to go off when Harold went 70 mph, and that took time to put in place on a Benz. He used the flat tires to gain that time.

"Let's go, boss," Alejandro joked. They were at Tamica's in minutes.

"Where are you going?" she asked, opening the door to get in as Harold stepped out.

"I booked your favorite room until my car gets fixed. I thought we could . . . Well, you know."

"Yeah, we can go spend some time, but not here. Why would we come here when you have your own place?"

"I thought you liked this place?"

"I do, but I thought we only came here because we were on our lunch break. I don't know what type of woman you think I am, but I'm *not* her, and we don't have to go into the office tomorrow. I thought that maybe I could spend the night for the first time."

"Stay the night? The whole night?"

"And make you an omelet in the morning."

"What about him?"

"Didn't I tell you not to make my problem yours? I'll deal with Frederick. I need you to focus on dealing with me!"

Alejandro cut his eyes at her. He loved the big-girl shit she was talking. He just wished she had been talking to him. The urge to kill Harold grew. He was done taking the backseat to a punk. If Tamika needed a shoulder to cry on when she learned of his death, Alejandro was prepared to tell her to cry on his dick.

"Alejandro, bro, you don't know no shortcuts to get us to Bartlett and you back in time?"

"Hell no, I am *not* dropping you off way in fucking Bartlett. Y'all need just to go in there and enjoy yourself. When the car's ready, I'll bring it."

"That's not what I want to do, Harold. I want to get in your bed," she whined looking Alejandro in his eyes, pleading that he gave her, her way.

"I'm sorry, sis, but I have to close out the day if Harold is leaving early. There's too much shit to do to prepare for Monday, and now it's all left on me to handle. Any other time you know I'd take you."

"I know you would, Alej. So, how do we get there now?"

Everyone in the car went silent as they racked their brains.

"Drop us off at the bus shelter."

"The bus shelter? It'll take all day to get to Bartlett from there."

Harold snapped his neck. Something wasn't right. There's no way in hell Tamica would be open for riding the city bus. Her only complaint was how long it would take to get there on the bus. That wasn't normal for Tamica.

"I meant so that we could take a cab. I'd never ask you to catch a city bus, and, frankly, I was under the impression that you would never ride a city bus."

She gave a nervous laugh. "Of course, I wouldn't ride the city bus. I was just stating facts. A cab works for me."

"Yeah, that'll work, but you will still need to get your vehicle today," Alejandro added.

"I know, but it'll buy us some time and buy you some to finish up at the plant, right?" Harold waited for a response. They both were talking differently.

"Right, I'm only trying to help."

Everyone in the car had a smile on their face . . . but for different reasons. Harold would get to wake up next to Tamica in his bed for the first time in nine years. Alejandro would regain his uncle's respect, and he'd have Tamica as his trophy, and as for Tamica, she'd be inheriting both of her men's fortunes and moving to New York like she'd dreamed of doing for years.

They were driving down Front Street in silence when Alejandro's phone rang. He had the AUX cord plugged, and when he answered, the voice came through the car's speaker.

"Primo, how are you doing, cousin?" The heavy Mexican accent could only belong to one person.

"Roberto? How are you, cousin? When did you get out?" The excitement in his voice made Harold and Tamica's smile grow. He leaned over and whispered to Harold, "This is the badass cousin I told you about that's locked up in the Feds."

"I'm doing well. How about you?" The voice sounded like his cousin, but the words didn't seem like they belonged to him. "As a matter of fact, where are you and who are you with?"

A puzzled look crossed his face. He decided to lie. "I'm with my girl. Who is this?"

"Where are you, Alejandro?"

"Is this Joe?"

"Wow, with a response like that, you better be alone because you just welcomed your new girlfriend to our party."

The car doors unexpectedly locked, and his cell phone powered off, but the voice was still coming through the speakers.

"Who gave you the authority to place a car bomb in Harold's car and set it up to look like Romano and the mob did it?"

Harold sat up stiffly in his seat. His jaw dropped as Alejandro pulled his gun from under his seat and pointed it at him. Harold put his hands up.

"Who do you think I got the order from? My uncle told me to do it. He thought Harold would snitch when everything was over."

"If that's true, why would your uncle call the board and tell them you're out of control? No, scratch that question. I *knew* he wanted you dead years ago. I guess this is his way of getting it done without doing it. Better question, when did I bless that move?"

"You didn't, but I don't work for you after today. I'm a Valdez."

The engine was losing power as it eased to a stop under the Hernando de Soto Bridge.

"Do you think I don't know what Harold has been saying in my building and to my board members? Joseph told me what he said over two years ago. That's why I have Tamica taking him out tonight. If you had followed protocol and reported your uncle's request, I could have used you to help her. Maybe you could have licked her pussy again like you did in your office that one time."

Harold turned around in wide-eyed disbelief and stared at Tamica, who dropped her chin to her chest in shame. "I know and see everything, and I handle all my problems. Maybe in your next life, you'll do better!"

"Joe, this Tamica. I'm in the car!" she yelled, knowing whatever Joe's next move was wouldn't be made with her being in the car. She was his lapdog, and everyone on the board knew it . . . but it was too late. Joe hung up the phone after saying his last words, and before anyone in the car could say another word . . . It blew up.

Chapter Twelve

Chicago, Illinois. Saturday, January 4, 1992

Ronald snuck Corinna in around 5:30 in the morning. The sex talk they had once Ethan was asleep had gotten the best of him, and his hand wouldn't suffice. It took a lot of convincing to get her to give it up with her student in the other room asleep, but they came to an agreement that doing it in the shower would be best. He told her to call him when she made it there, and he met her at the front door so she wouldn't knock. From the second he opened the door, he brought her in for a kiss that lingered through their walk to the bathroom in his master bedroom. He only released her tongue to lock his bedroom door securely. To be on the safe side, he pushed his dresser in front of the door. With Ethan in the house, anything was possible.

He hadn't noticed it until that moment, but Corinna was embarrassed from him seeing her fully naked. Now that he thought about it, she never took her clothes off with the lights on, and most of the time, he took them off for her underneath the covers. Ronald told her on many occasions how much he enjoyed every inch of her body, and no matter how much he said it, she was never listening. Tired of her assumptions of what he liked and what he didn't, he snatched the towel she tried to cover her body with and tossed it on the sink.

"Stop hiding from me. How can I even think about making you mine if you act like I don't qualify to be the person you plan to give it to? I told you, you are my type of woman."

"I heard you, but when we're out and about, your eyes don't roam on women who look like me." She giggled. "And that's okay. You have a right to like what you like, and I have the right to choose not to show it to you. Let's not kill the mood with this, please."

"The only thing killing my mood was that towel covering you up. You don't have to worry about me speaking about us again. I see I've been wasting my time trying to convince you that big, beautiful, plentiful women are my type, so I'll just continue to settle to fuck you whenever you can come through." He jumped in the shower, leaving her standing there. The sex he had in the shower at the gym was all right, but it wasn't her. The girl was slam and in perfect shape. There was nothing for him to grab on and hold on to as he enjoyed the ride. With every stroke, he wished she was Corrina. Now that the opportunity had presented itself, he was ready for the do over.

She stood there, lost in her thoughts. She didn't know if she should be upset or disappointed about what Ronald said to her. He had made it clear from the start that he didn't get into relationships, and he didn't believe in long-term anything. She was the opposite, but for the opportunity to sleep with her crush, she bit her tongue. Now, here they were five months in, and he was blaming her for being the reason they couldn't escalate the relationship. The part that upset her was that he used her self-esteem as the reason. How could anyone think they could force someone to feel comfortable in their own skin when the person hated the skin they were in? She didn't choose to be obese; she chose to let depression and her self-esteem keep her from doing something about it. If she were given a choice, she'd choose a healthier size without the work that was needed to achieve it.

She hesitated to open the back end of the shower. Slowly, she slid her hand through the opening to push the curtain back, and Ronald grabbed it. With care, he helped her step into the shower, and once the water fell onto her back, he began kissing her. It was the kind of kiss that said so much and meant even more. It was an apology and a compliment rolled into one. It said, I want you; I crave you; and I'm not perfect. She accepted his silent words and kissed him back with the same longing.

She wished her back was in a better state and that she had more strength in her legs because she wanted to get on her knees and please him. Her energy must have cycled around the shower because Ronald took a knee. With his help, she placed her foot on the rim of the tub and positioned her legs to the best of her ability, and he ate his breakfast under the flow of water. When his craving was satisfied, he stood up, pecked her lips, and turned her around slowly. He stepped back until the water bypassed his head and fell upon her back and stared at her. She was big and beautiful; that was a fact, but he couldn't understand how she couldn't see herself as sexy. Yes, she had extra in places that most didn't, but she also had it in places where most did. She was one of the few women that Ronald has slept with that not only had large, supple breasts, but she also had full, round nipples that matched. Her ass was dump truck status. In other words, a donkey bred with a horse couldn't touch her. Her legs curved thick like tree trunks and were smooth like they were dipped in hot caramel. Just staring at her was enough to send his swimmers down the drain, but he never let them go to waste.

He approached her like a lion and prepared to pounce on her. He had never been inside her without protection, but there was a first for everything. He slid inside of her, and instantly, her legs began to give way. It had been years since she felt an unwrapped penis, and it was obvious by the way she gushed. She attempted to look back at him so he could share her facial expression; however, he wasn't interested in it. He grabbed her hip with his right hand and pushed her head to the back of the shower wall with his leg mushing her face into the porcelain. Feeling sexier than a high-caliber porn star, she puckered her lips and kissed the wall. Once the shock of him being inside of her raw wore off, she helped by throwing it back. But Ronald wasn't ready. He instantly lost his footing and slid back. It made them feel defeated, and he wasn't comfortable with the loss. He regained his footing embittered and stroked her with force until her face began to slap hard against the wall. Honestly, he didn't give a damn if his strokes were causing her face to be abused. She earned it. In that lustful moment, he felt like she had earned a lot more, and he released inside of her. The consequences of his action weren't a concern at the moment, nor did he concern himself with the fact that he whispered in her ear that he loved her as he nutted. He would deal with the consequences of his actions another day. As of that moment, he did love her, and he had sex with her the way lovers do . . . He gave her his all.

They dressed, exited the bathroom, and walked out of the bedroom to cook breakfast . . . only to be met by Ethan patiently seated at the dining-room table, waiting for breakfast.

"I know y'all worked up an appetite. Hook us up, Miss Lawson."

She looked from Ronald to Ethan and then back at Ronald, who was standing there shaking his head.

"Ethan, boy, you, my son, are a mess."

"Thank you, so I guess I'm officially Miss Lawson's work son too, now, right?"

Ronald placed his arm around her shoulder and pulled her in to him. He placed a kiss on her forehead and then said, yeah, "I guess she is my work wife." He chuckled, she smiled, and Ethan looked content.

After breakfast, the makeshift family went to the department store to buy Ethan more clothes and shoes.

They also stopped at the hardware store, and Ronald had a house key made for Ethan.

"This is your key. You can come and go as you please; only one rule. Don't have anyone in my house. Are we understood?"

"If I can come and go as I please, then it's our house. And I wouldn't invite anyone to where I lay my head anyway."

"Ethan, this includes Martin. I don't trust him, and I mainly deal with him because you do. I don't want him in my house. There's nothing valuable in here, but it's mines."

"I understand."

He wanted Ethan to know he has somebody who cares and that he'd always have somewhere to go when he needed to get away from his life in the projects. He gave Ethan the okay to decorate the guest room and make it his. That's exactly what Ethan had done over the last two days.

The first day of school was scheduled for Tuesday, but all the teachers and staff had to report Monday in preparation. Ethan made himself a pallet on the living-room floor and watched TV. He could have stretched out on the couch, but after sleeping on the floor most of his life, the couch wasn't comfortable. He couldn't stretch out like he wanted to. Nothing on TV could hold his attention long anyway. He found discrepancies in everything he watched, including cartoons. He settled for watching the news, and the body found in the dumpster was still the number one headline. His days spent with Ronald temporarily made him forget that his father was dead.

The thought that he would never see his father in the flesh again turned his stomach, and he ran to the hallway bathroom to relieve his bowels, but there was no toilet tissue, so he used Ronald's bathroom instead. Sitting on the toilet, he stared around the room. The boredom that came with taking a long shit caused curiosity. He wondered if Ronald chose that shampoo and conditioner. He wondered why he stacked his towels in the corner instead of putting them in the linen closet, and mainly, he wondered what was in the medicine cabinet behind the mirror. He decided after the last log descended on its journey to the septic tank to check it out.

There were razors, a couple of toothbrushes, some Band-Aids, a bottle of peroxide, alcohol swabs, a few pill bottles, but one of them didn't have any pills. He grabbed it, opened it, and brought it to his nose. Forest mail . . . So, Ronald smoked that good stuff. His weed was greener than the Everglades. Ethan smoked from time to time but only to access the creativity portion of his brain. He researched the effects of marijuana, and that was the only one he wanted to verify. With the game plan he was creating for his future, he needed to access his creative side of his brain to ensure that he thought of every possible downfall, trial, or tribulation that could stand in his way like a hurdle. It worked, but the hungry and sleepy parts of it steered him away from using it frequently. He didn't like the feeling of having the munchies, especially when he had no money to feed himself.

He placed the bottle back in the medicine cabinet and made his way to the bedroom next. He looked under the mattress to see if Ronald was his own banker. He had heard and read of men stashing money underneath air mattresses. He looked under the bed for a secret box that would hold everything Ronald wouldn't want anyone to know about him. Ethan had gotten that idea from a movie he watched. From what Ethan could tell, Ronald was as boring as he reflected being. It wasn't until he ran across the file box at the top of Ronald's closet that he realized Ronald was hiding a lot.

The first item Ethan ran across was a death certificate issued by the United States Army for a Robert Hill Junior and a medal for his courage in combat. In that portion of the foul box, there were pictures of a younger version of Ronald with a boy who looked to be the same age. On the back of one of the pictures, it read, "Me and my brother Robert Junior on our first school trip." Not that Ethan and Ronald really spoke on family history, but he wondered why in their talks, Ronald never mentioned that he had a brother who died in combat.

Moving past the memories Ronald saved of his relationship with what seemed to be his only sibling, the next area was labeled "Mister Robert Hill Senior." Ethan was excited. He knew Ronald had daddy issues, and he also knew Ronald wasn't willing to talk about them. He used his deducing skills to figure out where their problem lay. Like his brother, it was obvious his father was in the military. From what the military records showed, he had done a little over three terms of service for the country. He was released from duty with an honorable discharge because of medical problems. Probing a little bit further, he found out Robert's father had been diagnosed with PTSD, and it affected every relationship he was in . . . by the looks of it, his relationship with Ronald the most. There was a handwritten letter where words had been scratched out and rewritten. It was a forged document, and it said that Ronald was going on some special undercover mission to track and locate his brother. The letter was addressed to Robert Hill Senior and dated after Robert Hill Jr.'s date of death. Behind it was a sealed professionally typed version of the letter, and the signature at the bottom matched the scratched form of the letter. Ronald had created it. Ethan wanted to know why Ronald would lie about his brother being dead to their father and why he would create a mission that would allow him never to see his parents again. Flipping through two more pages, he got his heartbreaking answer. There was a handwritten letter from a woman named Sharlene that read:

Hey, Handsome,

I heard you were looking for me everywhere a few years back. You even went as far as reaching out to a few names I gave you of my friends in Texas. I didn't want to be reached because of the nature of our relationship. I was supposed to be your good time, and after accepting that, that's all I was, so I was done with you. There were times that I missed you and thought of reaching out, but then, I was given a reason not to. I found out I was pregnant with your baby, and I knew if I shared that information with you, we'd be at the abortion clinic. So, I decided to birth and raise our son, Ronald Hill Junior, without you. It's been hard, but it's been worth it. The older he gets, the more he reminds me of you.

At 7, I started noticing something wasn't right with him and learned that our son was battling a few mental issues, one of which makes him very aggressive. I reached out to your father to find out if he knew how to contact you, and I learned you had enlisted in a private branch of the military to hunt down your brother. I instantly knew where my son inherited his mental issues. I don't know where you are, and I don't know how this information is going to make you feel, but our son needs his father, and I admit that I was wrong for making this decision to raise him without you. He is a Hill. That's something I cannot teach him to be, but you can. Enclosed, I've listed every possible method of reaching me, from my family and friends to my coworkers and even a few enemies. I pray that this letter reaches you in a sound mind. I guess I can finally say it. I love you.

Sincerely,

The woman who you should have settled down with,

Sharlene Gray

"He has a son!" Ethan yelled, shaken by the news. Ronald wasn't there to answer, but he was sure the answer was in the box. Pictures of the little boy came next, and he was Ronald's spitting image. He wondered why Ronald didn't acknowledge him as his son, and then he got his answer from the next handwritten letter.

> *You are pathetic,*
> *You made me wait two years for you to tell me you don't want or have any kids? I should track you down through the courts and force you to take a DNA test so RJ can at least get some child support out of you. You really need to grow up! How long did you think you could go without using condoms before someone reached out to you pregnant? This isn't about money; it's about time, Ronald. You told me your dad made your little brother his junior because he looked at you when you were born and said you were soft and a punk. That's exactly how I see you now. You're just like your father. You're crazy. I can't believe you said you would never claim a child with mental issues as yours. Burn in hell, that's if AIDS doesn't kill you first!*

Behind that letter were pictures of his son that were recently taken, but by whom? They were clearly taken in Atlanta, Georgia, but the cameraman was under suspicion. That area of the file box had receipts from hotel stays in the Atlanta area from less than seven months ago.

Ethan had a lot of questions he wanted to ask Ronald but decided he'd get the answers to them on his own. He copied the list of contact people Sharlene gave him, hoping that when the time came, the list would still be valid. He copied the address on the letter Ronald mailed his father and took a copy of his father's medical discharge and his brother's death certificate.

The shock of it all subsided and was replaced with disappointment. Ronald had become his favorite person in a short amount of time. To learn that he not only had daddy issues, he passed them out was heartbreaking.

With Ronald not due to return for another three hours, he took his time going through each page and discovered reasons he shouldn't trust Ronald with his heart. In his anger of discovering who Ronald really was, he laid all the hard facts across at the foot of Ronald's bed so he could see them when he returned and left a note that read, *I'm not your son. RJ is!* with a picture he confirmed Ronald took when he made trips to stalk the little boy. Ethan placed the key next to it and left with only what he came with. He made his decision without allowing Ronald to explain.

Ronald had gone by Ethan's house on multiple occasions, but the boy was never there. On one of his visits, Ethan's mother had the audacity to ask him, "What is it about my son that you like so much?"

"What is it about your son that I shouldn't like?"

"I'm just saying . . . The boy is smart, but we can't afford for him to go to college after high school. He has to get a job. I'm sick, and I can't work, and now that his daddy is dead, he's going to have to take care of me. I hope you not planting those thoughts in his head of him going to one of those richie-rich overpriced colleges. I already got him lined up to work at the plastic warehouse, and they're starting young men off at nine dollars an hour. That's more than enough for him to take care of himself and me. Don't you come around here stirring nothing up, you hear me?"

Ethan asked Ronald to never say anything to his mother without getting his permission first because he didn't have mama issues. Which could have been the truth, but his mama was definitely an issue for him.

"Why would you stump on the boy's dreams of being more than you and his daddy ever were?"

She laughed hysterically at his words. "Do you know what my son dreams of being when he grows up, or did you come up with your own plan for him?"

Ronald didn't answer her because, at the time, he couldn't remember what or if Ethan had mentioned what it was he wanted to be. He continued his questioning.

"Why does he have to go slave at a warehouse to supply you with your next fix? He doesn't owe you nothing. If anybody is in debt, it's you. You owe your son a lot more than what you are giving him."

"I don't owe him nothing. His daddy took care of us. All I had to do was to make sure the food was cooked, and that Ethan did what he was supposed to do around here. They took his daddy from me, and from what I can see, you trying to take him from me. I'm not going to let that happen, Mr. Hill. As a matter of fact, I don't care if Ethan holds your hand and escorts you in here. Don't you bring your ass back. I mean it, or I'm going to tell them people you got a thing for little boys, and I'm going to make sure it sticks!"

Ronald stared at the front door and made sure Ethan wasn't seconds from walking in before saying his next words.

"Let me ask you something, Mrs. Carruthers, and I want you to be honest. How much would it cost me to buy the rest of Ethan's life from you?"

She giggled uncomfortably. "What do you mean 'buy the rest of his life'?"

"Exactly what I said. You said he needs to get a job after high school to take care of you. I'm sure you've said this to him a hundred thousand times. When you said it, it made me think, that I cannot recall one time Ethan spoke on going to college nor what he wanted to do for a living. With the grades he's making, he should be headed to a university after graduating, but I think you already convinced him he couldn't go. So, what I'm asking is, how much will it cost me to get you to convince him that college is where he needs to go after high school? There isn't a dollar amount I wouldn't pay."

"I don't sit around thinking about how much that will cost." She rolled her eyes as she spoke. "Give me a day or two, and I'll give you a number. But look here, this talk we are having is between you and me. Don't go trying to brainwash my son against me. You're not going to like the outcome if you do!"

Ronald stepped into the hallway after closing the door and the urge to vomit almost knocked him to the floor. To think such a bright boy was given to two brainless drug heads for parents ripped at his heart. He had to find Ethan!

When he made it to school on Tuesday, the fourth period couldn't come fast enough. The class filled with students . . . all except Mimic and Ethan. Ronald didn't like the idea that they both didn't attend school on the same day. It didn't take any thought to decide that the boys must have been together. He went to the office to get Mimic's grandmother's telephone number out of his file and ran into Corrina on his way out.

"I just heard about the fallout you had with Ethan; I really hope you all can work things out."

Ronald was lost. He had no idea what she was talking about.

"What do you mean you just heard about my fallout with Ethan?"

"I was in there with Principal Pierce, and he said Ethan requested his class to be changed. He said he refused to be in a classroom with—"

"Don't bite your tongue. Say it. Whatever he said about me, I can take it."

"Ronald, now, you know I couldn't bite my tongue if I wanted to, and I don't want to. The depths of what Ethan said about you delayed my words. Hell, it was like getting a wake-up slap in the face. Your work son scheduled an appointment with Principal Pierce to inform him that he refused to be in the classroom with a man who couldn't stand up to any of his responsibilities, both personal and professional."

"Professionally?" he tittered. "I do my job!"

"Wait, that's not all he said. He refused to be taught by a man who chooses a good time over stability, and the man who didn't respect himself to have more in life when it was obvious that he could. That boy's words were so powerful, and I think he's right."

"So, you think Ethan is right about me?" he snorted.

"No, I'm *positive* that he's right about you. I'm speaking on his refusal. He's right to refuse to accept you as is when you could be a lot better. It has me over here thinking, why should I waste my time with a man who prefers a good time over stability?

"You know," she whispered, "when you told me you loved me the other night, it felt so good, but I knew it was a lie. You love everything about us. The control you have over when and where we have sex, how you can tell me what you want to eat two weeks in advance, and I have each meal ready for you, and how you decide if and when it's okay to sleep with other people. I appreciate your honesty about the little situation at the gym, but the first time I didn't answer my phone for you, you gave me an ultimatum. You told me if I can't answer your calls no matter who I'm in front of, then I don't need to dial your number anymore. And my silly ass heard the message and called you in the middle of class I was teaching so that I could prove to you I wasn't with nobody else. I don't blame you for that. That was a decision that I made, and this is a decision that I'm making again. Keep the Tupperware, or you can throw that shit in the garbage. I stand with Ethan on this one. You need to grow the fuck up!" She turned on her heels, and when she made it to the hallway, she looked back at him but only to shake her head in disgust.

Ronald wasn't used to the shitstorm that was brewing, and the only way he knew how to handle it was to visit his best friend, Mary J. He sat in his car and rolled his joint. He almost sparked it up right there in the school parking lot, but at the last minute, he realized what he was doing and drove off. He circled the block and inhaled her relaxing fragrance, and then slowly released it through his nose.

He had his reasons for everything that he did. He couldn't tell his parents their favorite son died. He loved them too much to break their hearts. Turning him into a special weapon for the military gave them something to brag about, and when he decided to go hiding from his past, lying to them about joining his brother on his mission made them respect him more than they ever had.

Second, it wasn't Ethan's or anybody else's business that he had a son he didn't claim and refused to raise. It didn't matter how they saw him; he knew the truth. Parenting wasn't for him, and he never wanted children. Sharlene should have told him so he could have paid for the abortion, and maybe they could have stayed together after that. He loved her, and it killed him to know that's why he cut her off. She had no right to decide to keep his child and then come back and try to force him to be a daddy. She fucked up his mind. From the moment he saw his son's pictures, he was torn on doing what was right. He fell in love with his smile instantly. It mirrored his, but what really tore him to shreds was that his son was his deceased brother's twin. It was just too much to bear, and Ethan had no right to judge him with only knowing half of the story.

Last, the shit with Corrina reminded him of what he had with Sharlene. The only difference was that Corrina reminded him of his mama, which was both a good and bad resemblance. She cared about every aspect of his life, which made him miss his mama, but she was too submissive like his mama, and that turned his stomach. He could call Corrina over in the rain, barefooted, and she'd apologize for hours for being wet. There were times when he was fucking her, he'd say things like, "You're my dumb bitch, ain't you?" or "Your ass would do anything to have a piece of me and this dick, huh?" and she'd agree and confess about everything she was willing to do for a chance to build something with him. Ronald went as far as to tell her about the slut he fucked at the gym while she was on her knees, blowing him in the living room.

"She wanted your dick, baby. Can you blame her?"

"I fucked her good too, but she wasn't you. Her pussy was garbage," he announced as he took another puff of his joint. "Look at all that dick I got to give. You can't get mad if I share it from time to time, okay, baby?" Corrina nodded and bobbed faster.

It made Ronald feel like a king while he was high, but once he came down, he apologized. He licked her pussy like a sad dog and then made love to her like the sex would determine if she would forgive him. Sharlene would have blacked his eye and then cried about it. She would have made him kiss her ass until his lips had a permanent indention on it. He had no business comparing the women, but he had never let go of Sharlene. Judging anyone he messed with against her standards came easy. Ronald was going through a lot, and nobody wanted to take a second to try to understand, so he left everything in his life the way it was and didn't attempt to fix anything in it.

On his way back to school, he saw Mimic walking out of the corner store in royal blue from head to toe and wearing a blue paisley rag tightly across his forehead like he was a modernized flower child.

"What the hell are you out here doing looking like a moving target? Get in the car, Martin!"

"And go where, nigga? Back to school? Do you know how much money I've been missing sitting in school eight hours a day? These junkies out here ain't loyal. They aren't sitting around waiting for me to get my education and putting off getting high. I'm done with school. I talked to my daddy over the weekend, and he hooked me up with his plug. All I got to do is bring him a piece of his money back, and he going to keep it flowing for me."

"And what does your grandma have to say about all that?"

"I don't know what she got to say about it. She put me out when she saw what Ethan had done to my face. I tried to tell her it was him, but she had already heard rumors that I was in the gang. She threw all my shit in the street and caused a scene, so it is what it is. I was tired of living with her anyway. I only did it because that's where my daddy wanted me at, but now that I've been put out, my niggas got me. My pops even said he preferred me with my niggas than my granny because she was making me soft."

"Your daddy is a fucking gangbanging loser and drug dealer!"

Before Ronald could blink, Mimic had his gun pointed at him. "Don't lose your muthafucking life speaking foul on my daddy. As a matter of fact, I'm itching to pull this trigger after you let Ethan do that shit to me in your car the other night anyway. How about you pull off, or I'll shoot you or have to beat your ass again? I ain't forgot how I whooped your ass in the school parking lot this summer. Ain't nobody scared of you, and tell Ethan I got a bullet for him when I see him."

"So, you're tough now, Martin?"

"Let that ass whooping I gave you decide."

Ronald sat there a second or two longer. He didn't know what it was about the boy that affected him, but he knew if he didn't fix things with Ethan, that Ethan could turn out ten times worse than what was standing before him. He gave Martin a dismissing head nod and drove off. Instead of going back to school, he drove home and called the principal saying he was under the weather and wouldn't return for the day.

Weeks passed, and he had only seen Ethan once. They were walking down the hall in opposite directions and crossed paths. There was so much he wanted to say to the boy, but Ethan's demeanor stated he wasn't in the mood to be fucked with, so he let it go. He reached out to Corrina and apologized, which she accepted. He asked about starting over, and she declined. He purposely drove by the projects every day to where he last saw Martin but never set eyes on the boy again. Feeling lonely, he reached out to his default.

"Hey, Mama, how you are doing?"

"Ronald, baby, oh, I'm so glad you called me. I know you're on that special mission, and it's hard for you to check in, but I wanted you to know that I'm proud of you, and your daddy is proud of you too."

"My daddy is proud of me too? How do you know that?" he said with a chuckle.

He never heard his mama say those words before and that was because if she had said them, she would have been lying.

"I know we can't say too much over this phone, but your daddy got the message, and he handled what was necessary. It's giving him a new beginning." She laughed. "He's been getting out of bed and even letting me take him to therapy. Can you believe that? After all these years, your daddy is listening to the words of a therapist." She cracked up. Her laugh was so contagious that Ronald joined in.

"Now *that's* a miracle! If you say he started celebrating Christmas, hell is going to freeze over, and the devil is going to change his name to Frosty," he laughed.

"It's been beautiful around here, son, and we are proud of you. Hurry up and find your brother and both of y'all come on home. I know you are skin and bones. Ain't nobody going to feed you like me."

"You ain't lying, Mama. These women ain't cooking. Half the time they won't even offer to buy you a meal. They mamas told them we're supposed to feed us. If I bring the bacon, she's supposed to cook it," he laughed.

"That tells me you ain't doing something right. A woman is always going to feed a man who's meeting her needs, but if he's slacking, she going to get amnesia in that kitchen. I hope you still ain't out there messing with a whole lot of women. It's time for you to settle down."

"Come on, Mama, I didn't call you to hear all that, and how am I supposed to settle down with a woman if you're my favorite girl?"

She laughed. "I've never looked at it like that. It's going to be hard for you to find somebody who holds a candle to all of this."

They both laughed and played catch-up. Ronald created so many fake military stories that he began to get excited from hearing himself tell them. He knew he would never be able to come clean and tell the truth about what he's been doing all these years because that meant he would have to tell his parents that his brother died serving the country. Talking to his mother seemed to be the right dose of medication that he needed. For the first time in months, he got up, got dressed, and headed out to the gym. He was at the door with his keys when Ethan knocked.

"Do I still have a room here?" Tears sat heavy in the wells of his eyes, but not one flowed over them.

"Only if I still got a son in you. I only let family in."

They embraced like a real father and son. He didn't know what Ethan had been going through, but he could tell times had been rough on him. It was four months since he left the key he was given, and Ronald thought of him every day.

"Come in. Put your bags down and let's go work some of this stress off at the gym."

"But I'm not 18 yet," Ethan said disappointedly.

"I haven't forgotten how old my son is. You just had a birthday in February. The gym will let you in at 16. After you work off whatever it is that's bothering you, we're going to go celebrate!"

They worked out and then had Chicago-style pizza at Ronald's favorite pizzeria downtown. Ethan had never had pizza from the restaurant, and now, he was hooked. They had small talk as they ate, but the conversation got heavy when they made it back to their house.

"Mimic, I mean, Martin, has been telling people to let me know that he has a bullet with my name on it. I didn't know killers made advertisements," he said, shrugging.

"Yeah, I ran into him, and he told me the same thing. But don't let that get to you. He's all talk; he's not a killer. It takes a lot to kill. It's more than just pulling the trigger and hiding the body. It plays heavy on your mind. Martin isn't equipped to kill a roach," Ronald chuckled.

"Yeah, killing does mess with the mind."

There was no way Ronald didn't feel the emotion in Ethan's words. His stomach turned at the thought of the question he was going to have to ask him next.

"You said that like you killed somebody before. Have you? Are you a killer, Ethan?"

"You did too, right? Have you killed before, Mr. Ronald?"

"Not flesh but I have killed dozens in other ways."

"Kill or be killed, right? Sometimes, people threaten your life, and it doesn't mean that your flesh will perish. Some threats to our life stop you from growing. Or they are done to make you feel like you will be stuck in situations we don't want to be in. People can kill you that way too. I can't go out like that. I got to have more, a lot more."

"But you didn't answer my question, Ethan. Have you killed before in any way, son?"

"I got rid of my daddy issues," he said boldly, looking into Ronald's eyes for a nonverbal response.

Ronald's heart stopped. He couldn't breathe. Ethan had just confessed to murder. Not just any murder, but he left his father, who was shot eight times, and tossed his body in the dumpster like day-old trash. All he could do was stare at the boy in return and not be the first to break. When Ethan doubled blinked, Ronald exhaled.

"Go ahead and get yourself ready for bed. You got school in the morning."

Ethan stood to his feet, and instead of walking toward his room, he walked over to Ronald and hugged him tightly. Ronald didn't have to see his face to know that he was crying.

"I'm sorry for leaving like that because you're the best pops anybody could have. Don't let your son grow up without you. If you do, he's going to hate you, and if he tries to handle his daddy issues the way I handled mine, I'ma shoot his face off. That way, there won't be anybody that looks like you who can take my place, and I'll be the only son you got. Period!"

Once again, Ronald was at a loss for words.

Chapter Thirteen

Memphis, Tennessee. Thursday, January 31, 2019, cont.

Roman's trailer swayed as he crossed the Hernando de Soto Bridge, leaving Tennessee to enter Arkansas. The gust of wind was a lot stronger than usual, and he was forced to grip the wheel to balance his load. Unbeknownst to him, a car occupying the people who furnished his load had blown up beneath him, and the "wind" he assumed he was battling was really a hit to the structure of the bridge.

The blast sent his food to the floor. He was given a choice to save his rig or the free food he was given at his first refrigerator drop-off. Although the fast-food franchise was his personal favorite place to eat, the extra fries he was given took a backseat to saving the lives of those around him . . . and his as well.

To make matters worse, his boss was in his ear, fussing at him about his oversight at MediTech. Apparently, Alejandro called the company and ended their contract. For whatever reason, he made Roman's small mistake the reason why they were severing ties.

"You should have called dispatch if you found a discrepancy in the order. It's not your job to speak with our clients!"

"I said, my bad, and it won't happen again." Roman was listening to him while acting on the two-second rule. He leaned over his seat and tried to save as many of the fries as he could. When he picked up all that were in his reach, he was officially in Arkansas.

"Your bad doesn't fix the loss you caused us. When you're done with the deliveries, bring it in. We will finish this in person."

The call ended, and he was happy it did. His new occupation changed the way he made a living; it didn't fix his attitude. He was a hothead, and the slightest thing would piss him off. It didn't start with the criminal behavior, more than likely, so it's why he went that route. As a kid, he was the boy no one wanted to play with because they feared when he won or loss, he'd whoop their asses. He was hard to please, even harder to satisfy. Roman snapped off about any and everything. His boss saved his job for him by hanging up.

Now that he was seated upright, he gave his attention back to the road. Checking his rearview mirror, he saw that he was being pulled over by the highway patrol.

"What seems to be the problem, Officer?"

Besides a nasty attitude, Roman was allergic to the police and did his best to keep them away. Whenever they were in his presence, he'd sweat bullets. He didn't fear jail; it was no longer a possibility for him, unlike many others. He wasn't going back—period—and he'd go above and beyond to ensure that was his truth. Unlike most men who feared the police, they just made Roman anxious and question suicide. He did not know how many officers he'd have to take out to cause his own death. One night spent in jail was one night too many, and this traffic stop could be his last moments of life. He planned to take out the first officer that mentioned placing cuffs on his wrist, and he prayed that his own death would be fast.

"You didn't stop at the weigh station. Is something going on?"

Roman was bent over the seat as the red light prompted him to stop at the weigh station entering Arkansas. He missed it, and now he was being pulled over. It was his fault that he wasn't paying attention, but being the hothead that he is, he blamed it on the officer having a problem with him being black.

"No, there isn't anything going on. I missed the red light because I had to pick up some shit I dropped. So, when did the highway patrol start pulling over truck drivers immediately after they failed to stop, or could you see my face and decided to make me your priority?"

These were the stops Officer Noble could do without. Cops were killing black men; he wouldn't deny it and had even heard other cops' joke and make light that they would do it too. Those are the officers he stayed far away from, and the only reason he didn't report them is that they were ranked higher than he, and though the policy stated no retaliation, he knew it was bullshit.

There were many times Officer Noble wanted to pull out his phone and show pictures of his family when he was accused of being racist. His wife was black, his twin sons were half black, and the woman who adopted him at birth was black. Although his mama tried hard to keep him aware of the important differences between races, he was raised black. The only reason he never flashed a family picture is that he felt it was cliché. You know, how racist white people like to point out they have one black friend or the black causes they make donations to. He refused to spend his life defending his skin color. There were some fucked-up white people in this world, and he could say the same about blacks. He would do his job and hug his family tighter when he got home.

"I don't know which patrolman is here when you normally refuse to stop at the weigh station; however, when I'm here, I'm stopping everybody."

"Yeah, right," he mumbled.

Officer Noble took a few steps back and requested backup.

"Let me take a look at your paperwork and your driver's license. Once everything has been verified, you'll be good to go. Just don't miss the next weigh station!"

Noble got back into his car and ran the driver's license. No warrants, no outstanding tickets; yet, there were a few past small possession charges and a drug trafficking arrest. Secretly, Noble hoped that wouldn't be the case today.

Within a few minutes, he was joined by two squad cars. Once he briefed the officers of the situation, he walked back up to the truck.

"Mr. Roman, here is your license back. I'm going to hold on to this paperwork. Please open up the back. We just need to take a quick look; then you'll be back on your way."

Roman jumped out of the cab and walked to the back of his truck, aggressively swinging his arms as if he didn't have a care in the world or cared if he hit someone. Once he opened it so they could have their look, he stepped back and stood by two officers.

"I see all of these refrigerators are plugged up. Do you know what's inside of them?"

"It's not my job to know. All I do is open the trailer, they load up, and I drop it off."

"Where do you drop them off at?"

"Normally, I pick up the refrigerators from fast-food restaurants. Today, they got me dropping them off to the restaurants. The normal driver on this quit yesterday."

"So, you pick up your load on Shelby Drive. Shelby Drive and what?"

"No, where did you get Shelby Drive from?"

"That's the address on the paper."

"That must be their corporate address or something. I picked up my load in President's Island. The address is preset in my GPS."

Officer Noble looked at his captain and then walked to his car.

"Dispatch, I need an address run."

In minutes, he returned to the group with the information but spoke to the truck driver first.

"Mr. Roman, I know you're just out here doing a job, and so are we. I have to ask you to have a seat in the back of my car while we go through this load."

"Why? What's going on?"

His anxiety was starting to build. He didn't have a weapon on him, and the highway patrol officers had their pistols out of his reach. All he would be able to do is fight, which meant they would probably jump him, cuff him, and throw him in the back of their car anyway. Good thing his baby mama called so his daughter could hear her daddy's voice. He calmly walked to the squad car and got in the back.

"Hey, what are you doing, beautiful? Daddy misses you. I can't wait to get off and see you. What are you doing, angel?"

His daughter was his world, and he couldn't wait until her speech developed to respond back. Whenever the world got too heavy, he had her to lighten his load.

Dispatch couldn't confirm the address on the shipping slip, but they did confirm the address he had in the GPS.

"It belongs to that large pharmaceutical company Med-iTech. I looked to see if they had any ties to the fast-food industry or what pharmaceuticals they could be providing for them and came up empty-handed."

"Everybody wants to be a detective," one of the officers mumbled. The guy was a jerk, and his dislike for Noble was because he felt like Noble fraternized with the enemy.

In a heated argument at a bar when they were off duty, he called him a nigger-lover. The punch Noble sent to his mouth should have been followed by many more, but the fight was instantly broken up.

"In other words," his captain said, "it's time we checked this bad boy out."

Each refrigerator not only had a bolted lock on the side of it but also there was a linked chain wrapped around it with a padlock to loosen it once the code was put in place. One of the patrol officers had bolt cutters, but ultimately, they called firemen to the scene with a portable Jaws of Life. In seconds, the first refrigerator was unlocked and opened.

"I think these fast-food restaurants have found a way to make Happy Meals for adults. Instead of toys," the captain spoke to the group with a handful of different street drugs stretched in front of them, "they're giving them a happy high. Noble, this may be the biggest drug bust in Arkansas history. Congratulations. I guess you'll be my boss soon. While I call it in, get the rest of these refrigerators opened," he ordered.

The drug bust did start on Interstate 40 headed westbound. However, it extended to Kentucky, Georgia, Mississippi, Alabama, Arkansas, Oklahoma, and, of course, Tennessee. Within hours, the federal courts issued multiple search and arrest warrants. The trucking company Roman worked for was taken over by the Feds. They needed it to uncover every shipment they delivered for MediTech. All the fast-food restaurant franchises tied to the delivery addresses were shut down.

MediTech was labeled as the headquarters of Joe's operations, and as many as six government agencies immediately covered the warehouse. The chemists Joe arranged to be killed over the next few days were arrested, and all were willing to sing loudly to cut a deal. Everyone in the building wanted to pull rank and argue over evidence found. It was chaotic.

It wasn't long before the license plate was also being run on the car that exploded under the bridge, and it too was being investigated. The remains found in the car made the ten o'clock news. It was announced that some of the head personnel of MediTech were burnt to death in a car minutes before the Arkansas bust. In no time, police found evidence at Harold's and Alejandro's houses and inside of Tamica's disabled vehicle left on Madison, and everything linked back to Joe, including the murder of the deputy director of the TBI, who was Tamica's husband.

By lunchtime Saturday, the investigation was international news. The board, public and private investors, the mob, cartel, and two government agencies had been linked to the pharmaceutical company. A suitcase of evidence and proof of collusion was found at an address linked to Harold's name. It was a small cabin outside of Pigeon Forge, where he used to go and clear his mind from time to time. He used the cabin as his backup plan. He left enough information lingering in his house that would force anyone investigating his murder to have a look-see at the cabin. They had hit the jackpot. All those billionaires, murderers, and drug traffickers were under Joe's umbrella, which made Joe the number one Most Wanted Man on Earth. As hundreds of arrests were being made, Joe's world was shrinking by the second. Everyone wanted him dead. The cartel and the mob worked together and put a billion-dollar bounty on his head. With no one knowing what he looked like, where he was from, or even where to start their search for him, the world braced for many murders and the deaths of countless innocent people.

For the first time in history, everyone seemed to be in cahoots and agreed that Joe must die. Even the media wanted to help in his capture. They not only posted a blank gray silhouette with the words "Most Wanted" written across the bottom and the list of government agencies who sought his arrest, but they also took it a step further and announced the billion-dollar bounty that was on Joe's head. They even gave instructions on how to turn in his dead body to collect the reward.

In all the years of Joe's reign, he made his first mistake, and it was going to cost him dearly—his life. There wasn't a place safe on earth where he could hide. Once people started peeling away the layers of his identity, he'd make more enemies by the hour.

How did he make such a huge mistake?

Start Over

Chapter Fourteen

Memphis, Tennessee. Friday, February 2, 2019

It was colder than a polar bear's frosty ass in snow as Aric walked down the street, but he had to get to his mama's house. He needed to shower, and he knew she was up early cooking a big-ass breakfast to start the day off right.

His stroll from downtown to Frazier didn't look any different than it had the last time his Nike's acted as his Uber. Beer bottles and cigarette butts paved the dirty streets and bullet shells garnished them.

He tried to pretend he was back at home in Cali as Nipsey Hussle blared through his headphones blocking out all the sounds that reminded him that he lived in the country now, but his eyes wouldn't accept the sights as home. Besides the random junkies in their designated spots in front of the gas station panhandling for loose change and cigarettes, the shit was a ghost town this early. The fly-ass whips with lifters to accommodate the switches on low riders were replaced with monster-size tires on King Ranch pickup trucks. However, those were occupied with white faces. No Mexicans out hustling their breakfast foods for a quick dollar or two and the pit bulls in the south were locked down by chains and didn't cause him to get to his destination faster by chasing him. It was the meaningless bullshit like that Aric missed the most.

The country living shit was getting old, but it was keeping him free. After the police kicked in his mom's door to snatch his half-naked ass out of bed for the third time in his life, she decided to relocate to give her son better, but were cheaper rent and more restrictions really better? In Aric's opinion, the only differences between the two cities were that Memphis liquor stores didn't stay open until the wee hours of the morning, and instead of gang-bangers, the city was filled with goons, savages, pimps, hoes, and wannabes.

"What's good, boo? I thought that was you."

He didn't have to face the street to know that Shatika's raggedy ass had finally caught him slipping. She begged him the night before to spend Sunday with her and her three boys. He declined because her real man drove 18-wheelers and Aric wasn't in the mood to sleep in his clothes, just in case he needed to make a mad dash to the window if dude popped up. Her pussy was good, and her head game was strong, but she lived foul. Her house catered to rats and roaches as she made sure never to clean up, and she constantly dragged her kids into her side nigga's business. She wanted Aric to play with them and help with homework because the nigga she convinced to be their daddy was always on the road. Those badass kids did need some male bonding time, but that shit wasn't in his side nigga contract.

Shatika made her boys call him uncle, and whenever she'd get caught talking to him on the phone when her man was home, the bitch would call him big bruah. She seemed to get a kick out of fucking off on her man. However, the game she was playing was deadly. That's why Aric spent the night fucking her best friend Regina instead.

"Shit, nothing much, sweetie. Headed to Mom's house. Can I get a ride to Frazier Blvd.?"

"Damn, your accent's sexy," she laughed. "Hell yeah, hop in. I just gotta drop this milk off to the boys first."

Five minutes later, she had Aric in the kitchen making bowls of cereal for the boys, and three minutes after that, she was rewarding him for the small task with her throat full of his dick. He didn't have a condom, but he trusted baby girl. She was cheating on her man, but she had always been faithful to him.

Shatika tried to gas Aric up to lick that beastly man trap in between her legs by doing a spectacular job blowing him, but it hadn't worked. He wanted to get inside of her and relax in her natural flowing stream. Her stream flowed smoother than the Mississippi River after a heavy rain, but something about the pussy wasn't right today.

"Damn, baby, let me get in there."

"I'm not stopping you. Go deeper, Aric."

"Shit, I'm trying, but yo' shit feels like it's blocked and closed."

He scissor legged her open, but that didn't work. He seesawed up and down and then from left to right, and that didn't work either. Finally, he made her get on all fours and rammed his way in. He got in about twenty good strokes before an ice water feeling hit the tip of his dick and almost sent him into shock.

"What the fuck?" He pulled his dick out and inspected it. "What the fuck was that?" The dumb country bitch didn't know what he was talking about.

"That's good pussy, but you already know that shit," she giggled, but a flag was already thrown on the play. He had to challenge that last play by sliding two fingers inside of her to find the source. He was digging around but couldn't find anything, all the while she was moaning louder than she did with his dick in her. He wasn't trying to please her, though she was a second away from coming, so he kept going. As her flare gates opened, a sour-smelling condom came flowing out, and the smell made him call Earl all over her stomach. With his pants and drawers around his ankles, he rushed to the nearest sink, which was in the kitchen. Her boys looked at him and went right back to eating their cereal like the shit was normal. He stood on his tippy toes letting the warm water run over his dick as he cased the scene for dish soap. There wasn't any.

"Aye, one of y'all little niggas go get me some soap from the bathroom."

"Ain't none," her youngest one said.

"We been using laundry detergent," her oldest one added.

"Well, get me some of that, then."

He came back with the powdery substance just as Shatika walked in covered in her bathrobe.

"I swear I didn't know that was in there, Aric."

"Why in the fuck were you begging for my shit if yo' nasty ass got some last night?"

"I didn't get any last night. That had to be in there from three days ago when my friend came by to check on the kids and me. I promise I don't get down like that."

He wanted to knock the bitch smooth out, but his meat wasn't finished sanitizing yet.

"Man, just drop me off."

"I will . . . when you finish what you started," she said, rolling her eyes.

"Bitch, you stupid!"

He made it back to the main street before she pulled up on him, begging him to get in. The shit was crazy, but he was feeling betrayed. He couldn't believe she was fucking off on him, although she was doing the same to her man. Aric felt like he should have been treated differently because he spent time with her, and every nigga slang dick knew that's what all females wanted.

You can be broke, but if you can lay up under a woman all day, the shit is priceless to them. Aric seemed like he was stuck in his feelings about the incident as she apologized wholeheartedly, but after chin checking himself for catching feelings for another man's bitch, he saw it for what it really was . . . an opportunity to hustle.

He was up one on her and decided to take advantage of it. "You got a few dollars?"

"For what, nigga?"

"I'm down until tomorrow, and my moms needs some shit from the grocery store."

"I don't have any cash, but my food stamps hit this morning. I'll take you to the store."

"That's okay. I wanted to take her and let her grab whatever she wanted."

"Okay, that's cool. I'll just follow y'all there and swipe the card when she's done. I got about a hundred and fifty dollars I can spare."

"Don't worry about it. I'll figure the shit out on my own. How I look letting you come to the store with us and my moms ask me who you are? After that foul shit you just pulled on me, you should be more than happy to let me take the card."

"I know you're not talking about foul shit when you spent the night fucking my cousin Regina. Yeah, the ho called me talking about how you ate the booty, shit breath. I haven't sucked nobody's dick but yours. Not even my baby daddy's when he come through, so you can't get mad at me."

Damn, I thought they were friends, was the only thought going through his head as she kept giving details of his night of horror with her cousin. The head and pussy were garbage, but he didn't find that out until he sealed the deal to get it with his tongue. She was playing tight with the goodies, and he had to find a way to loosen her up, so he put it on her. He licked her from her belly button to her spine, and when he strapped up to get inside of her, he was left disappointed. He tried to walk her through on how to tighten up her muscles so she could grip his dick, but that didn't work. He spent the night ramming his meat down her throat as he fucked her with the bottom end of his Sprite bottle.

"Oh, so you think you're the only one who gets lonely? I can't even get fully undressed and lie in bed with you because your man could pop up at any given moment. Yeah, I fucked her no-walls-having-ass but wished it was you the entire time. Check yo' missed calls. I called you as soon as I got done fucking her."

She checked her call log but came up empty-handed like he knew she would. He didn't call her; he called his mom to see if she was awake. He needed somewhere to go.

"Here . . ." she said after blaming her cell phone provider for not getting the call. "Only spend $150 on it because I have to do our shopping too. Its nine hundred on there."

"No, keep your stamps. I'm good on you and them. As a matter of fact, drop me off at that McDonald's across the light. I'm done fucking with you."

He could smell the bacon before he hit the steps to the house. His mom was up putting in work, and he was thankful for it because his stomach had been talking to him from the time, he left McDonald's parking lot.

"You got it smelling good in here, woman." He planted a kiss on her cheek since her hands were too full to hug her.

"When those cinnamon rolls get done breakfast is ready."

"Cool!" he said, leaning against the refrigerator. "Aye, Mama, do you know anybody who needs some food stamps? My friend is about to get evicted, and she's trying to sell $900's worth for five hundred."

"Hell yeah, I do. You know no-walls-having-ass is 18 now, and they cut off the crumbs they were giving me for your sister. They claim food stamps are for the working Americans, but if it weren't for having her, they wouldn't have given my working ass shit. And speaking of working, my job is hiring for a janitor. I know it's not construction work but having a job is better than the shit you got going now."

"I'm not cleaning no bathrooms or taking out trash unless it yours. You already know that, Mama, but after breakfast, can we go do these food stamps so I can take her, her card, and her money?"

"Uh-huh, we can go, but I know you, Aric. That card going in the trash, and that dingy chick isn't going to see a dime of that money. You're an ain't-shit nigga with good looks like your daddy. I ain't stupid. Now, go wake your sister up and wash y'all's hands so we can eat."

There wasn't a reason for him to dispute the truth, so he went to do as he was told.

"Aye, sis—"

Talk about being stopped in his tracks. He walked into his little sister sucking dick like it was her only chance at survival. It took shock too long to wear off because before he could make his way to beat the nigga down, she had been pleasing fast enough. The nigga was out the back door and in the driver's seat of his car when Aric could finally move.

"Damn, you don't know how to knock?"

"Knock for what? This is why Mama took the fucking lock off your door in the first place. I told her ass as long as that back door was in your room, that shit wouldn't work. Man, you out here hoping harder than yo' ass was in Cali. Those trips to the abortion clinic haven't taught your stupid ass shit, I see."

"Fuck you, Aric. For your information, that's my man, and if you hadn't come in this bitch *Diary of a Mad Black Woman* style, I would have introduced you to him."

"With a dick in your mouth? Whatever! Get yo' ass up. It's time for breakfast and make sure you brush them chops first. Mama don't need dick breath on all of her utensils."

He probably should have said more or told her mom on her so she could hit her with one of those Iyanla Vanzant intervention talks, but who was he to judge? He had his own shit going on, and to be real, she probably got that extra freaky shit from him. For years back in Cali, they had to share rooms. Being seven years older than she, he used to fuck a plethora of bitches on their bedroom floor, and every now and then, he or the chick would catch her little ass hanging off the side of her bed watching. He didn't mind at the time because he thought he was teaching her how a man is supposed to treat a woman's body, but the shit backfired. Alicia saw him fucking a lot of bitches and took that as the norm, and when she made it to 14, she began fucking a lot of different niggas. He knew the words of her teacher wouldn't mean shit until he could lead by example, and that wasn't going to happen no time anytime soon.

"Aric, your friend is at the door for you," his mom yelled.

"What friend you got?" Alicia asked as she grabbed her toothbrush out of her top drawer.

"Same shit I want to know."

He took his pistol off the safety and headed toward the door. Snatching it open, he said, "Who in the fuck are you?" The gun was in his hand, hidden behind the open door.

"A job opportunity, if you're the right nigga for the task," Joe asked.

Aric never forgot a face. He'd seen the guy twice. Once at the gas station when he was buying cigars to stuff his weed in, the dude behind the register had thrown the package toward him, and Aric snapped.

"Hold up, my nigga. Did you just throw these hoes at me?"

"You take long time. Look, long line!"

"I don't give a fuck how long it is, bitch; you don't throw shit at me."

"Get out! I no sell you nothing. Get out my store and no come back!" the owner yelled.

"Man, just sell me the shells, and I won't. You're the only bitch-ass nigga on this side of the town open right now. I don't have a car to go somewhere else."

"I no care. Get fuck ass out, or I call the police!"

"You gon' call the police? Man, I bet not catch yo' ass outside nowhere. Who in the fuck do you think you are to threaten me?"

The store owner grabbed his cell phone and called the police. Almost everybody in the store walked out.

Almost everybody.

"Hang up the phone."

Aric and the store owner looked at the man like he had lost his mind, and he proved that they might be right as he snatched the phone out of his hand.

"Get the cigars and go. If you really feel that disrespected, don't ever step foot back in here. I'll handle him."

Aric scanned the nigga from head to toe. He was the poster boy for the Average Nigga Campaign. Standing five feet eleven inches and weighing about 197 pounds, he was evenly proportioned. The navy blue and gray

New Balances he wore were about a size 10, and he had a normal faded haircut. He didn't have any facial hair shielding his looks, which made his almond-shaped eyes his most memorable feature besides the old scar that went across the bottom of his chin. He was dressed nicely but not flashy. A nice navy blue long-sleeve button-up possibly from the Gap or Banana Republic and relaxed front-fitted jeans.

"I appreciate it, big homie," Aric said, giving him a second once-over before walking out the door. Once outside, he scanned the parking lot to see what the dude was driving. Parked at pump number two was a gray Buick LeSabre. The car was nice and plain like its driver. No rims, no tint, and after looking in it as he walked by, no visible signs of being beat. He didn't know who the nigga thought he was, but to Aric, he seemed normal.

The second time they had crossed paths was at Jack Pirtle's while he was buying chicken. He wanted a two-piece and some fries once he got off the bus on Democrat Rd. He was on his way to apply for an overnight position at FedEx ground and needed to put something on his stomach. Last in line, the guy from the gas station walked past him on his way out and gave a head nod. Again, he didn't notice anything special about the dude. This time, he was wearing a white V-neck T-shirt, a pair of gray joggers, and some black slides with no-show ankle socks. Not that he was looking for something to visually make the man. It wouldn't have been necessary to know that there was something different about him then. When it was his turn to place his order, a girl at the counter told him the dude in the V-neck had already paid for it and told him to keep the change. She handed him the change from the hundred-dollar bill the guy left after he ordered his two-piece. Aric ran out the door to see which direction the guy went, but he was ghost.

***

"Are you following me or something? How did you know to pull up at my mama's house?"

"The funny thing about it is that I keep running into you. I was riding around trying to figure out how to handle this little problem of mines, and there you were again. By the time I could turn around, you were already walking in the door. I sat in the car, debating knocking on the door, and here I am. Are you looking for work or not?"

"What kind of work, and how much are you paying?"

Joe looked over Aric's shoulder into the house if anyone inside was listening. He nodded for Aric to step out on the porch, and he did, making sure Joe saw the pistol in his hand.

"The job pays $200,000 in cash. I'll give you 25 percent up front, and the rest on delivery."

"Hell yeah, who I got to kill? And I'm going to need 50 percent up front. Just because you like chicken and brought me some cigars don't mean I know you. I'ma need to see that you are legit."

"I'm legit, and I'm down for the 50 percent up front. That means I don't have to go into the consequences of you not finishing the job, right?"

"Look, I'm not one of these savage-ass Memphis niggas who don't know nut from piss. Any nigga that offers you $200,000 to do anything already got you marked; probably my moms and sister too.

"Yep, and the bitch house you just left with all the kids, she made that list too."

"So, are you going to keep talking about the consequences or tell me how I can get to this money? What do I got to do?"

"Have you ever been to Chicago?"

Chapter Fifteen

Chicago, Illinois. Saturday, February 2, 2019

Ronald knew the news was coming; yet, he still wasn't taking it well. To know that the disease attacking his memory had finally made it to the stage before it would take his life was disheartening. Whenever he could remember his doctor's new diagnosis, he'd cry but not for long, because he would forget what he was crying about.

Depression set in when he remembered he was depressed, and he found comfort in silence. He kept his television off and requested to keep the lights in his room dim. He declined visits unless they were from his son. The nurses stopped bringing him trays with solid foods and began bringing him soups and purees that they would spoon-feed him. He was given a catheter because the urge to use the restroom was forgotten. In the two weeks he had been hospitalized, his health was rapidly declining.

"Hey, Pops, how are you feeling?"

When RJ got the news, it hit him harder than he had assumed it would. The relationship he swore he didn't want with his father seemed to intrigue him as he realized death meant that there would be no opportunity to reconcile.

"Son, I'm not sure if I even remember how I feel," he chuckled. "But I know it's nice seeing you. How's my grandson doing?"

"He's fine; he's actually at the house spending time with my mama. She and her husband are in town for a few days."

Ronald hadn't thought of Sharlene as his woman in years. It was funny that RJ mentioning her and another man made him feel funny. It was she he reached out to on RJ's twenty-first birthday. She had every right to hang up on him and to withhold any information on how to be in contact with their son, but she hadn't. She even sounded happy to hear his voice when he called. She not only arranged the visit where they would meet, she flew with RJ to Chicago. Ronald hadn't seen her since RJ's twenty-fifth birthday party. That was the night that RJ announced he would be moving to Chicago and leaving the South behind.

"How's your mama doing?"

There was a first for everything, and that question had made the list of first. Years ago, Ronald had made the mistake of trying to talk to RJ about his mother, and RJ immediately shut down the conversation.

"She's fine; just getting old," he laughed. "She's just like everybody else dealing with aches and pains, but she's hanging in there. She actually told me to tell you hi."

"You make sure you send her my love. I know you don't want to hear this, and you probably don't believe me, but your mama was a hell of a woman. I never met a woman that held standards like hers, and I even used her character and personality in teaching young boys to know what to look for in a woman."

To say that RJ was uncomfortable was an understatement, but he let his dad talk. The anger, hurt, and disappointment he held on to only so he could rub it in Ronald's face from the moment they met was gone. He was about to bury his father. All he wanted was for his dad's final days to be peaceful.

"So, have you been watching the news lately? There's a lot of stuff going on. It's crazy to know all of it is real."

"Like what? What's going on?"

"There's this drug kingpin, pharmaceuticals, logistics guy. I don't know what to call him, but there's this guy who has had his hand in over twenty companies for years. And he employed billionaires to mob bosses to build and invest in his company's growth. Anyway, the shit hit the fan, and all the companies were really cover-ups for this wide scale drug operation. The Feds have found his fingerprint on companies in twenty-eight out of fifty states, all the U.S. territories, Mexico, Canada, South America, Cuba, and I believe there are like two other countries involved. He apparently made some money internationally or something like that. Truth is, Pops, they don't know how he did it. They don't even know who he is or what race he belongs to. It's like a mad manhunt going on for him, but nobody knows who they are looking for."

"That sounds like a plot to a really good book," Ronald laughed.

"I was thinking a really good movie," RJ joined him with a snicker. "You should see how many people are wearing T-shirts that say, '*I am Joe.*'"

"I don't get it. Why do the shirts say that?"

"Well, some detectives in Memphis were able to find out the name he was using, and now, some big company copyrighted or trademarked the saying, 'I am Joe.'"

"Wow, sounds like he did make it big."

"Are you kidding me? He's *huge*. This guy is the cause of the stock market plummeting 10,000 points last week. When they started investigating his companies, many of them were Fortune 500 companies, and they are being shut down. If it keeps going like this, it'll be like reliving the Stone Age around here. Cell phone companies, logistic companies, pharmaceutical companies, airports . . . I mean *anything* you can name, he owns and operates."

"They think the guy is from Memphis?"

"I actually heard that they think he's from Chicago, but depending on what city and state you live in, people are saying he's from where they are too. Hold on, let me turn on the TV. I'm sure it's on. It's *always* on!"

He powered on the television and flipped a channel and found what he was looking for.

"Okay, here goes something about him."

The reporter was using words that Ronald couldn't remember the definition to. Listening to her talk was frustrating, and he lost interest in learning the information his son was trying to share with him. It wasn't until they flashed a piece from the *60 Minutes* special that Ronald remembered he had been following the case.

"Yes, yes, I've heard about this. What's going on? Give me an update!"

The haste in his voice caused RJ to raise his eyebrow. His father seemed a little *too* interested, which was strange because moments earlier, he didn't seem like he was interested at all.

"Okay, it all started with a *60 Minutes* special on kingpins. Some dude from Chicago was on the show and said he knew who was making the moves down South because the boy told him when they were in school together. The boy he named as the kingpin had been missing for years. One of the news stations reached out to the detectives who were on the missing person case, and they said they assumed he was dead years ago while the investigating was going on, but his remains were never found.

"Anyway, that guy from the show ended up committing suicide, or so that's what the coroner said. The show, however, Memphis police took seriously and investigated what the guy was saying. Much of what he said was verifiable as fact, and there had been two detectives working the case for years. The dude Joe or whatever spoke up and started saying everything was true but didn't give any information on who he was. He got sloppy and killed somebody or blew somebody up. I don't remember which it was, but the people he killed were the heads of the largest pharmaceutical company in the Western Hemisphere, and once the Feds started investigating the company, they found out all types of billionaires and cartel bosses we're on the board at the company. The chemists were arrested, and they started telling everything. The company was making the medicinal *and* street version of every drug available. Everybody wants this guy now. The mob and cartels have a billion-dollar bounty on his head, and everybody is out trying to get it. I'm only keeping up with the story to see who finds him first. Will it be the Feds, the mob, or just somebody random that caught him slipping? Everybody is suspect," he laughed.

Ronald was at a loss for words. He forgot the depression he temporarily was under; he could feel again. He didn't like the update he received on Ethan's situation. Life turned that boy into a monster in Ronald's eyes, and no one, including him, did anything to help. When the boy had first gone missing, the detectives not only questioned him, they served him a search warrant to check his house. Ethan's mama was doped up and saying random shit, including that she thought Ronald was a pedophile and had been molesting her son. It was that accusation that made him decide not to go on his own search for the missing boy. No one seemed to understand why he was so invested in the child, and since Ethan's mother threw that dog bone in the air, the dogs went after him. When he offered to help search for Ethan, they asked him if he was missing his lover. Whooping a detective was looked upon as a crime, so he walked away and let it go. He wouldn't allow Ethan to go through it alone again.

"I know that you know I'm losing my memory, and I know that you think it's already gone. I won't lie to you, RJ; I have spells throughout the day. I don't feel or get an urge to use the restroom. Half the time, I don't know where I am or who I am. You see these straps on the bed? That's when they have to lock me up and tie me to it because I panic and have accused the nurse of being any and everything *but* a nurse. I need you to listen to me and believe me when I tell you this. That Joe that is on the news, that's your *brother,* son, and I need to get to Memphis to help him."

RJ laughed. There was nothing to think about.

"Pops, are you losing your damn mind again? What new drugs do they got you on?"

"Reach that book, RJ, reach it for me . . . that . . . um, what's it called?" Ronald's mind was drawing a blank canvas. "You know, the book they give you when you're in school, and it has you and your friends' pictures in it? It's one of the books I had you send me from when I used to teach. Do you know what I'm talking about?"

That pulled on RJ's heartstrings. His pops could give the complete definition or description of the yearbook and said everything *but* the name of it. Without saying anything, he grabbed the book and handed it to him.

"Do you know how to work your phone to pull up the name of the guy who was on the *60 Minutes* show? I can prove it to you."

The nurses advised RJ that it was healthy for him to play memory games with his father to keep him from feeling completely useless. He pulled out his phone and searched for the guy's name.

"The guy's name is Martin?"

"Is there a way on that thing where it shows you what school he went to?"

"Maybe, Pops. Let me put his full name in the search bar and see what come up."

He tried a variety of searches, and finally, he found what he was looking for. The results made him sit on the bed with his father.

"It says he graduated from the school you used to work at. Are you serious? You *really* know this guy?"

As RJ asked his question, Ronald slid his finger over a picture in the book. RJ didn't have to read the name under it to know it was the same person from the *60 Minutes* episode. On the show, his face had been blacked out, but after his death, they released his picture, and it was him. Flipping to the front cover of the book, Ronald thought he might have had a signed message from the boy but remembered this wasn't his copy of the yearbook. This was the copy given to Ethan's mom, and she gave Ronald all the books Ethan had in his room.

"And this boy here, *that's* your brother. That's your big brother. I didn't birth him, but he's mine. *That's* the Joe that they're looking for."

"Man, get the fuck out of here! You show me a picture of a guy that you taught and expect me to believe a cat who went to raggedy-ass South Side Heights is the same cat everybody is looking for? And that this said cat is your *son,* who really ain't your son? Did your doctors change your meds recently?"

"You don't have to believe me, RJ. You have never believed anything I've said to you, so why start now? I'm not in the business of convincing anybody to believe my truth. It doesn't pay enough. I'm not going to ask you to walk down memory lane with me, but I am going to ask you to walk me the fuck out of this hospital so I can go take care of my boy."

"Hey, Pops, you're a cold-blooded muthafucka. You abandoned me and didn't reach out until I was 21. You sit in my face damn near distraught over a cat you used to teach, and you tell me that you got to run to this nigga's aid? I don't care if it's true or not at this moment, but you're dead to me. Fuck you, old man!" He grabbed his keys off the table and exited the room, never looking back.

It may sound fucked up, but Ronald didn't care. He tried to salvage that relationship too many times than he would have tried in any other relationship, and he was done. He was months, if he were lucky, away from dying, and he was going to live his last days however he wanted to. All he had to do was find a way to get out of that hospital and make it to Memphis. He'd help Ethan any way that he could.

His room door opened, and he wondered what RJ had come back to say. If it were anything less than an apology, he'd kick him out.

"Mr. Hill, Mr. Ronald Hill. I believe you."

Ronald didn't know who the guy was standing at the foot of his bed, and he couldn't remember if he knew him or not, but he already earned the respect he had just lost for his son.

"You *should* believe me because I'm not lying. Will you help me? Will you help me get out of here?"

"Shit, that's what I'm here to do. Your son Ethan sent me here to bring you home. He said you're dying, and he wants you with him in your final days. He gave me $200,000 to make sure you make it back to Tennessee, and that's what I'm here to do. What you want me to pack?"

"I don't need anything out of here; let's go."

"What about your meds? You want me to grab those?"

"No. I got a feeling I'm not going to need them anymore once we make it to Memphis. Just grab my shoes out of the closet behind you."

He handed Ronald his shoes and then said, "I'll be right back." When he came back, he was in scrubs with a face mask and blue hair net with a chart in his hand. He disconnected Ronald to all the machines, and immediately, his nurse came in.

"Where's my patient going?"

"The doctors want another CAT scan of his brain, so I'm about to take him up to go get it."

"You mean you're about to take him down. We are on the twelfth floor. That's the seventh floor."

"It's been a long day. Yeah, the seventh floor."

"You can say that again. I've been working a double, and I'm ready to pass out. When you bring him back, check him in with me at the desk. I'ma have to get him connected back to all of these machines. Did you remove the catheter?"

He didn't know what the hell a catheter was to think about removing it, and Ronald couldn't remember what one was either.

"No, I left it."

"Good. It was hard as hell to get him to relax to insert it the first time. Let me check it to make sure it's empty, and if he goes, I'll give you a new bag to attach to it." She walked over to a drawer and handed him an empty bag. "Just change it if he gets it over this line right here. You don't want to let it get too full; you know what I'm saying?"

"Yeah, I do."

She stepped out of the room, and he grabbed the bag next to Ronald's bed and took all the empty catheter bags and put them inside. Instantly, Ronald remembered something that he did need.

"There's a sealed letter in that box with the books. Can you grab that and that yearbook? I want to take that with me."

"No problem, Pops. I got you."

They walked out the door into the elevators without causing any suspicion. Aric had the rental car parked outside of the emergency entrance. He put Ronald in the car and drove off. They had a seven-hour ride ahead of them, and Ronald planned on smiling the whole way there. He was going to see his son.

Chapter Sixteen

Memphis, Tennessee. Sunday, February 3, 2019

Memphis, Tennessee, was more beautiful than any picture Ronald had seen of the historical city. He had always wanted to travel to Memphis for a hot plate of BBQ with a beer on Beale Street and to take a tour of the National Civil Rights Museum, but that was a list he never got around to using. There were many places he dreamed of visiting in his life, but once he reconciled with his son, playing catch-up was the only item on his bucket list that he wanted to fulfill.

Ronald couldn't remember why the young man was taking him to Memphis, but in spite of that, he was enjoying the ride.

"You think after we handle this business in Memphis, you'll be able to take me to Atlanta? It can't be too far away from here, right?"

"Nah, it's close as hell. If your son says he wants me to take you to Atlanta next, then that's where we headed. That's one of my favorite places to go kick it anyway."

"I don't know, son. RJ treats me like I'm his child. He will probably say no to you taking me to Memphis."

"You mean Atlanta, and who in the fuck is RJ? I'm not taking you to meet up with some hating-ass nigga named RJ. I'm taking you to see your son Ethan, remember?"

And like that, Ronald remembered.

"Yes, you're taking me to see Ethan. You got me from the hospital in Chicago, and we are on a seven-hour trip to Memphis. All I got to do is sit back and chill." Ronald repeated Aric's words verbatim, and it made both men smile. Along the trip, Ronald had two large fits where he screamed for help to get away from Aric, and those were the words Aric made him repeat to get through them. "I can't wait to see him! You've been so helpful to us; I'm going to tell him to pay you once we get there."

"He did pay me, real good too. If he's getting you a nurse, tell him I want the job. With all the money he gave me, the first six months are free," he said matter-of-factly. "Your son is real generous. Can I ask you a question?"

"Sure, if you're a friend of his, then you're a friend of mine."

"Okay, so, what does your son do exactly for a living? He gave me $200,000 to bust you out of the hospital and drive you to Memphis. It wasn't hard, and I would have done it for $10,000. Why do you think he offered me so much?"

"I don't know what my son does for a living. I haven't talked to him in years. My guess would be he paid you because you were handling one of his fragile packages, and he wanted you to take good care of it. And you did, son. You took damn good care of me."

Aric ran his mouth the entire drive. Ronald wasn't able to confirm it, but he thought Aric might've continued to talk while he was asleep. Although Aric's California gangbanger mentality got on his nerves, the boy was heaven-sent. He stopped and bought him some extra-large sweats, a T-shirt that read, "*I am Joe*," and an elastic band. He used the band to strap the catheter to Ronald's frail leg so it couldn't be noticed. Once he had him dressed, he fed Ronald mashed potatoes without asking if he were hungry and used a squirting bottle to force him to drink.

"When we make it to Memphis, I'll make sure to tell my son how well you took care of me. I can't promise you a bonus check, but I will put in a good word."

"It's no problem, man. I didn't do it for that. When your pops told me what was up with you, I knew why we kept running into each other. This shit was meant to happen." He bit into his sandwich and didn't speak until he had chewed the food in his mouth and swallowed. "My mama took care of my grandma with Alzheimer's until she died. It was hard on all of us, you know, seeing her go through it. But, fortunately, for us, we found a way to trigger memories, so we felt good knowing she knew who we were on the day she died. How long have you not been able to eat shit?"

"Hold on, son. My memory ain't that messed up. I know I never eaten shit." Ronald laughed, trying to lighten the mood. He wouldn't ignore the question, though. He just wanted to be able to talk about it comfortably. "I haven't been able to eat solids since I made it to the hospital two weeks ago, but I was thinking about it. I can't remember the last time I ate anything solid."

"My grandma couldn't remember to chew or swallow, so they ran this tube down her throat to her stomach or whatever and fed her that way. If I would've had the power to make decisions on her life, I would have made those folks put her to sleep. That's a cold way to see somebody you love die. Your son must really love you!"

Ronald smiled at him. He was excited to see Ethan again after all the years that had passed. The last time he saw him was the night he took him to the gym and celebrated his birthday over pizza. It was the night Ethan confessed to murdering his own father. Thinking of how brutally he murdered him was nothing less than a sign of the pain his father caused him. Ethan didn't give an explanation on why he did it or what happened that made him feel that he had to do it, though he was visibly hurt that he had.

That was the last time he saw Ethan, but that wasn't the last time he had to deal with things surrounding him. The next morning when he woke up, Ethan had broken his heart.

Chicago, Illinois, Saturday, May 2, 1992

Loud knocks pounded on Ronald's door. He knew who they belonged to before he could slide his pants on and make it to the door before it was kicked in.

"Good morning. How can I help you?" He yawned in the detectives' faces.

"Are you Ronald Hill?"

"Yes, I am. How can I help you?"

Three uniformed officers appeared from what seemed like thin air as the detective handed him the search warrant.

"Have you seen this boy? His name is Ethan Wade Carruthers."

"Yeah, that's my godson. He's in there in the guest room asleep. What's going on? Why are you looking for him?" He hoped the early-morning intrusion didn't have anything to do with him being tied to his father's murder or that the reason he mentioned Martin's death threat was that he killed him first. He tried to remain cool until the police showed their hand first.

Both detectives and all three officers immediately went toward the bedroom. Ronald followed closely on their heels.

"Hey, Ethan, these officers need to speak with you, son. Get up." At the last second, Ronald decided the boy deserved a chance to run and tried to notify him the police were about to walk in, but it wasn't necessary. The room

was empty, and the bed was made up like it had never been slept in. The room was spotless, and you could smell the bleach and other cleaning products that had been used in the air. Ronald ran to the closet. Everything he had bought Ethan was gone, and so was the key he placed back on the dresser while he slept.

"He was here last night. He got here around 7:30 or 8:00 p.m., and we went to the gym for about an hour. After that, we had pizza, and then he showered and went to bed. I stayed up a little late watching TV and knocked out around 1:00 or 2:00 a.m. He was in bed when I went to my room because I checked on him, and he was asleep."

"We didn't ask you for any details, sir. Why the need to give them?"

"I'm giving them because he was here, and now, he's not. He didn't mention leaving. What's the search warrant for anyway?"

"Ethan Wade Carruthers, a 16-year-old African American male, was reported missing three weeks ago by his mother. We've been keeping an eye on all your moves, and we never found any connect between you and Mr. Carruthers."

"Why would you be keeping an eye on me?"

"You are the only person his mother listed as 'suspicious.' She told me she had been uncomfortable with your relationship with her son. We got an anonymous tip this morning that you and him argued outside of your house in the wee hours of the morning. What were y'all arguing about?"

"We weren't arguing about anything. I told you I hadn't talked to him since last night. The last time I saw him, he was in that room, under those covers, asleep. Before last night, I hadn't spoken to him in four months."

"We need you to throw on a shirt and come have a chat with us at the police precinct."

"No problem; let me grab my shirt."

They didn't let Ronald drive his own car when he asked if he could. They placed him in the back of a squad car uncuffed, but he still felt as if he had been arrested. For hours, they asked him the same question in as many different ways as their minds could create, and for hours, he gave all the same answers. One of the detectives asked him to create a list of suspicious people, and the first name he wrote was Martin, and the only name he could add, which was more out of spite than anything else, was Ethan's mother.

"So, if this Martin boy told you he was going to kill Ethan, why didn't you come and tell us?" the detective over the missing person case questioned. The detective worked in homicide and was the detective on Ethan's father's case as well. He picked up the missing person case in the event it was tied to the unsolved murder of Ethan's father.

"I didn't say anything because I knew he wasn't going to do anything."

"That's funny you should say that."

"And why would that be funny?" Ronald was irritated and nervous. He wasn't nervous for his own outcome but for the safety of Ethan.

"It's funny because not even five minutes ago, you wrote Martin's name down as a suspicious person, and here we are five minutes later, and you are saying he's not suspicious."

"I never said he wasn't suspicious. I said he wasn't going to kill him. If Martin has anything to do with Ethan going missing, he's under somebody else's orders, and he's not going to pull the trigger."

"Pull the trigger? I said Ethan was missing. I didn't say he was dead. Is he dead? I mean, you seem to be the last person to say that they saw him, and that anonymous tip says you were too. Did you kill Ethan?"

"Ethan isn't dead; he's somewhere hiding."

"Why would he be somewhere hiding? Is he hiding from you?"

It took Ronald longer than it should have to realize anything that he said was going to be twisted. They wanted him to be guilty, and they wanted him to think he was guilty. After more than three hours of questioning, Ronald finally asked for his lawyer to be present.

The investigation went on for months. After the court granted the detective access to the video from the gym and the restaurant, he ruled out foul play involving Ronald. By the videos, Ethan looked like he was having the time of his life, and since the anonymous tipster decided to remain anonymous, they had nothing to fall back on. Once he was completely cleared of suspicion, he created his own missing person reward and planted Ethan's picture on every available wall space in Greater Chicago. With all the hours and work he invested in finding the boy, it was to no avail. In six months, he and the detective on the case, Detective Washburn, became close friends. At a private meeting between the two men a year later, Detective Washburn told Ronald his true thoughts on the case.

"I hate to say it, especially to you, but that boy is dead."

"Why would you say that? Did new information come in or evidence that suggests it?"

"No," the detective said, shaking his head. "When you've done this for as long as I have, you just know these things. His dad was found in a public dumpster. Whoever did it didn't attempt to hide his body. It was almost like there was a lesson they were trying to teach,

*and they used him to get their point across. I don't know
too many 16-year-old boys."*

"He's almost 18 now. He'll be 18 this upcoming March."

*"Excuse me, 17 years old, in this day in age that could
survive with no money, clothes, or food. This isn't a ransom situation, or we would already have heard what
that ransom was. His family is poor, and his mother is
strung out. I guess what I'm trying to say is, nothing
is adding up to Ethan still being alive, especially not after all this time. You might want to get some sleep and
let this case go."*

*"Never! What father would let go of a case or even give
up hope on the return of his son? He's coming back, and
when he does, he's going to have a hell of a story to tell."*

*Ronald drank himself to sleep that night. He had
picked up the habit of drinking himself to sleep many
nights now. He had prided himself on smoking weed
only and stayed away from alcohol, but now, it was
the opposite. He couldn't smoke weed because of the
cost and paranoia. It made him feel like he was next. If
they came for Ethan, they surely would come for him.
Although Martin had checked out to be clean, Ronald
refused to believe that the people he affiliated with didn't
have something to do with it. If it ever came out that
Ethan was killed by the hands of some Crips, he'd killed
Martin himself.*

*The next morning, he woke up to breaking news. Co-
lombian drug lord Pablo Escobar had been killed. He
didn't know why the story demanded his attention, but
he gave it to the TV. Of course, with his death, other
drug lords', traffickers', and kingpins' names were being
thrown around. It took him back to the tattoo parlor,
and that's when it finally happened. That's when Ronald
finally broke down. He cried for hours, only to get himself together and head out to the liquor store. He bought*

*light, dark, and some Caribbean Brown. Then he drove
by the guy's house who supplied his weed and gave
him $100. He wasn't sure of how much weed he had
bought, but he was certain there wouldn't be any left in
the morning. When he made it home, he called Corrina.
They had rekindled their friendship as she teamed with
him on a hunt to find Ethan. They had crossed the lines
a few times that led to some damn good meals; however,
it always was staged to be "accidental." This time, he
was going to be up front.*

"Are you busy?"

*She could hear the hurt in his tone, so there was no
way she'd tell him she was. She put her piles of laundry
to the side and headed his way. He met her at the door
with a glass.*

*"Will you sip with me tonight? Can we be work hus-
band and wife just one more time? If you can't do it for
me, can you do it for Ethan?"*

*She snatched the drink out of his hand and swallowed
the whole glass in one loud gulp.*

"Keep them coming!"

*They drank, smoked, and fucked all night. In the
morning, he asked her to join him in the shower. And as
he made love to her from the back, he asked her to move
in with him.*

*"I know you've been out looking for a place," he said,
pulling his meat out of her before either one of them was
finished, but he wanted her to know he was serious, and
it wasn't the goodness of her pussy that had his mouth
running. "There's more than enough room here if you
need your own space, and, well, I thought we could be
official."*

"Official what, Ronald? I need to hear you say it."

*"Officially together, officially engaged, officially faith-
ful to each other for the rest of our lives. You become*

mine officially, and I become yours officially. I don't have a ring right now to propose with properly, but this is where I'm going with this. I know I can have more, like you and Ethan said, and I want everything that I can have. I want everything that's mines!"

They kissed, and she said, yes. Repeatedly. He was lost in the moment but still heard his bedroom door close.

"Who's there?" he asked, listening attentively for another sound, but there wasn't one, so he left off where they had paused, stroking in and out of his wife-to-be.

Two weeks later in preparation of her moving in, he destroyed the contents of his file box, page by page. The only thing he planned on saving were the pictures of his son. As he scrolled through the memories, he prayed he could forget. Then he ran across an envelope that read, Mr. R. Hill. He didn't know what it was, but the writing was familiar.

Mr. Ronald,
Don't you think it's funny how they brag that they finally killed Pablo? But I bet the autopsy will reveal there was a bullet in his right ear. He said he'd kill himself that way; he wouldn't give them the pleasure of doing it. You see, before you can dig into a lifestyle like his, you have to plan. You need a plan to win and another plan of all the ways that you could fail. You will need to put more focus on failing than into winning if you really want to win. I've done that, and if it ever starts looking like the end, you *will* see me again. Congratulations on the engagement and decision to settle down. It looks like you finally found you a new Sharlene. Hopefully, we will never see each other again, but if we do . . . Let's call it the "to be continued" of all of this.
Your son

With tears running down his face, he read the letter at least a hundred times and sealed it in an envelope as his most valuable keepsake.

"Okay, we're here," Aric said, looking up and down Riverside Drive. "Your son said for me to drop you off at the bench near the statue at the park. When the cabdriver comes to get you, you go with him. Tell him to take you to the closest bus stop on Shelby Drive near the Nike warehouse. Do you think you can remember that?"

"Bus stop closest to Nike on Shelby Drive."

"Yeah, but I probably should still write it down. Here," he wrote it on the back of the sealed envelope Ronald had been clutching on his ride. "Don't forget, if you need a nurse, I'm your man!"

He was supposed to take the rental car back to the airport but put the rear passenger tire on flat instead and would call the company to have it towed. The rental wasn't in his name anyway. He found a junkie with an unexpired driver's license and gave him $1,000 to open up an account at the bank inside of the discount department store. They printed him a debit card on the spot, and three days later, Aric and his friend were at Save A Buck car rental picking up the vehicle. He didn't know anything about the guy who hired him to trust that there wouldn't be any backlash from their arrangement, but seeing that he was $200,000 richer, why not invest in his own freedom? He was sure the hospital in Chicago reported the plates to the police when they watched the cameras to see what he did with Ronald.

In one of the condos across the street, a sniper waited for Joe to tell him to pull the trigger. Joe wasn't sure if Aric would break under pressure when the nationwide hunt for Ronald began, but when the sniper walked him through what Aric was doing, Joe decided to let him live and hung up the phone.

"Are you here for the Silver Sneakers Park Walk?" two 60-something-year-old women asked Ronald, and he couldn't remember if he was or not.

"If I'm a Silver Sneaker, I guess I am."

They reached out their hands to help him up and then walked him to the sign-up table on the other side of the park. When the cabdriver came looking for the passenger he was supposed to pick up, he was gone.

The walk with the seniors was exactly what Ronald needed. He was the youngest in the crowd but had the worst memory. After the walk, the participants strolled over to Beale Street and had dinner. Being that it was Ronald's first time on the world-famous street, a few of the women made a detour before heading to the restaurant.

"B. B. King and Lucille sat on a stump and played right here?" he asked excitedly.

"Yes, sir, and hundreds more," Dolores added. "What a lot of folks don't know is that Robert Church purchased all the blocks around here when that yellow fever epidemic started taking folks' lives in the area. Nobody wanted nothing to do with downtown Memphis, and that's how he ended up becoming the first black millionaire from the South."

"That's amazing. I want to say I knew that but can't remember if I did or not. When I had my youth, I was a history teacher. Keep talking, Dolores, I'm enjoying this."

She gave him a history lesson at Church Park about the presidents and black leaders who gave speeches there and gave another lesson when they made it down to the Beale Street Baptist Church.

"You'd never know how much history was jammed in these two miles by looking at it at nightfall. The streets are packed with half-naked women, drinking, partying, and dancing."

"Then you should bring me back later." He laughed, but she didn't join in. She continued like she hadn't heard his foolishness.

"They do hold a Beale Street Blues Festival that brings people out from all over the world, and during that weekend, the history of the street is acknowledged again. Times have changed so much," she said, looking at her wrinkled hands, and Ronald caught on to it.

"Yes, they have, but wine gets better with time, and I know a good glass of it when I see one." He grabbed her hand, and they walked back to the restaurant to rejoin the group.

"I don't think I have money to pay for my food," Ronald said to the ladies he had been sitting with. "I think my son took everything. They made me sign some papers making him my power of attorney, and I don't think I've seen a dollar since."

"Don't worry about that, sugar. I'll pay for your dinner *and* your breakfast," Dolores chimed in.

"Run, Ronald, while you still have a chance. That dinner and breakfast she is paying for is going to cost you more than it's worth," one of the men at the table across from him said. Both tables went up in laughter. Well, everybody at the tables laughed except for Dolores. She didn't find anything that he said funny.

"I believe you said your name was Doris, is that right?" Ronald asked.

"Dolores, sugar," she replied, taken aback. They had a moment where they bonded, and here, he was talking like she was no different than the rest of the group.

"Ms. Dolores, I thank you, and I appreciate your kindness. I haven't enjoyed myself like this in years, but if it's not asking for too much, can we please go now? I'm very tired."

"But you haven't gotten your food yet. Trust me when I say you don't want to miss the chance to taste their black-eyed peas and buttermilk corn bread."

"Is that what I ordered?" he asked with a smile.

"Yes," she said, laughing nervously that he had forgotten that fast. "And beef brisket, baked macaroni, and candied yams. Do you not remember?"

"I remember I'm hungry!" he said, and everyone laughed.

Ronald didn't remember walking to her car or the ride in it because he fell asleep in his chair at the restaurant. He hadn't stayed awake over two hours in weeks, and the three and a half hours he stayed awake tired him out. Their waiter and a few men from the walk loaded him in Dolores's car, and when she made it home, she had her grandsons bring him in.

"I found the drainage bags for your catheter and changed it. I have a box of adult diapers if you would prefer to wear those instead."

Wearing a long sleeve, high-neck nightgown with her silver hair flowing down her back, Dolores stood over Ronald as if she were visiting him in the hospital.

"I don't get the urge to go. Not for number one or two. They do something every morning to make me, you know," he said, pointing toward his rear, "and they put the catheter in there to force it out."

"You're dying, aren't you? Sorry to be so blunt about it, but I was an RN more than half my life, and I spent the last ten years before retirement working in a nursing home. Your Alzheimer's is at the ending stages, isn't it?"

"Yes, ma'am, I'm dying, but a part of me already feels like I'm dead. I don't remember anything, and when something does come to mind, I can't hold on to it long enough to make out if it's real or fake. I was one of those stupid people who thought they knew everything. Everything I touched I fucked up, and instead of righting my wrongs, I prayed for years that the God who I didn't believe in would erase the memories of all the pain I caused in my life and others', and he did."

"If you can remember all of that, your memory seems pretty sharp to me."

"Thank you kindly. If you saw one of my fits, you wouldn't think so. I'll be honest with you, pretty lady. I don't know who you are, how we met, or where I am. The only reason I'm not panicking is because of the way the light is peeking around your shape. You look like an angel from God. Now, who could be scared of an angel?"

She smiled at him.

"What about a wife or kids? Do you have either? I really want to know who would let you out alone this far in your disease. It's like committing homicide."

"I almost had a wife. Her name was . . . Sharlene or maybe Corrina, I can't recall. It's one of those memories I asked to be erased, but she died five days before our wedding. I can't remember if it was stomach cancer or a heart attack, but I do know I never gave love a chance again."

"I'm so sorry to hear that. I lost my husband ten years ago to lung cancer. He loved his cigarettes. I tried to get him to quit when I noticed he picked up a bedtime cough, but you can't tell a doctor anything. They have all the answers. We had a son, but he was killed by a stray bullet at a house party out in Westwood as a teenager. A few months after his death, a young lady came knocking on our door saying she was pregnant with his twins. We had a test done or whatnot, and they belonged to my son. It was like being given a double dose of him to hold on to. Their mother could never get it together, so we have been raising them since they were 3 years old. That's who helped me get you in the house. They're in college and were supposed to live on campus but didn't want me to be here alone. I fuss like I don't want them here, but I don't know what I'd do without them now that Robert is gone."

"My brother's name is Robert. He's in the military on a special secret mission." The lie he told for so many years flowed out of his mouth because after all of the years he told it, he finally believed it. "I have two sons. My youngest is my brother's spitting image. He gave me a grandson, and my oldest boy chose to stay away from me. I don't know if he has any kids. Maybe one day I'll get to find out."

He went back to sleep as if they weren't in the middle of a conversation. Recalling the few memories that he had tired him out.

As he slept, Dolores dug through his bag but didn't find anything that said who he was or where he was going. She found a sealed letter with instructions for him to give a cabdriver and wondered if he had followed them. She'd offer to take him there after she fed him in the morning.

"You can at least eat your grits, Ronald. You have to eat something."

"I'm not hungry, and I don't trust you. Show me proof that I'm in Memphis, Tennessee, right now, dammit!" He flipped her table over, and she screamed. Her grandsons had already left the house for school, and there was no one around who could help. Ronald picked up the butter knife she set before him and charged at her with it.

"Help, somebody help me!" she screamed. She tried to run into the living so she could make it out of the front door, but Ronald dived at her, and they both fell to the floor.

"Who are you, and how did I get here?" he bellowed.

"I don't know how you got to Memphis. I met you at a bench in the park. I'm Dolores. I brought you home with me because you said you needed somewhere to stay until the Shelby County Assessor of Property opened in the morning. You said you wanted to buy the biggest warehouse here that was on sale the longest."

"Why would I come to Memphis to buy a warehouse? I don't have any money!" He started fumbling with her hair to reveal her neck. That's the spot where he'd cut her.

"I don't know why you said it, but you kept chanting, 'You're taking me to see Ethan. You got me from the hospital in Chicago, and we are on a seven-hour trip to Memphis. All I got to do is sit back and chill. You're taking me to—'"

"to see Ethan. You got me from the hospital in Chicago, and we are on a seven-hour trip to Memphis. All I got to do is sit back and chill." He dropped the knife and got off her, crying. Everything in his head was blurry. He remembered the chant but couldn't remember who made him recite the words. He remembered the hospital but could have sworn it was in Atlanta, not Chicago. He continued to chant the words because there was something about them that made him feel calm.

While Ronald occupied himself, Dolores stood to her feet and stepped closer to the front door as he stayed there on the floor crying and chanting. After the tenth time he chanted the words, she asked him in the calmest and softest voice she could muster, "Do you want to go to the assessor of property office or the bus stop closest to the Nike warehouse on—"

"Shelby Drive! That's where I'm supposed to go! That's what my nurse told me. He said my son would pick me up from there. Will you take me?"

"No, I'm not going anywhere with you after you pulled a plastic butter knife on me, but I will call you a cab and pay for it. Come on; let me get you dressed, and that drainage bag changed so you can get to your son."

The cab was there in twenty minutes, and she had him packed and ready to go. She didn't like sending him off without feeding him, but she couldn't get him to eat. She couldn't believe anyone would leave him by himself in the state he was in, and that they found it funny. He had three shirts that all read, *"I am Joe"* in his bag, which made him look like he was begging to be young in the high top sneakers and sweats he had on. If he wore a gold chain, you'd think he was preparing to speak on a then-and-now hip-hop documentary. She waved him off, hoping he'd be OK but glad he was out of her house.

Chapter Seventeen

Memphis, Tennessee. Monday, February 4, 2019

Joe couldn't sleep. He drove past the bus stop every fifteen minutes looking for Ronald, and he wasn't there.

"I gave you one fucking job to do, and I even let you live because you seemed smart enough to survive after this, and your ungrateful ass lost my fucking package!" he yelled, vowing to have Aric, his mother, and sister killed for his blunder. How could his plan not to fail keep failing in ways that would prevent him from recovering with a win?

Since the age of 14, he studied everything he could on drugs from those who grew them, distributed them, sold them hand-to-hand, and those who used them both medicinally and for pleasure. He needed to understand why his parents loved dope so much and made it a priority over raising him. He concluded that they were dumb and unwillingly decided to be on the wrong side of the drug industry. His parents were on the team that housed the losers, which was the team of the addicts. Nothing that he came across highlighted a drug abuser in a good light. From health issues to homelessness, everything he read about those battling addiction was depressing.

When he moved up to the hand-to-hand sells, he saw little to no profit there. Yes, some street dealers made enough money to drive a nice car or live in an expensive house, but the hours they devoted to achieving it wasn't

worth the pay, nor was the time they lost in jail and battling possession cases. If the hand-to-hand deal managed
to stay away from all of that, then he only had to worry
about being robbed by the next dealer, territorial wars, or
a junkie who was desperate enough to stab him in order
to get their next fix. There was always a hater watching
with an itching trigger finger over the 911 button, ready
to snitch because they didn't have the nuts to get what
the dealer had, so they wanted them stopped, and sometimes that call was made by a woman who said she loved
him, but in anger, she showed that method of revenge.
Ethan couldn't see himself waiting around for someone
who supplies him to go through any of the above.

The supplier seemed like a nice spot to start, but you
had to gain the trust of the distributor to do that, and
they weren't taking applications or giving out character
tests. In order to gain the trust of the distributor, you had
to come with vast amounts of money and be ready to buy
more product when he needed you to. There wasn't any
room to complain about having an overstock of drugs
because a distributor didn't send out a notice of termi-
nation for not creating a growing demand. He killed you,
which made being the distributor one up on Ethan's list.
Each level of the industry had its cons, but his research
proved the farther up the levels he went, the more protection he would receive.

He spent months studying the moves of Frank Lucas,
Harlem's drug kingpin, and what sat on his mind the most
was the success he accomplished by removing the middleman. The protection around him grew because so many
were invested in his product that they couldn't let harm
come his way. Before you knew it, he had the mob and police on payroll, not excluding the bankers on his roster.
Ethan could see the flaws in the kingpin's moves, but, hell,
it was the 1960 and 1970s. He didn't have the same worries

that Ethan would have today. It was Ethan's job to point out flaws; he was supposed to learn from them. Besides, men like Frank Lucas were the reason for most of the rules that were put in place today.

Ethan needed to find a way to become the distributor while he yearned to be the manufacturer. He began reading pharmacology books and the active ingredients in most addiction-causing legal prescriptions, and he found some common denominators: cocaine, heroin, marijuana, and opium. He locked his focus on the companies making those drugs. It seemed too simple. Would it really be that easy to get on the board of these companies with an alias, reach out to some current drug lords, convince them to buy the companies using the same alias the board was familiar with, and let him run the operations of producing both legal and illegal drugs out of the same plant so they could keep their attention on the operations they already have in place? It was that simple, but it would take years of planning to win, and at the minimum, a decade of planning to fail before he could make his first move.

Ethan Wade Carruthers was a son of two drug addicts who both had been arrested for drug use and entered drug rehab a dozen times combined. He had to find a way to cut the ties with his parents in order to give them more in life than what they were willing to give themselves.

"What do you mean, give you up for adoption?" his mama yelled.

Ethan had tried to get Child and Family Services involved multiple times by winning over the heart of a teacher and then telling that teacher about the hell he went through at home, but when investigators came out and gave his mama a deadline to get things in order, she always did. It made him feel good that she could let the drugs go long enough to pretend at least to put her son first, but it wasn't helping his progress. Instead of continuing a broken cycle, he decided to sit them down and share his plan with them.

"If you gave me up, I'd be given a new name, and the background I had before with y'all as my parents, I can request it to be sealed," he reasoned.

"Boy, anything the government seals can be opened when the government wants it opened," his daddy noted. "Your plan is damn good, and I can hear the thought and time you put into it, but look at your grades. Why chase being a drug lord when you can change the world?"

"I want to be the organizer of drug lords, the bosses' boss, and let their egos make them believe that we're partners. I'm trying to be a kingpin and the first ever of this kind. History would have to compare me to Escobar, and that would be a farfetched comparison."

"What about us? You'd just throw us away, baby?" His mama knew he had a soft spot for her, and that was because, through her addiction, she made it her business to be her son's best friend. Ethan was different, and when 5-year-old boys were making dump trucks collide, he was lining them up to create a transportation system for rocks that he pretended were diamonds. She didn't know where his gift came from, but she made sure he'd never hide it. As her drug addiction worsened, she didn't change her goals for him; she just added herself to the list of things he needed to make a priority.

"What do you mean, Mama? When I'm straight, you and Daddy will be straight too. I'm going to change your life. You just got to trust and believe me now."

"I do believe you, son, but you need to keep planning it out because I'm never going to give up my rights over you, and as your daddy said, the government can open up anything they want to. It sounds to me like you need to find a way to play dead."

It was the perfect idea, and that sent him running out the door to the library to research people who had played dead. Everyone he was running across eventually came clean or had gotten caught, which meant he had only scratched the surface. He needed to find those who weren't discovered until their real deaths. He kept coming up empty-handed, so he gathered his research and decided to be the person he was looking for around the time he met Ronald. By the age of 16, he'd be gone and should be financially ready to start his plan by 28 years old, and then came his first hurdle.

"Ethan, come over here, boy."

His daddy was high as hell and standing in a group of nine small-time dealers. Ethan didn't like any of them. Not because they sold his parents their poison. He understood that to be a business transaction. He didn't like them because of the length of time they had been small time. With more than thirty years in the drug game standing before him, he didn't understand why none of them opted for a promotion.

"What's up, Daddy?" he said, emotionless.

"I was out here talking to Byrd and them about that secret plan you're putting together. Tell them how you plan on cornering the drug market. I was trying to remember that shit you were saying about Pablo Saint Lucas Escobar and them, or whatever the fuck you said their names are." He turned his back to his son to face the men he was entertaining as Ethan checked out his surroundings. *"Listen to his plan, y'all. It's failure proof. The little nigga even asked me to give up my rights over*

him so he could put his shit in motion. I'm telling you now, one day, y'all are going to be working for him."
Everything else went fast.

Ethan snatched the gun from Byrd's waistband, snapped off the safety, and shot his father in the back of his head. Seven shots later, he returned the gun to Byrd.

"I don't take my business being told lightly, understand me?"

"Shit, I wasn't paying his high ass no attention anyway. Come on, niggas, we got to go, and you better hide too, little nigga. Somebody calling them boys right now."

"I'll dip in a second. Y'all didn't see shit out here, tonight, did you?"

"I'm Ray Charles to everything that doesn't involve me," Byrd said, walking off, feeling his way around like he was blind. Ethan looked down at his father, and a lone tear fell.

"Dumb-ass nigga!" He picked up his daddy's body, tossed it in the dumpster, and headed to Mimic's house. He didn't go over there as an alibi. He needed to use his water hose to wash himself up and put on a pair of clothes he knew his grandmother left folded on the back porch from a day of doing laundry. The back door was never locked, and though he could have knocked on the door and she'd let him in to eat and shower, he didn't need her or Mimic to know he had been there.

Two hours later, when he made it back home, his daddy's body was still hanging out of the trash can, and the police hadn't been called. No one cared about hearing shooting. They were used to it. He walked in the house, showered again, and put on his clothes. He carefully folded Mimic's and took them back.

"Baby, is that you?" his mama shouted from her bedroom.

"No, Mama, it's me," he shouted back.

"Did you see your daddy out there? He was supposed to try to get us a loan and bring his ass back. Looks like his ass detoured again."

"Yeah, I seen him," Ethan said, walking toward her room.

"Run back downstairs and tell him I want him, baby."

"He can't come, Mama."

She saw the look in her son's eyes and sat up. "Why can't he come, Ethan?"

"Because he went out there and tried to tell Byrd and those other fools my plan and then asked me to break it down to them," he said, hallow voiced.

"One of them must have fronted him a hit. He was high, baby. You know he'd never leak your plan."

"But he did, Mama."

"Okay," she said, giggling to lighten the mood, "but why can't you go back and get him for me, Ethan? Why can't you tell your daddy that I want him? I'll get in his ass for telling your business."

She knew why before he said, and tears rolled down her face before he did.

"I already handled it. I'm only telling you so you won't blame anybody else for it."

"You're big-ass Ethan, the future kingpin. Why are you pussyfooting around what you did? Say the shit!" she was crying erratically.

"I grabbed Byrd's gun and blew his fucking brains out. I threw him in the dumpster outside, if you want to go pay your respects."

She flipped out of the bed and slapped the shit out of Ethan, but he didn't move. He let her hit him until she could no longer swing, and then she fell on him, crying.

"Why, baby, why?"

"If I can't trust y'all, who do I have, Mama?"

"But that's your daddy!" she yelled.

"*No, that's* your husband. *My daddy would have never opened his mouth. I got a question for you now that he's gone. Are you my mama, or are you his wife?*"

She slapped him again and then wiped the snot from her nose.

"*I'm your* mother *before anything, but you owe me, nigga. You owe me that life you were talking about. You already took your daddy's life over this kingpin shit. You better live it out because if you don't, I'm going to show you what his* wife *would do. Is that fair?*"

He hugged her tightly.

"*That's all I wanted to hear. Sit on the bed so I can update you on my plan. After what happened tonight, I don't have long, and I need you to play a few parts in this too.*"

Ethan had planned it all out perfectly, and all his adult alter ego Joe had to do was execute it properly. As of late, that seemed impossible.

Joe wanted to reach out to a few people on his payroll and have them search the city for Ronald, but who could he trust? Everybody wanted him dead, and he didn't know who was out for that billion-dollar reward. He thought about reaching out to Aric, but he wasn't sure if the boy had caught on to who he was or if Ronald and his failing mind had told him. At this point, he wasn't sure if Ronald knew that he and Joe were one and the same. The last time he checked on Ronald, he was losing his battle to Alzheimer's, and he moved into an assisted living facility. These were situations Ethan couldn't plan for at 16, and these were situations Joe couldn't handle because he lived his life by Ethan's plans. Trying to freestyle anything this far into the plan could be his demise. He was the richest man on earth . . . and the loneliest too. He had no one to turn to, not even his mama because of that shit Mimic told the people at 60 Minutes.

His mama's phone had been ringing off the hook with questions about her deceased son with one of the questions being, "Does a part of you still feel like he's alive somewhere, as if whoever kidnapped him didn't kill him, and he doesn't remember who he is anymore?"

He wouldn't be able to check in with her until it blew over, that's if it ever did. He needed his daddy by his side to help him through his rough time, but instead, he was lost somewhere roaming Memphis's streets. Joe decided to keep his eyes on the news and his ear to the radio to see if he heard anything about Ronald over the airwaves. If Ronald didn't turn up in seventy-two hours, he'd take the bulk of his fortune and flee for his life. Where he would go was a mystery because everyone was on the hunt to find him.

"We're here! This is the closest bus stop to Nike. You have a good day and welcome again to Memphis," the cabdriver said, smiling because the woman had overpaid him for the trip.

"I didn't know this was Memphis. Doesn't look like the Memphis I was at yesterday," he said, squinting his eyes as he tried to remember the other version of the city he saw. "Do you have a pen and paper to write something down for me? Can you write, 'Don't get off this bench,' please? I don't want to get lost again."

"Sure, pal, no problem."

He handed him the note written on a yellow carbon copy receipt slip. For the first hour or so, Ronald scanned his eyes over the paper. He remembered what it said more than he could read it. The letters look like drawings, and he couldn't comprehend what the drawings together meant. It was like putting Shakespeare right in front of a 4-year-old and not only expecting him to be able to say the words but also to know the definition of them. His mind was withering away by the second.

He had fallen asleep and didn't know for how long but when he opened his eyes, it was dark out. He looked at the note again, and it was useless because he didn't know what it said. He could feel anxiety building inside but knew now wasn't the time for a panic attack. He was sitting at that bus stop for a reason. There were hundreds of bus stops in all major cities, but this one was chosen for a reason. Yes, the reason could have been that he was supposed to meet someone here, but he wasn't sure. He stood up and looked around. He could see the sign for the Nike Warehouse, a truck stop, and some train tracks up ahead, but the one thing he noticed was that he was in an area full of warehouses and logistic companies. He decided to walk around. He would walk no more than a mile in all four directions and take a seat back at the bus stop in between walks just in case there was a reason he was supposed to be sitting there.

He walked to the north and then came back and rested for thirty minutes. Next, he walked to the south, and because of the rocky road, he needed a nap when he made it back. An hour and a half later, he headed east. On his way back to the bus stop, there was something about the south he felt he had overlooked. He tried hard to remember, but nothing rang a bell. There was a sign planted in the concrete in front of the building that had numbers and letters on it, but he couldn't make out what it said. It was outside of the gate of one of the largest warehouses Ronald had ever seen. From where he stood, there had to be at least fifty truck loading docks. The longer he stared at the warehouse, he realized it hadn't been in use for years, but there was a light on, on the right side of the building. He decided to go there and see if anyone could help him. He needed a hotel for the night because sleeping on the bus bench wasn't an option.

The warehouse gate was closed to vehicle traffic, but he could easily duck under the railing to get in. As he lowered his neck and head under the bar, a sign caught his attention and this one, he could read, *"Welcome to Memphis, America's Distribution Center."* He'd remember to ask someone what it meant.

From the gate to the door where the light was located had to be at least two miles. It felt longer than that with the cracks in the surface and the tall grass growing from them. Two rats crossed his path on his way back, but he didn't jump because he no longer remembered what rats were. He was starting to pant hard and get light-headed with every step, and when he thought he would pass out, he made it to his destination . . . and there was a bench. He decided he would catch his breath and then knock on the door for help. Ronald was asleep before he could realize he was sleepy.

Something woke him up, but he couldn't think clearly to know what it was. Where the light was on there was a door open underneath it. He tried to get his strength together to lift his body from the bench so he could go inside the building, but he was too weak. He stumbled back to the seat and was immediately lifted.

"Come on, Mr. Ronald; I got you."

Chapter Eighteen

Memphis, Tennessee. Tuesday, February 5, 2019

The bed was so comfortable, Ronald could barely keep his eyes open. He had never slept on memory foam, and in his rapidly decreasing condition, enjoying it was a cliché. By morning, he thought it would be a good idea to change the bag connected to his catheter, but it was no longer there. He was in a pair of boxers and the most expensive pair of pajamas he had ever worn.

He fought to get out of bed because the memory foam kept causing him to sink into it, but after five minutes of trying, he was victorious and slid his feet into the house slippers that waited for him on the side of the bed. The room was gorgeous, and for some reason, it gave him the feeling that it was set up for him. There were large pictures all over the wall full of familiar faces. The face that he recognized first was of his brother, Robert. It was a picture of them as kids. He smiled and walked over to the picture.

"Oh boy, what a life that I have lived, and I can tell you this, Robert Junior, you lucked up and got to leave this zoo early." He rubbed his hand across his brother's face before moving on to the next. There was a picture of his mother and father side by side, dressed up. He wasn't certain, but he assumed it was their wedding day. He gave his dad a quick look, his mama a loving smile, and then moved on to the next picture. His heart pounded against his chest. It was a picture of him and Corrina at their wedding rehearsal dinner taken just days before her death. He couldn't recall if he had ever seen the picture, but staring at it made his knees weak. He never grieved her; he wasn't strong enough to. Instead, he convinced himself to believe that their marriage was never meant to be, and he included her in the prayers of things he didn't want to remember. Staring at her, all he could do was cry. Once he got it out, he turned to a picture of two boys, and he smiled. He knew exactly who they were. There wasn't a negative thought that crossed his mind looking into their youthful faces. Ethan and Martin . . . his boys. He turned around sure there would be a picture of his son RJ and his grandson the third and got thrown off by the man standing in the door frame watching him.

"We were so young then. Through all the craziness, I still like to look at us as if we were best friends. Come on, old man, you got to eat something."

"This is a really nice place you have, young man, but do I know you? Are you another one of my son's friends here to help me out?"

Joe's feelings were crushed. He was sure out of all people Ronald had forgotten, he would never forget him. Instead of forcing him to remember who he was, he decided to play along.

"Yes, I'm another one of Ethan's friends. My name is Joe. Nice to meet you," he said, extending his hand out for a shake. Ronald grabbed his hand and shook it and then wrapped his arms around him and cried.

"You think I don't know my son when I see him? Boy, this is a dream come true. I've missed you all my life!" Ronald hugged him so tightly that the love Joe was feeling caused him to drop a few tears. It had been years since he had anyone close enough to him to love him, and it felt good, a little too good. He made Ronald let him go.

Taken aback, Ronald said, "I guess this isn't the happy ending I've been longing for." He looked around for his bag, pulled the sealed letter out of it, and held it in the air. "This must be the 'to be continued' you were talking about." Joe nodded his head. "Well, let's eat. I guess we got a lot to talk about."

Ronald followed Joe out of his room, and immediately, he was walking through a work of art. Nothing gave a hint that they were in less than a fine art museum. From wall to wall, paintings from all over the world done by famous and not-so-famous artists covered his walls. He passed a row of grand pianos that were connected in a circle. Each piano had belonged to some famous musician. The one that caught Ronald's eyes used to belong to Stevie Wonder. When Joe caught him staring at it, he said, "I won that one at a charity auction."

They made it to the end of the hallway, where a golf cart was waiting. He helped Ronald onto the passenger side and then drove it three miles to get to the eating area. An IV station was set up and a plate of food was on the table.

"I looked into a few things to know how to take care of you while you are here, and I found this thing called a TPN, or Total Parenteral Nutrition. It's a way to feed you that bypasses the stomach. Food is given to you through your veins and will give you most of the nutrients your body needs to keep you functioning."

"How do I know this isn't the way you're going to kill me for knowing your secrets, Ethan?"

"Let's get something straight. Ethan is dead. I'm Joe, and why would I kill you, old man?"

"No, dammit, you're Ethan, and Joe is the man everybody is looking for. You need to find a way to separate Ethan from Joe. That's what you need to be working on. If you can kill Ethan off, killing Joe should be just as easy." Ronald stuck his arm out in preparation for the feeding, and Joe couldn't help but chuckle.

"I see you still got a lot of fight in you. You still haven't learned anything yet, have you?"

"Oh yes, going through the hurt of losing you, I learned a lot."

"So, how do you think I should get rid of this Joe?"

Ronald looked at him like he was stupid before responding. "You made the plan over twenty-six years ago. It took me a long time to read in between the lines, but I'm here, ain't I? Let's get this party started."

Joe began hooking Ronald up to the machine, and when he was done, he ate his breakfast.

"When we're done having breakfast, there's something on TV I need you to see."

They rode the golf cart half a mile and turned into what looked like a drive-in movie theater. There were three rows of seats; however, Joe stayed on the golf cart and had it pointed at the screen. He touched a button on the wall, and a recording of the *Chicago News* came on.

"This has to be taken from a scene in a scary movie. After the escape of Ronald Hill from hospice care at the hospital, he called his storage unit and offered the front desk agent $500,000 to empty the contents of a unit that he's had for almost thirty years. He had never missed a payment on the unit. Well, the agent didn't take light to the offer and immediately called the police after seeing someone named Ronald Hill had escaped from the hospital on the news. He was sure it had to be the same person who was calling making that strange request."

The scene switched to the outside of the storage unit where it was taped off and full of detectives.

"The storage unit was empty. The only thing inside of it was a deep freezer filled with solid ice. We had forensics defrost the ice, and they found blood, a lot of blood belonging to a young man who had been missing for over twenty-six years. At this time, we have not received

authorization from the family to release his name, but
they have been notified. We are not sure if Ronald Hill
is armed, but he is completely dangerous. Please, if you
come in contact with him, call your local authorities. He
can be anywhere between here and Memphis, Tennessee.
Thank you."

The detective walked off, and Joe paused the show.

"I didn't own a storage unit."

"Yes, you did. When I went through your file box, I
found the letter you forged to your father from the U.S.
government, and I thought, how gullible could your
father be? So, I forged another letter from the U.S. government telling him that he needed to rent a storage unit
in his name and to add you as the only other person who
could enter without a key. The letter said he would only
need to pay for it when he opened it and to never go to
the storage unit again. It directed him to leave both keys
to the unit in his mailbox, and the military police would
be coming by to pick it up. Your daddy loved this country,
and he loved you and your brother a hell of a lot more.
He would have done anything to help you bring your
brother back. I paid on that storage for years. I brought
the deep freezer when I was 18. Just so happened days
before I was to have it delivered to the unit, I overheated
and passed out. When I woke up, blood was everywhere.
I had busted my chin." He showed Ronald the scar that
stretched from one side of his chin to the other. "I used
a sponge to soak up as much blood as I could and then
wiped it around the bottom of the deep freezer before
putting blocks of ice in it so it wouldn't smear the blood.
That blood and ice have been in there ever since. Ethan
Wade Carruthers is officially dead, and my mother just
received the death certificate."

"You set me up to kill you? Do you know the hell I went
through with the police suspecting me of kidnapping

you? I lost my job! Did you know your mama told those detectives that she was uncomfortable with our relationship, and for months, they followed me, watching every single thing that I did!"

"Yeah, I told my mama she had to do it. Ronald, I planned this out since I was 16, and I was only supposed to have to follow through with this plan if I was about to fail. I'm failing. Everything around me is crumbling all because I made the same mistake that I made at 15. Do you remember how I responded after going through your file box?"

"I don't remember shit!" Ronald was too upset even to try to rack his brain. He couldn't believe that he was just named dangerous by the police, and the whole world would be looking for him in the murder of his most favorite person on earth. He didn't know if he should be heartbroken or angry.

"You're pissed. Okay, I get it, but here we are now, and there's no turning back. You don't want to remember, that's fine. I'll remind you. When I found out you had a son, a dead brother, and was lying to your parents, I lost respect for you, and in my anger, I made a very hasty decision. I left the stuff you bought me and the key without hearing your side to anything. I did it before that day I killed my daddy. I was so pissed that he betrayed my trust that, again, I made a hasty decision, and now it's the reason why my world is crumbling and falling on my head.

"I got pissed again that someone I employed went behind my back and made a move without my blessing. I started feeling like God, and I felt like he had to have the ultimate consequence, which was his life, but there were other people in the car. Very important people in the car and one of them I was sure was my Sharlene. I was shutting down the shop and needed her to do a few more things to make the transition smooth, and instead of letting him speak, I hung up in his face and then blew up the car with her in it. The suspicions it cost sent a ripple. There was a truck driver who got pulled over with a lot of my product. His statement said he had no idea what was in the load and the only reason he missed the weigh station was that the car exploded. It shook the bridge, knocked his food over, and he was in the process of picking it up when he missed the prompt telling him to go through the weigh station. The guy who I blew up was the nephew of a very large cartel boss, and even though he set his nephew up to be killed, it was easier for him to blame me.

When all the government agencies ran into my pharmaceutical building and the homes of the deceased, they uncovered everything. That's how they linked the legal and illegal drugs to me, government officials, Wall Street billionaires, cartel leaders, and mob bosses. Instantly, everybody who I had been working with for years now wanted my head. Their banking accounts were being seized, and their worlds were crashing all around them. They found the chemists who I scheduled to be killed later that weekend and questioned them, and, of course, they told everything they knew. I became wanted by the good, and the number one wanted on the list of the bad. The plan that I made all those years ago had a clause for something like this, and that clause involves you."

"Yeah, that's the part I figured out from reading this letter. You said we would never meet again unless your plan didn't work out, and at that time, we would call it the 'to be continued.' That's what this is, to be continued, isn't it? I'm Joe, ain't I?"

"Yeah, you're Joe," he confirmed.

"Are you going to let these people kill me or throw me in jail because your plan didn't work?"

"My plan worked, and this was my ticket out. *You* are my ticket out. And I'm not going to let anybody put a hand on you. You're my pops!"

"My memory ain't what it used to be but didn't you kill your last pops? What makes me so special?"

Joe could have slit his neck for the remark he made, but he understood the place it was coming from.

"You're dying; you've been dying from the moment you were born. You just received your countdown, that's all."

"What if I weren't dying? You wrote this letter when you were 17, and there's no way you or I knew I'd have Alzheimer's, and it would be taking my life back then. What was your plan when you wrote it? I'm dying to know!"

"Same plan. You take the fall for me. You become Joe; I sail off into the sunset."

"That was really cute how you planned that, but you didn't answer my question. Would you have killed me to make me Joe if I weren't already dying?"

"I would have done whatever I needed to do."

The truth felt like knives to the chest. Ethan said it without a crack in his voice.

"When I first met you, I saw it. I didn't know what it was, but I knew it didn't have a place in a boy your age, and here we are, all these years later, and it's never left you."

Joe laughed hysterically. "And what is it that you saw in me so many years ago?"

"A vessel without a soul. Take me to my overly decorated room you tried to use to make shit seem right. I need my rest."

"You do what I say—" Joe started, but Ronald cut him off.

"No, from here on out, *you* do what the fuck *I* say. *I'm* Joe; don't forget it and find a way to put a fucking medium well New York strip steak in my IV!"

Joe cranked up the golf cart and drove Ronald back to his room. He sat in his living room, watching Ronald on the surveillance video as he slept. He couldn't let go of the thought of Ronald calling him a vessel without a soul; however, he couldn't disagree with the analogy. He always felt like something on the inside was missing, and he couldn't remember a time when it was there. He was cold, and Ronald had always expected more from him, but he couldn't understand why. He did try to butter up the situation with nostalgic items and made it overkill, but he wanted him to die comfortably. The emotional roller-coaster ride he would be on during Ronald's stay had to be expedited. He'd find a way to speed up his death without Ronald detecting it.

Three hours later, he saw Ronald sitting on the bed, flipping through the yearbook and smiling, so he decided to join him.

"Hey, Ethan, come here. Do you remember that teacher there?"

"Yeah, I think his name was Mr. Johnson. Why? What's up?"

"I watched Martin break into his car, and that fool stood in the window watching." Ronald was laughing. "I went outside and tried to defend him, and Martin whooped my ass." He laughed even harder. "I never shared this with you, but I was so glad you beat the shit out of him in my backseat."

Joe laughed. "I should have got rid of him a long time ago. I never thought he would say anything to anybody. He always acted like he didn't believe anything that I was saying, so when I saw him on *60 Minutes* running his mouth, I was shocked. I had some people find out how much they paid him for the information. And then I paid the director of the show's assistant to kill him and stuff the amount of money they offered him down his throat. Everybody in the building except for the lady doing the interview and those higher up knew what was going to happen, including the police they had securing him. Paying off all those people could have bankrupted me. That's *if* I was the average Joe, that is."

"Well, good thing I'm not the average Joe," Ronald chimed in. "Now, how about telling me all the stuff that I've gotten into over the years? You took my catheter out, and you're forcing me to eat, which should make me shit, and we both know I can't do that. I don't have to have my memory to know you need me dead sooner than later, so here's the deal. Humor me just for today, give me a true father-and-son experience, and then tomorrow, you can figure out a painless way for me to go. I'm sure you already had one in mind. I don't know much about you and your relationship with your father, but the Ethan I knew loved me. There's no way he'd put a bullet in me."

"You're right. I'd never put a bullet in you. Tomorrow it is. Now scoot over, Pops. I got some crazy shit to tell you."

"I shouldn't have to say this to you, but you have a brother and nephew and—"

"You don't have to say anything. Are you ready to play catch-up on what you've been doing as Joe all these years or what?"

They talked and laughed all night. Joe told him story after story, and Ronald couldn't believe the life he had lived. Joe should be sitting in somebody's electric chair being fried; instead, he was making his arrangements to spend his life on a beach with more money than anybody in the world will ever touch, and the only sacrifice he had to make to do so was blaming it on Ronald. They ate again and watched the 10:00 news. There was a familiar face talking.

"Shit, I got a call from some nigga saying he had a gun at my mama's and sister's head, and if I didn't

get to Chicago right then and there, he was going to kill them. So, I pulled up at my mama's house, and they seemed straight, but I didn't want to test it 'cause dude was still calling my phone. I got a rental car, and I shot out there. When I got there, the old dude had like $50,000 for me, talking about he needed to get to Memphis and shut some shit down. I asked him why he chose me, and the nigga said he typed in Memphis on one of the social media sites, and my profile came up. Crazy shit, right? For seven hours, he told me how he got over on the government for years. How he worked with the cartel and fucked them over and how the mob was his bitch. He was talking big shit, and I was staring at him like, damn, nigga, they gon' kill you. That Ronald Hill guy, that's that nigga Joe."

"Did he say he was coming to see anyone in Memphis?" the reporter asked, taking the microphone back from him.

"In all honesty, the nigga was just stopping here to pick up some money. He really wanted me to take him to Atlanta. If you look at the video from the parking lot at Tom Lee Park, when he got out of the car, I went back and put both rear tires on flat, so I wouldn't have to take him, and then I dipped. I can't believe I got to meet the real Joe!"

"Do you have any idea where he's at now?"

"Yeah, in Atlanta. He said that's where he wanted to die. And I don't know if it will help the mob bosses or not, but he didn't try to fuck shit up at the pharmaceutical plant. He was really dealing with Alzheimer's, and he made a bad call. I don't know if that's going to stop y'all from killing his ass, but dude's memory is fucked up. I don't know how y'all worked for him without knowing he was old as hell, and his memory was shot, but he fucked up on accident."

"Aric, what did you do with the money he gave you? Did you turn it in to the authorities?"

"Hell yeah, I gave them what was left. I gave him like $47,000. I spent three trying to do everything he told me to do to get to Memphis from Chicago, and then the nigga needed some clothes and didn't give me no money to go inside the place to get it. If you look at the videos from that mall, I think that was in Kentucky or something. I copped him some clothes, and he's wearing them same clothes at the park. I told the police as soon as I made it back, and I didn't have his ass in my face. I knew I was turning that money in when he gave it to me, and that's exactly what I did."

Joe and Ronald roared in laughter.

"Damn, he gave me more than my money's worth," Joe said, trying to catch his breath.

"And he was a hell of a good nurse too."

In the middle of the night, Ronald had another fit. This time, he was more violent than he had ever been before. He was trying to claw his nails in Joe's face, and he was screaming that Joe was the devil. Joe was shaken up and didn't know what to do. He ran out of the room, and when he returned, he had a cigar stuffed with weed.

"Here, smoke this and calm down." Ronald snatched it and hit it hard. He coughed like he had virgin lungs, then smoked some more. He hit it one more time and then calmed all the way down.

"Are you all right, Ronald?"

"I've smoked weed all my life, and I never tasted any like this." Ronald smoked the whole blunt with Joe sitting at his side. He closed his eyes and never opened them again.

Joe didn't know what the cause of death was. He wondered if the weed was too strong or if Ronald had forgotten to exhale. He wasn't sure, but he had a lot of work to do before sunrise. He put Ronald in an "I am Joe" shirt and then put him on the golf cart. They rolled to his room where he retrieved a box that had all the company names Joe ran in them and proof of how he got them. The trades he made out of the country were done in Ronald's father's name, and so were the first few businesses he opened. Robert Sr. thought he was helping his son and did everything the secret government letters asked of him, including burning the letters in the grill after the task was done.

Going through Ronald's file box is what made the fictional character Joe possible to live a nonfictional life, and he'd ever be in debt for that life he was able to live because of them. His plan worked perfectly, and he'd retire with more money than he would ever be able to count.

Once Joe had everything he needed, he drove off the back dock and went across the street to the bus stop he had Ronald meet him at. He propped Ronald up like he was awake with the box on his lap, a lighter in his sweat pockets, and the blunt he was smoking in his hand. On the front of the box, he wrote, "*Kingpin of Memphis*," and then drove off without fear of being spotted. Joe owned every business in the intersection and had the cameras disabled before taking his long nap at the bus stop.

Long live Joe!

The End

Epilogue

"Tonight, I have the pleasure of sitting down with the biggest victim of Joe's famous reign, Evelyn Carruthers. The mother of Ethan Wade Carruthers, the 16-year-old that went missing and whose remains were recently found in a storage unit less than ten blocks from her home at the time. Evelyn told detectives when her son was first missing, that she felt there was something strange and abnormal about his relationship with Mr. Ronald Hill, his history teacher that we now know is the infamous Joe."

The camera flashed to Ethan's mother sitting in a chair draped in diamonds, her gray hair flawless, and her makeup fresh off a magazine photoshoot. She looked better in her golden years than she had at any point in her life, and it was Ethan she had to thank for it. He promised her he would achieve the goal, and he did. Once he put her in rehab for two years in California, she enrolled in school and received her AA in office administration. She worked for a law office to cover up the monthly allowance Joe was sending her, and she lived her happily ever after alone. She was prepared to get on the show and lie her ass off. That's why she clutched the tissue box. Ethan had kept his word, and she never once doubted that he would. Now, it was her turn to put in work for him. It was time to let Ethan rest in peace.

"I'm Stacey Wilcox. These stories and more, tonight on 60 Minutes. Tick, tick, tick."

The beachside bar was crowded, and Revo needed the noise. He had an important call he had put off for too long to continue to wait. He dialed the number and then inhaled.

"Can I speak to RJ?"

"Damn, I've been waiting almost three years for this. What's up?"

"I was calling to tell you—"

"that your nephew is straight, and after the shit you pulled, family comes first. Is that what you were calling for?" The aggression in his voice is why Revo hadn't picked up the phone. He deserved it, so he let his younger brother shoot his shot.

"Yeah, that's exactly what I was calling for."

"Cool, but you need to know my wife just pushed out another son."

"Is that right? Congratulations. Sounds like I got another nephew to spoil."

"You do, and his name is Ronald Joe Wade."

"Is that right?"

"Yeah, that's right. I had to name him after my deceased brother and dad. I know we didn't get to talk, but you need to know something. When my pops, my bad, *our* pops told me about you, I knew one thing for sure . . . He loved you more than he ever loved me."

"Don't say that. Different times, different circumstances. You got caught up in the old young pop's days, and I just lucked up and got the pops who felt guilty about what he did to you. That's all that is."

"You're real good with words. Now I know how you got Pops to agree to take the fall, but know he did it out of love."

"Yeah, he did, and that's why I'm calling family first, right?"

"Right. As long as you remember we are family and the sacrifices that were made for family!"

"Y'all good; say no more!" Revo said with too much bass in his voice.

"I didn't plan to!" RJ hung up the phone. He wouldn't say anything more, and that would be the last time he answered an unknown, private, or international number. He'd play cool on the line, but if he were ever in the same space as Big Brother Revo, he'd try to knock his head off his shoulders before hugging him.

Placing the phone back on its cradle, he overheard a woman on his left talking. She was trying hard to whisper but couldn't because she was too invested in making sure that she was giving somebody a dose of Memphis blues. Revo tried not to listen, but she was talking so much shit, and he couldn't help but laugh.

"You're a muthafucking fool if you think I'd let all of those bastards back in the States attempt to kill me and not get my revenge. I'm coming back, and before I start over, I'm tearing shit up first. I'm bored with living a straight and narrow life. Fucking up a few already miserable lives is just what I need to feel like me again. I'm tired of being Vanessa Moore, the new American face on the island. Although it's been fun, and this island dick has been refreshing," she paused to take a thirsty swallow of her pineapple-coconut juice infused with rum drink and then held it in the air as if she were making a toast. "It's time for me to show my ass and them bitches you call friends who back home gave me more than enough reasons to. Let the games begin!" she slammed the phone down and did a little dance.

She walked over to him when she noticed he was locked in a stance her way.

"I was talking to my fiancé's best friend because my fiancé tried to kill me awhile back, and he helped me get away until he calmed down. But I think it's time to go back and play ghost. There's some people I need to haunt, and you're nosy as hell!"

"You were speaking my language. I had to listen."

"And what language is that?" she purred as she ran her hand under the scar underneath his chin.

"I heard you say start over."

"That's what life is all about, right? Fucking up, learning from your mistakes, and starting all over."

"That's a different outlook on life."

"Then how do you see it?"

"Shit, I see it like this. We mess up a whole lot, but every mess up ain't worthy of a new start. Some things we have to suffer for, other things we got to learn from, and until we go through it all, how could we even think about getting a new start?"

"Okay, I see you're on some deep shit," she said, laughing. "Are you buying me a drink, or are you just running your mouth?"

"You talk to everybody like that, don't you?"

This was Revo's longest conversation with a woman in years. In the past, he'd walk through a club, see something he liked, caked her the entire night, and then took her somewhere where he could beat her cat up . . . and bounced. He liked the sassy woman in front of him, but her mouth needed a filter.

"Yes, I do, so are you going to answer my question or keep hitting me with more of them?"

"Aye, waitress!"

The waitress looked in his direction, and though she hated to be yelled at, he looked like a tipper. After she finished delivering her drinks, she'd make her way to him.

"So, where's your wife?"

"I don't do them."

"Why not?"

"It takes a whole lot of faithfulness and a whole lot of openness, and I'm not either one." He shrugged.

"Honest, I like that. But what if you meet the right one; what if you meet your Sharlene?"

"Sharlene?"

"You don't listen to Anthony Hamilton?" she giggled.

He chuckled, feeling slightly relieved, "Yeah, I listen to him, but my daddy told me something about a Sharlene when I was younger. I just thought you heard it too."

"I have heard something about a Sharlene. I heard every man gets one, and if he lets her go, his ass is going to be crying like Anthony Hamilton on that song too."

They laughed in unison.

"Is it your theory that every man only gets one Sharlene in his life? What if she died unexpectedly?"

"Then he might get another one. That's up to the higher powers that be."

The waitress arrived to take their drink orders. He allowed her to place hers first, and then he placed his. When the waitress got up from writing in her notepad, she looked at him and said, "Anything else?" and gave him a seductive smile. He smiled back,

"Nah, that's it for now."

She turned on her heels and went to retrieve their drinks. She was gorgeous in the sunlight, and he wondered if that glow brightened in the dark. She could have been no more than 30, and there wasn't a blemish in sight on her made up face. Her legs looked like two bow and arrows conjoined by the strings, and the heaviness of her butt kept her balanced. Standing five foot six, about 165 pounds, and the color of a bale of hay slightly burnt by the sun, her energy was sweet and sexy. Her long hair fell over her shoulders in tight coils, which he could tell was her everyday look, and it gave you a reason to steal a peek at the fullness of her breasts. He wanted her, but not bad enough to end his conversation with Ms. Feisty.

"Damn, you just goin' flirt with that ho in front of me like that?"

"Sure, you ain't mines, and you look like you're just in this for a good time," he said matter-of-factly.

"You better know it! I'm somebody's Sharlene, but like I said, he tried to kill me, and I have to make him remember who I was to him first, so, yeah, all I'm looking for is a good time," she laughed.

"What's your name, Good Time?" he said with his jaw dropped as the waitress made her way back with her eyes on him. Her name badge read Sharlene Hill, and he almost walked away from Ms. Good Time to place his focus where he knew it would count. He decided to fuck the dog shit out of the Kim-Kim in front of him tonight and lock things down with his Sharlene tomorrow. *"Sharlenes will always wait; just don't keep them waiting long."* He heard Ronald's voice spitting wisdom in his head.

"It's Savannah, Savannah James, and you are?" she asked, extending her hand.

"Revo, Revo Al Tarts."

"Is that French?"

"Something like that," he said with a smirk.

The waitress handed her drink first and then bent over and whispered in his ear as she handed him his, "Revo Al Tarts, backward, that means, 'Start All Over.' Maybe when you're done playing with the island whore, you can tell me what you're starting all over from. Maybe I can help."

She gave him a napkin and walked off. Her number was written on it, and the *i* in the word "Hill" was dotted with a heart. He knew he would be marrying her.